VOL

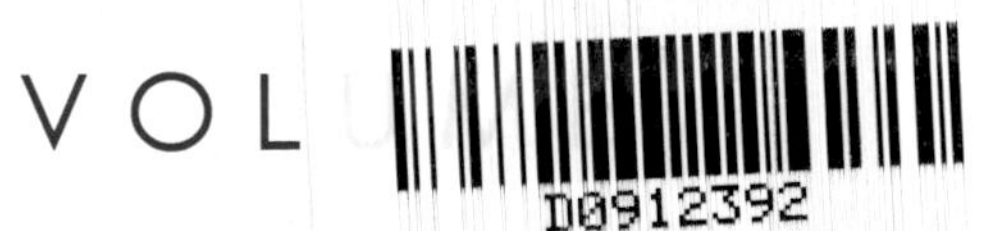

CHARACTERS, CRAZIES And The CULTURE Of Northeast Georgia

For Don Linnartz —
special friend and "eye
consultant" at Lanier Village
Gordon Sawyer
June 3, 2011

GORDON SAWYER

ABOUT THE COVER: Northeast Georgia's mountain region reaches from peaks along the state's northern border (several more than 4,000 feet above sea level) southward to Gainesville at 1,200 feet). Pictured on the cover is Tray Mountain (4,419 feet) as viewed from the Skylake Community (1,800 feet).

ISBN 13: 9781453864791
10: 1453864792
LCCN : 2010915054
Published by: SawyerHouse Publishing
439 Historic Green Street
Gainesville, GA 30501
770/534-7642
Printed in the USA

OTHER BOOKS BY GORDON SAWYER

Northeast Georgia: A History (The development of Georgia's mountain region)

Gainesville – 1900 to 2000 (a photographic history)

JAMES LONGSTREET: Before Manassas and After Appomattox (Lee's "Old War Horse" is buried in Gainesville, Georgia)

RICHARD KIDDER: World War II Survivor – Manila to Bataan, To Corregidor. To Cabanatuan POW. To a Hell Ship. To Umeda Bunsho POW in Osaka. To Tsuraga POW. To Home Alive ... (the true WW II story of a Gainesville resident)

The AGRIBUSINESS POULTRY INDUSTRY: A History of its Development. (Gainesville Georgia is the "Poultry Capital of the World")

ACKNOWLEDGMENTS

This has been a much larger project than I had anticipated. After all, I had 10 years of "Common Sense Chronicles" already in the can. But this is Volume I of a two volume set, and to my patient wife, Jean, and to my understanding family, thank you for your patience and endurance, To my daughter-in-law, Cathryn Sawyer, thank you for being my editor-in-chief. To Fay Martin, my thanks for downloading and giving structure to the whole thing. A special thanks to John Jacobs, Jay Jacobs, Joel Williams, Bill Wilson and the whole staff at Jacobs Media for allowing me to do my thing by airing my "Common Sense Chronicles" to draw from and use in this book. And to all of you who have contributed historical information, and history tips, my sincere thanks. As they used to say in the Golden Olden Days of radio: keep them cards and letters a'comin'.

— Gordon Sawyer

TABLE OF CONTENTS

CHARACTERS, CRAZIES, And The CULTURE Of Northeast Georgia

PREFACE

How many times have you heard "we did so-and-so IN THE GOOD OLE DAYS?" This book started as a collection of stuff about those "good ole days" taken, first, from some market studies our advertising agency did in the 1960's, and mostly from my "Common Sense Chronicles" which were broadcast on Radio Station WDUN. My research and writing started as a fairly serious search for the CULTURE of Georgia's mountain region, from the North Carolina line down through, and including, Gainesville.

Working in tandem with Olin Jackson, then editor of the *North Georgia Journal* (now *Georgia Backroads)*, I quickly learned that Northeast Georgia had more, and more colorful, CHARACTERS than the rest of Georgia combined. Not only that, but I soon came to the realization there were an unusual number of high-octane Characters who were a bit on the crazy side ... but GOOD CRAZY. On the flip side of that coin were some colorful people that were about as BAD CRAZY as one can get.

I define the GOOD OLE DAYS as the period from the first settling of Georgia's mountain area until the 1960's when all America's culture began a dramatic change, taking Northeast Georgia with it ... but only part way.

So ... right here at the beginning, let's define what is meant when I say Characters, Crazies and Culture.

First, CULTURE. To talk about culture is NOT to speak of cultured people who are highly sophisticated, overly educated, and delight in letting you know it. I haven't come across many of these people in Northeast Georgia ... a few, but not many. The culture of most regions is heavily influenced by geography, and Northeast Georgia is a prime example. This is an area with God-made mountains and man-made lakes. No matter where we were born, we are mountain people, much closer to the hard-scrabble culture of the Blue Ridge Mountains than the historic plantation culture of coastal Georgia or Carolina. Besides the geography it is the people who set the tone for the culture of an area ... how they think, how they live, how they look. And the more I researched, the more I came to realize we have a bunch of characters around here. Always have, still do.

About those CHARACTERS. Wasn't it Gov. Zell Miller who said: I don't know how you would define (a mountain character) but I know one when I see one? For the purpose of this study, Characters are people who tend to think, speak, and act outside "the customary beliefs and social norms" of the mass of "normal folks" around them. In Northeast Georgia, to say a person is "a real character" is almost always a compliment.

Then the CRAZIES come on the scene. These are people who go way beyond being a character. There are two types.

GOOD CRAZY. These are super high octane Characters. They are always up to something, but their intent is to build things up, not tear them down. Most often you will find them among the "movers and shakers". Some lead in politics, some in business, some in the church, some in civic organizations. But some come out of nowhere and have, or have had, a major influence on the culture of their community.

BAD CRAZY. These also have an impact on our culture ... usually bad. Some are notorious law-breakers, and others just overdo things. Very often there is a very fine line between a Good Crazy and a Bad Crazy, but I think you will know 'em when you see 'em.

The pattern of this book is to START EACH CHAPTER with a SERIOUS THOUGHT or story about the Culture of Northeast Georgia, FOLLOWED BY SNAPSHOTS taken from 10 years of my brief "Common Sense Chronicles" aired on Northeast Georgia's radio station WDUN.

I hope you enjoy this view of Northeast Georgia from a window on historic Green Street, and may the wind always be at your back.

— Gordon Sawyer
2011

CHAPTER 1 — God Giveth and God Taketh Away

The culture of every region is heavily influenced by what the Founding Fathers of these United States called "Nature's God." It is well known and fully accepted that people are drawn, as by a magnet, to large bodies of WATER and high MOUNTAINS.

The Culture of Northeast Georgia was, and still is, dramatically driven by the Blue Ridge Mountains, a part of the Appalachian chain. More than anything else, it is the mountains that historically have set Northeast Georgia apart from the rest of the state.

Northeast Georgia is also the location of the HEADWATERS of several major rivers, streams where the water flows fast, or as Sidney Lanier said in his famous poem about the Chattahoochee River "rush amain to reach the plain." The deep valleys were ideal for the building of dams to tame flash floods and to generate electricity. Thus, as man built the dams, a necklace of large lakes was formed, so now the region has both highlands and islands.

But the highlands and islands were only the beginning of the historic natural wealth to be found in this rugged corner of the state of Georgia. There were trees; ah, the great Chestnut Trees, that were already here when man first arrived. And with a rainfall of 50 inches per year, the trees and everything else grew lush and green.

Wildlife was abundant, especially the deer, which became a major cash crop for the early Indians, and still draw serious hunters. Trout also populated those cold, fast-flowing streams. Among the Indians, these were things worth fighting for, and ancient battles between the Creeks and the Cherokee have left names like Blood Mountain and War Hill.

The red clay soil was good for making bricks, and there was ample wood for firing the kilns. There were also deposits of another type of clay, good for making pottery, used for jugs and churns and other hard-to-get frontier items. There were other minerals, and asbestos … all for the mining.

And yes, there was Gold, but for the early Indians, that was merely a curiosity, and the earliest settlers did not know the Gold was here. That came later, after the Europeans arrived..

But most of all, as America was being settled, the land in the mountains was cheap, some there for the taking. The poorer people who came from Europe and landed in Eastern ports like Philadelphia and Baltimore migrated through Pennsylvania, and then turned South on the "Great Wagon Road" that ran along the Eastern edge of the Appalachian Mountains. When they reached South

Carolina, the adventuresome and the poorest turned West at 76 (yes, 76 is the name of the village, even today). They crossed the upper reaches of the Savannah River and poured into mountainous Georgia to settle.

These were God-fearing, hard-working people seeking the American dream – a home on land of their own, but most of all, freedom. They understood liberty, and were willing to pay the price to get it.

But not only had their God given them a paradise, He also had given them some severe challenges.

The land was ill suited for farming. It was hilly, and the soil was poor. As farming evolved in the South, cotton became King. And mountain land and cotton didn't get along well. Life was hard, but these settlers "made do," for they were proud, and they were free. They could plant what they wanted to, and where they wanted to ... and they didn't have to share their wealth with a king.

The mountain terrain made it well nigh impossible to build or maintain roads, and good roads would be a long time a'coming. Good roads and railroads still haven't come to some areas.

And about that rain: God sometimes gave them too much in too short a time, and the water would scream down from the high mountains, tumbling rocks and wearing smooth the rough edges, then flooding the rich bottom land, often just plowed and planted. There was always the fear of fire, for lightning loved to dance across the high points of any man-made structure. And did I mention tornadoes?

As time went on, the boll weevil migrated into the area, and took its toll on cotton farming. But the greatest loss came in the 1920s and 30s when the Chestnut blight killed all Chestnut trees that had not already been cut and taken to the sawmills.

✲ ✲ ✲

The point is simple: God giveth, and God taketh away. Nature's God has played a major role, and continues to be a major influence, in the CULTURE of mountainous Northeast Georgia.

✲ ✲ ✲

Northeast Georgia's Natural Advantages

(Excerpts from the 68 page promotional booklet produced by Gainesville businessmen in 1888)

"Gainesville is 1,300 feet above the sea level. Thus, like the surrounding country, while it is a part of the Sunny South and suffers from no rigorous winter, it is lifted far above the malaria and extreme heat of many portions of the South. On the other hand, its elevation is not so great as to subject it to the chill and dampness and sudden changes so often experienced in the higher altitudes"

MINERAL RESOURCES. The 1888 booklet logically focuses on Gold. The Gold rush ended about 1849 when the Gold diggers moved to California, Colorado, and even Australia. Says the booklet: "A new era is doubtless beginning for gold mining here. It has been discovered that unlimited beds of free-milling, but low grade, ore exists here (and) can be treated with very profitable results." It is amazing how people react at the mention of Gold.

In addition to Gold, the 1888 brochure points out that Northeast Georgia has deposits of Iron, Manganese, Plumbago, Soapstone, Mica, Kaolin, Asbestos and other minerals, not to mention limestone, clay, gems and other "precious stones".

(The 1888 booklet has been reprinted, and is available at the Northeast Georgia History Center at Brenau University)

☆ ☆ ☆

Early Indians And Their Land

Early on the Indians were friendly to European newcomers ... more friendly than with other Indian tribes. In the Indian culture the land belonged to everybody. Only if an Indian, or Indian tribe, was "using" a piece of land was it "theirs." The European culture insisted land "belonged" to someone, and the owner could put stakes in the corner of a piece of land, and it belonged to that person. In the early days of mountain settlement, with land as far as the eye could see, land ownership was not a problem. Later on it would be.

☆ ☆ ☆

Conflicts Among Indian Tribes

The history of Georgia would be incomplete without the stories of the Creek and Cherokee Indians. They were two of the five civilized tribes seen by Spanish explorer Hernando de Soto in 1540 and English explorer James Edward Oglethorpe in 1733.

De Soto found them clad in skins of animals, believing in evil spirits and calling on their "witch doctor" in preparation for life after death.

The long-standing differences between tribes meant constant war.

Georgians recognized Creek Indian Alexander McGillivary as a double-dealing chief who nursed a bitter hatred for the white Georgians. McGillivary was of mixed blood – Scotch, French and Creek. He influenced the Georgia Indians not to abide by any treaty ceding their land to the white men. He said: "We want nothing from the white people but justice. We want our hunting grounds preserved ... they were ours from the beginning of time." In 1790 he signed a treaty that the Indians called a "sellout," and they labeled McGillivary "the Prince of Scoundrels."

The internal Indian dispute brought President Washington and his friend General James Jackson to Georgia in 1791, and a treaty was made with the Creek Nation. This famous Creek quote was recorded: "The hatchet is now buried and we smoke with our Indian neighbors the calumet of peace."

In 1796 another treaty was signed, but the list of grievances pushed the differences to a bloody climax. Two factions grew up among Creeks. Georgia Governor George Troup insisted that the United States remove the Indians west.

The Indian Springs treaty of March 24, 1832, broke the Creek power, and 23,000 were on their way west. An old Indian said, "Now our people are on the road to disappearance; we are at the end of our trail." (History teacher Ruth Waters, in the Times 4/14/96.

Naturalist John Muir Visits Gainesville

I suppose I remembered that John Muir's famous book *A Thousand Mile Walk to the Gulf* mentioned Gainesville, but had long ago forgotten what he said. So, it was with delight that Dr. Harvey Newman loaned me his copy of that great book, and encouraged me to again view North Georgia through Muir's eyes in the late 1860's.

It was in 1867 that young botanist John Muir set out from Indianapolis on his one-thousand mile trek to the Gulf. He knew from the beginning that he would visit Gainesville, for he told his family to address letters there. In his journal he noted: "Passed the comfortable, finely shaded little town of Gainesville. The Chattahoochee River is richly embanked with massive, mossy, dark green water oaks, and wreathed with a dense growth of muscadine grapevines, whose ornate foliage, so well adapted to bank embroidery, was enriched with other interweaving species of vines and brightly colored flowers."

Said Muir, "This is the first truly southern stream I have met." And as a botanist, he said: "...it is here on the southern slope of the Alleghanies that the greatest number of heady, enterprising, plants from both the Northern and Southern climates can be found." That was John Muir, in Gainesville, in 1867.

A Mail Route For The Frontier

I was down in Savannah the other day, digging out some information from the reference room at the Georgia Historical Society. One thing I was looking for was the difference between the way people in South Georgia thought and lived as opposed to the way North Georgians thought and lived.

I picked the year 1802, about the time the Old Federal Road was cleared to go from Gainesville and Flowery Branch into Cherokee Indian territory ... an era when this area was pure frontier and Savannah was already a trading town. So, I started reading the Savannah newspaper of the time, the *Georgia Republican and State Intelligencer*. Most of the news was about business and trade ... ship arrivals and departures ... news about government and army assignments. One store had received 16 trunks of shoes; another 500 iron pots and ovens; another a shipment of window glass.

There was no news about INLAND Georgia, none, until I came across an announcement by the Postmaster General asking for proposals for carrying the mails of the United States. One route they wanted served was "From Augusta to Elberton, Franklin, Clarksboro" (which I assume meant Clarkesville). Mail delivered once a week, leaving Augusta on Monday, reaching Clarkesboro on Thursday, then returning. That was mail service on the frontier in 1802.

* * *

Trees As Wagon Brakes on Mountain Roads

Several years ago, people driving through our North Georgia mountains noticed there were large clearings at the highest points where a road crossed the mountain, almost, some said, as if it had been clear cut for a farm. And they wondered: why?

It was one of those things that practical mountain people caused, for when the early settlers of this region first cut a wagon road across the North Georgia mountains they had a problem ... not going up the mountains, but coming down. You see, the brakes on even the best of wagons were not too good, and mules backing against their harness were not nearly as sure-footed as when pulling. A runaway wagon was a sure disaster; you could count on that.

So the wagonmaster of the late 1800s when he got to the top of the mountain road, got out his axe, cut a tree and tied it on behind the wagon to slow it down. The heavier the load, the bigger the tree. Then came the early automobiles and trucks, and they continued the practice, for a trip all the way down the mountain, riding the brakes, would burn them out. There was another benefit, too. Pulling the brushy trees along the road helped keep it graded and smooth. But it sure didn't help the stand of trees at the top of the mountain.

Hall County and Its Historic Roads

Gainesville has always been the major transportation center for Northeast Georgia. Before the white man came, at least seven Indian trail systems passed through Hall County. Two were major routes, one going north to south from Virginia to the Gulf, and the other east to west from Augusta to Chattanooga and beyond.

The north-south road was generally known as the "Peachtree Trail" or "Ridge Road". It came into Hall County from the Northeast and closely followed present day Route 13. It left Hall County in the Hog Mountain area, near Flowery Branch.

The east-west road went through Athens and entered Hall County near Chestnut Mountain. This was referred to as the "Cherokee Trading Path," and after it became a wagon road about 1802, as the "Federal Road".

These two superhighways of the frontier crossed near Young's Tavern, very close to the new Atlanta Falcon's football complex. Many were not roads at all, but four-foot wide pack-train and post-rider paths. Their exact location is now shadowy, but the Indians, and the wild animals before them, selected their routes well, for most of today's major Hall County roads closely follow one or the other of those seven original trails.

New Year's Ice Storm Circa 1900

I've admittedly been holding back on this one. I kind of wanted all the millennium foolishness to get behind us ... to get reasonably past New Year's 2000 before reporting what the weather looked like in the South on January 1, 1900. Actually, a cold wave had hit most of the eastern part of the United States, but it was the South that took the greatest damage ... and Gainesville was pretty well shut down.

To tell you how bad it was, the front page of the New York Times had several stories about the 1900 New Year's storm. It reported Macon, Georgia, had snow that was "fully six inches on the level." The Macon story reported that "the heaviest snowstorm within the memory of the oldest inhabitants" had fallen that day. And Savannah had snow and sleet. In Charleston, snow fell most of the day, and then it turned into an ice storm. One story was headed "Frozen to Death In Georgia" and told the story of a lumber mill hand in Stillman, Georgia, who was found frozen to death in the justice court room.

After all the hullabaloo we had about the millennium, can you imagine what the media would have said if that kind of storm had hit us on January 1, 2000?

✲ ✲ ✲

The Tornado of 1936

It was April 6, 1936, and it was what one would call a "muggy" day. Overcast. Dreary. Some said it not only was dark for the time of day, but also had a greenish cast. Even so, Gainesville was waking up as usual; people were going to work; kids were on their way to school. And then, at about the eight o'clock hour, came the great noise. Some said it sounded like a dozen freight trains travelling at full speed, right over you. There was no warning, just chaos, as windows blew out, walls tumbled, and all kinds of things – large and small – were flying through the air. Then quiet, and fires began where red-hot coals from coal-burning stoves were like roving torches, and sparks from downed electric wires lit splintered lumber.

At that time, in 1936, it was the most devastating tornado in American history. Actually, it was three tornadoes. The first missed Gainesville itself, but did severe damage to New Holland mill, on the north edge of town. The real damage, however, was done by twin tornadoes that converged right on top of the Gainesville square ... one approached coming up-hill along Dawsonville

Highway, and the other moved in from the Old Atlanta highway.

There is still debate about how many were killed and injured, but shortly after the tornado the count was 213 killed, and more than 900 seriously injured. It only took three minutes for the monster storm to pass through Gainesville and move on, but in that brief span of time, more than 100 homes that today would qualify for the National Register of Historic Homes were destroyed.

Remembering the Tornado of 1936

The Gainesville tornado of 1936 was, at that time, the most destructive tornado in American history. More than 200 people were killed, and more than 900 injured to the point they needed physical care. Actually, two tornadoes converged squarely on top of the Gainesville square. They hit at about 8 a.m., and only took three minutes to travel almost one mile.

The school was only one block off the square. Some children were already there, others on the way. It was described as turning black as midnight, and sounding like a thousand locomotives moving through. Trees were uprooted, cars blown over, homes moved off their foundations. The brick walls of Gainesville High withstood the blast, but windows were blown out, doors blown in. The pictures show it was a mess, looking like a war torn city.

C. J. Cheeves was Superintendent of Schools at the time, and in the quiet that followed, he was walking through the debris in the hallways, going room to room, finding kids, and hoping for the best. As he stepped into one classroom, covered with glass shards and split lumber, Clifford Martin (yes, the one who now owns Martin Furniture) stuck his head up from under the teacher's desk, where he had taken refuge, and said: "Mr. Cheeves, does this mean we won't have to take exams today?"

✲ ✲ ✲

The First Car Crash In Banks County

We had some ice on the roads the other day, and sure enough we had some fender benders ... and it brought to mind one of my favorite bits of history about the arrival of automobiles in Northeast Georgia. It was about 1910 ... give or take a few years ... and there was considerable excitement in Banks County, and especially in Maysville. You see, automobiles were catching the fancy of all America and Banks County had two of the popular but noisy monsters. Not just one, but two.

Boone Suddath had one and "Stig" Morris the other, and these two cars were the talk of the town. For some people they were merely a curiosity. For others they were proof positive that Banks County was as modern as anybody, anywhere ... sort of like having a telephone or electricity. For most, however, cars were considered a nuisance for they cut ruts in roads in wet weather, blew up huge clouds of dust in dry times, and scared the be-geebies out of horses in any kind of weather ... and that was a time when horses were the primary mode of transportation for most folks.

But it wasn't the arrival of the new cars that had the whole community talking and laughing this particular time. It was the fact that Boone Suddath and "Stig" Morris, driving their new-fangled cars just outside Maysville – one going East, the other West –had just had a head-on collision. Got the picture? There were only two cars in all of Banks County, and they had just had a colossal wreck. I think it is fair to say it took a few years for Northeast Georgia to get accustomed to automobiles.

✲ ✲ ✲

Gainesville Street Railroad Posts Summer Schedule

It was July 1886, and the Gainesville Street Railroad had just posted its summer schedule. At that time, Gainesville's trolley cars were pulled by horses, and they were noted for being on time. In fact, residents insisted they stuck to their schedule so precisely that you could "set your clock by them." The weekday morning schedule went this way:

Leave the square for the depot at 6:40, 8:30, 10:03, 11:05 and `12:00

Leave depot for public square at 7:04, 8:45, 10:36, 11:35, and 12:25

Leave Gower Springs for public square at 9:35, 11:30 and 12:30

The afternoon schedule was similar, with the last trips leaving at 7:30, except for a final car from the depot to the square which left at 8:30. And what about Sundays? The printed schedule had one of those old-fashioned hands pointing to special type that stated: "Cars run to and from church on Sundays."

The fare between the public square and depot was five cents; between the public square and Gower Springs, 5 cents; and a complete round trip could be had for 15 cents. There was one extra: baggage cost from 15 to 25 cents, depending on the amount being carried.

It was signed by R. E. Green, proprietor.

Gainesville Had Public Transportation A Century Ago

I was amused the other day at a story in the local paper that referred to the "Red Rabbit" as Gainesville's FIRST public transportation system. The fact is Gainesville had a rather complete street trolley system more than 100 years ago. In the late 1800s, a private enterprise got an okay from the city to run tracks along the then-unpaved streets, then acquired horse-drawn trolleys, and started a profit-making public transportation system. This new transportation system was a major factor in bringing electricity to Gainesville. It was the need for power for the trolleys and lights for homes and businesses that launched one of Georgia's first hydroelectric power plants after Dunlap Dam was built across the Chatahoochee, backing up Lake Warner.

Gainesville's public transportation system, circa 1900, ran from Riverside Military Academy along Riverside Drive, right by my window on Green Street to the square, and then down Main Street to the Railroad station. Another line was added going to New Holland, and still later there was a bus line to Chicopee.

✲ ✲ ✲

Airline Service for Gainesville?

It was 1950, and Gainesville's Chamber of Commerce was busy. The established business leaders were promoting the town, and the young tigers who had recently returned from World War II were in the midst of things. Many felt they had lost a few years from their careers, and were willing to work long and hard to make up for that lost time.

Anyway, one of the major projects was to try and get regular, scheduled airline service for Gainesville. After all, we had a good airport ... the field and tower built here by the Navy during the War. And a lot of Southern cities similar to ours had airline service - towns like Anniston, in Alabama, and Hattiesburg, in Mississippi. The bigger four-engine commercial airliners flew the long routes to the big cities, but it was the workhorse that served the smaller cities of America - the magnificent old DC-3 - and if a town was really going to get ahead in this brave new world, it flat-out needed airline service.

The Chamber of Commerce petitioned the Aeronautics Board for a stop in Gainesville between Charlotte and Atlanta, pointing out that we were the largest city in Northeast Georgia, with a metropolitan population of 22,000 people.

☆ ☆ ☆

The Coming of Buford Dam

There was growing concern in Gainesville in 1949 about this dam that apparently was going to be built down the river near Buford. When the Grand Jury wanted more facts, it came out hat 539 Hall County farms would be covered by the new lake. Only three bridges would be built to replace 16 being covered. About 25,000 of the 45,000 acres in the reservoir were to be in Hall County. To quote the Gainesville News: "An Enabling Act passed by Congress several years ago allows the government to flood an area by merely giving property owners notice that a dam is going to be constructed ... and to settle with the owners at the leisure of the government." This was getting serious.

Atlanta had been promoting the dam and lake, for flood control reasons, they said, so the local Chamber of Commerce invited the Honorable. Elbert Tuttle, President of the Atlanta Chamber, to be the featured speaker at its 40th Annual Banquet. The whole theme of his talk that night was that the dam would be good, and that Atlanta would assist with any problems it might cause in Hall County.

It had not been named Lake Lanier yet ... but that lake was the main topic of conversation in all Hall County in 1949.

✲ ✲ ✲

Gainesville's Springs and Water, Water Everywhere

The present-day flap with Alabama and Florida about the use of water from the Chattahoochee River is just one more chapter of a longstanding saga of water and its impact on our area.

Early trading roads into the southern frontier came through Gainesville, and there were two main reasons. First, travelers could cross the Chattahoochee River nearby, and second, there were at least seven major springs in the area that made ideal camping spots.

During the late 1800s, the springs of Gainesville gained a widespread reputation for their health-giving power. Each spring had its own unique qualities. People from the coastal areas came here to get away from "the fever" (malaria) and to partake of the pure water and the cool mountain air.

Gainesville was one of the first towns in the area to have a public water supply. Water rates in the early 1900s ran 80 cents a month for a residence housing a family up to five people, and a dime more for each person above five,. If you watered a horse, mule or cow, that also cost you a dime an animal. But if you had a bath tub, that was serious – that would cost you 40 cents a month. Do you reckon the city would cut back on our water rates today if we cut back on our bathing?

✲ ✲ ✲

Alabama Owns No Part of the Chattahoochee River

We keep wondering what Alabama is doing in the water wars ... you know, the debate between Georgia, Florida, and Alabama about how the water in the Chatahoochee River is to be used. The reason Alabama should not be in the discussion is because the state line between Georgia and Alabama is on the West bank of that great river. The west bank.

What brought this to mind was a thing I found in Joe Cook's book about the Chattahoochee called "River Song." Says Cook,

"Although no permanent white settlements existed along the Chattahoochee at the time, Georgians James

Jackson, Abraham Baldwin, and John Milledge knew that whatever authority controlled the river would also control commerce. River travel was the swiftest means of transport, and hydropower was essential to any industrial endeavor. With this point in mind, the statesmen claimed the Chattahoochee for Georgia and set the (Georgia) boundary as "running thence up the said River Chattahoochee and along the western bank thereof." That's what they said: the Western bank thereof. So, Alabama owns no part of the Chattahoochee River and should have no part of our current river wars."

All that took place in the early 1800s when the state of Georgia traded its land west of the Chattahoochee to the United States government in exchange for the land in North Georgia claimed by the Cherokee Indians. There's an irony to all this, though. It was the University of Alabama Press, and not the University of Georgia Press, that published "River Song," Joe Cook's magnificent book about the Chattahoochee River.

The Lure of The Blue Ridge Mountains

You haven't lived till you sit on a porch on a Blue Ridge Mountain and experience a summer storm. At times in the mountains it gets as stifling hot as in flatlands ... late afternoon temperature near 90 degrees, no breeze. At times like this you know a storm is brewing. You watch as a white-out occurs between you and Chimney Mountain, across the valley. Rain is on its way.

A light breeze begins, the temperature begins to drop, and for a half hour or so it is conversation quiet. Then in the distance you hear thunder, the kind Grandmother Ruth referred to as "God moving the furniture around upstairs." It takes a while before the first raindrops hit ... then the wind ... and more thunder, close by.

Then comes the fun, the activity that sends the timid off the porch and inside. Gusts of wind, not the kind that merely makes the leaves stir, but wind that makes the tall trees sway to and fro, accompanied by blasts of thunder close by that rattle the dishes in the kitchen cabinet. That's when bolts of lightning pick a tall tree, and you hope it won't follow a root to where you are. It's interesting ... when lightning hits close by, the static electricity will make the hair on your arms, or even the hair on your head, stand up. Then comes the rain ... a true rainstorm ... a half inch or so in a very short time. As it passes, you can see lightning dance along the ridge called Grimes Nose.

Suddenly it is quiet again. The last light of day reflects off the standing puddles blown on the porch. It is sweater-cool. Quiet. And somewhere down the mountain, comes the lonely hoot of an owl.

☆ ☆ ☆

The Legend of Sautee and Nacoochee

Many pre-history legends of the Indian tribes of Northeast Georgia can be found, but none is more enduring than the legend of Sautee and Nacoochee. The Cherokees controlled much of the mountains, and the valley land, and they often clashed with the Chickasaws. At one point the Chickasaws asked the Cherokees if they could peacefully cross Cherokee territory. The request was granted, so long as the Chickasaw band stayed on the Unicoi Trail, and only stopped at designated places.

One of the camping spots was where two beautiful valleys merge, at the location of the Great White Oak. As the Chickasaws rested, a number of Cherokees slipped close to the camp to get a look at their traditional foe. One was Nacoochee, a teenage daughter of Chief Wahoo, and as she peered at the dreaded Chickasaws, she spotted one particularly handsome young man. Their eyes met. It was Sautee, the son of the Chickasaw Chief. That night they met under the Great White Oak and slipped off together. Chief Wahoo was livid; he ordered that Sautee be thrown from the rock face of Yonah Mountain, and that Nacoochee be taken to watch the execution. Just before Sautee was to be thrown from the cliff, Nacoochee broke free and ran to him, and they jumped to their death together. A distraught Chief Wahoo had them buried together under the Great White Oak, naming one valley Sautee and the other Nacoochee. The Indian names for these two valleys remain to this day.

✲ ✲ ✲

Welcome to the Beauty of Northeast Georgia

If you haven't taken a ride in the mountains or a cruise on Lake Lanier lately, may I suggest you do so this month? Just go out and see the Mountain Laurel. It is in full bloom, and our mountains are covered, and that, along with the pink-white clusters along the shores of Lake Lanier, remind one that this, too, is mountain country. 'Midst all the negative news we are constantly bombarded with out of Washington, the beauty makes it abundantly clear we have a lot of blessings in our lives.

For instance, have you noticed the local news lately about the number of people being honored for their good works ... presentations by the Jaycees and recognition by the Hearts of Gold group. The presentation of $15,000 in scholarship money by the local Kiwanis Club to the top winners in their annual high school competition for achievements in visual art, writing, and the performing arts, and the stunning level of talent these students presented. And our athletic teams ... all showing that we have a great generation of people coming along. Beauty, they say, is in the eye of the beholder, and I ask you: how can you possibly look at all the good that is blooming in our area right now and not see beauty?

Look at the economy. There are headlines saying bad things are happening in the economy, but here at home you are seeing Help Wanted signs, and the Dow just went sailing past 13,000 without even looking back. And there is the war. We hear charges out of Washington that our troops have lost the war, but we know our troops and we proudly stand on their side. The headlines out of Washington also insist the entire world now sees us as ugly Americans, and yet the French ... the French of all people ... have just elected a new President who is an uncompromising pro-American conservative. And I ask you, where in the world is there a place more beautiful than right here, right now?

CHAPTER 2: From Whence Did They Come, These Mountain Folk?

The history of Georgia dates back to 1733, when King George II granted a charter for a new colony on coastal America, and it was named Georgia for that King. Its port of entry was Savannah. Through treaties with the Indians, settlement of Georgia pushed inland, first covering the coastal area and then the Piedmont belt, including Augusta up the Savannah River.

During the American Revolutionary War, mountainous Northeast Georgia appeared on maps as Cherokee territory, and the Indians sided with the British. At the end of the war much of the property owned by English Loyalists was confiscated by Americans, and Georgians insisted the Indian land should be treated the same way since Indians had actually killed American frontier families.

The new United States government followed English law, and insisted the Americans could not claim title to Indian territory until a treaty was signed with the Indian tribes that were affected. Then, in 1777, during the Revolutionary War, the Cession of 1773 was agreed to by Indians, and the Northeast Georgia land rush was officially underway.

The Indians rebelled at the onrush of white settlers, and battles broke out, lasting until 1785 when the Treaty of Hopewell brought peace once more. In 1790, when the first United States census was taken, the former Indian territory showed a population of 31,000 people (not including Indians, of course). Most of the new settlers were small farmers from the Carolinas or Virginia who saw the opportunity to get fertile land along the river "bottoms." Migrants from the coastal areas were relatively few.

These first settlers were all steeped in the culture of Europe. And yes, as we shall see later, the Scotch-Irish Presbyterians brought with them an ability to make fine whiskey.

There was a strong Presbyterian culture among those first settlers, soon to give way to Methodist and Baptist. Along the coast, Episcopal churches remained from the early English settlers, many who were loyalists during the Revolutionary War and returned to England when the war ended.

In 1802 the United States government made an agreement with Georgia to the effect that "... all Indian titles within the territory of the state (would be) extinguished as soon as it should become practicable." Then in 1803, the United States, with the approval of Indian tribes, began construction of the "Federal Road" from present-day Flowery Branch to Rossville (just South of Chattanooga), a road that went through the heart of Indian mountain land.

The Unicoi Turnpike was delayed by the buildup to the War of 1812, but was cleared in 1813, providing another major artery into the mountains.

Things were happening fast in North Georgia, and the Compact of 1812 cleared the way for more settlement in the mountains. The Compact of 1812 was an agreement between the state of Georgia and the United States government in which Georgia got clear title to all lands in its present-day boundaries, and the United States got Alabama, Mississippi and lands west. (Some say trading off Alabama and Mississippi was one of Georgia's greatest achievements – just kidding.)

In order to stifle land speculation, Georgia established Land Lotteries which remained in effect from 1805 until 1832, and two of those lotteries covered former Cherokee lands in Northeast Georgia, in 1820 and 1832. The trickle of frontier settlers seeking land became a flood as settlers poured into Northeast Georgia.

The names on land records and in cemeteries tell "from whence they came." Scotch-Irish, English, some German. These were hardworking "common folk," neither royalty nor wealthy. They were Protestant, and had risked everything they had – including their lives – to live and worship in freedom. Their word was their bond, and they were highly distrustful of government power. And yet ... when war came, they were among the first to volunteer.

✲ ✲ ✲

Lyman Hall - Who Was He?

We refer to this as Hall County, and many of us know it was named for Dr. Lyman Hall, one of Georgia's three signers of the Declaration of Independence. But what else do we know about that good man?

Dr. Lyman Hall was born in 1724 in Wallingford, Connecticut, and in 1742 graduated from Yale. Three years later, he became a Congregational minister. That didn't work out, however. So three years later, he turned his attention to teaching and medicine. He came South, living first with a group of roaming Puritans, then acquiring land along the Georgia coast and practicing medicine in Savannah. He became well-known and respected; he and two others (Button Gwinnett and George Walton) represented Georgia in the Continental Congress, and as an outgrowth of this service, signed the Declaration of Independence.

In 1778, the British landed on the coast of Georgia, and confiscated everything Lyman Hall had. They destroyed his plantation and burned his home in Sunbury. He fled and survived personally, if not financially, and after the Revolutionary War ended, he became one of the early governors of Georgia. It was in 1818 ...28 years after his death ...that the legislature honored Lyman Hall by naming a new frontier county for him ... Hall County.

☼ ☼ ☼

Hall County Is Formed in 1818

The year was 1818, and the State of Georgia was getting ready to hold a lottery ... this lottery was to award frontier farms to land-hungry settlers. Today's Hall County was part of the frontier then, and already many settlers had moved into the territory.

The Georgia Legislature, fully expecting a rush of people when the lottery was held in 1820, formed a new county. It was carved partly from Franklin County and partly from Jackson County. Basically, they did a pretty good job, for early maps show a Hall County with nearly the same shape and size as we see today.

But there were a number of small refinements to be made as the exact location of county lines were determined. In 1819, the lines between Hall and Gwinnett, and Hall and Habersham were settled. Cherokee County got a chunk of Hall in 1831, and Hall got a lot of land back from Habersham in 1845. Hall and Lumpkin drew a new line in 1852; Hall and Banks in 1859.

Back to 1818, when Hall County was first laid out .... The decision was made to name the new frontier county for Lyman Hall, one of Georgia's three signers of the Declaration of Independence.

☼ ☼ ☼

Gainesville Is Named for General Edmund Pendleton Gaines

Gainesville was named for General Edmund Pendleton Gaines, a crusty-tough military man who made his mark on the American frontier. Apparently, he was highly admired by his troops, for it was on their recommendation that he was honored by having a town named for him.

General Gaines lived from 1777 to 1849, entered the Army at age 17, was commissioned at 22, and rose rapidly to the rank of Major General in the War of 1812. In 1815, he was given command of the Southern Division, and became known as one of the few commanders who felt sympathy for the plight of the Indians. In 1825, he was chosen to arbitrate a dispute between the Creek Indians and Georgia Governor George Troop, and he and Troop clashed angrily and often. Gaines and General Winfield Scott also disagreed openly.

One biographer, Jane B. Peacock, said General Gaines was a "... strong-willed and irascible commander who moved decisively without waiting for approval from his superiors ..." But she also said he was a "... capable and resourceful commander during the Creek uprisings in Georgia ...", and she went on to say he was "... never a timid leader."

In 1821, his men and the Georgia Legislature honored General Edmund Pendleton Gaines by naming a frontier town for him: Gainesville, Georgia.

✲ ✲ ✲

The Great (Philadelphia) Wagon Road

Parke Rouse Jr. in his book *The Great Wagon Road*, says "the Warriors path became the principal highway of the colonial back country." To quote:

"The endless procession of new settlers, Indian traders, soldiers, and missionaries swelled as the Revolution approached. 'In the last 16 years of the colonial era', wrote the historian Carl Bridenbaugh, 'southbound traffic along the Great Philadelphia Wagon Road was numbered in tens of thousands; it was the most heavily traveled road in all America and must have had more vehicles jolting along its rough and tortuous way than all other main roads put together.'"

✲ ✲ ✲

Hall County's First White Settlers

We tend to think of all Georgia getting started when Oglethorpe founded Savannah, but it wasn't until the 1780s, after the American Revolution, that Northeast Georgia got its first white settlers. Franklin County, part of present day Northeast Georgia, had been carved out of the frontier and opened up for settlement under the "headright" system.

One of the first areas to be settled in today's Hall County was a community called "Stonethrow," near present-day Gillsville. Stonethrow also was near War Hill, so-called because of a major battle fought between the Creek and Cherokee Indians to determine who had exclusive right to the old Lacoda Trail, the principal route between Augusta and Toccoa.

War Hill had another distinction that helped draw settlers to it ... it was the site of a blockhouse, a rugged log fort, built by the State of Georgia to protect settlers from the Indians who still lived in the territory and occasionally went on a rampage. With the blockhouse nearby in case of trouble, settlers began to move into Indian territory that later became Hall County. It was because of a treaty with the Cherokee Indians in 1817 that Hall County was officially formed and surveyed for distribution to new settlers. And in 1818, Hall County was made official.

✲ ✲ ✲

A Lot of Settlers Came Through Jackson County

The other day, I was digging out some historical information about how Hall County was originally settled. I knew the pioneers who first came here to stay had come from the East, across Franklin and Jackson Counties, and I was skimming through an old book called *Historical Collections of Georgia* dated in 1854. And deep into the book, on page 499, in fact, I found a sketch of Jackson County. It starts out by stating, "This county was formed in 1796; part set off as Clarke (in) 1801; part added to Madison, 1811; part to Walton, Gwinnett, and Hall, 1818."

So, if my math is correct, Jackson County was founded some 22 years before Hall County. The report says, and I quote here: "It was called after General James Jackson"" – and I will admit I don't know who General James Jackson was.

The 1854 report says "Jefferson is the seat of justice, situated on the wasters of the Oconee River, distant from Milledgeville 87 miles." At that time, Milledgeville was, of course, the capital of Georgia, and everybody measured everything from Milledgeville. Jefferson was made the county seat in 1806 and incorporated in 1812.

One comment was interesting. "Much of the soil of this county is unproductive," the book states, "although there are some good lands on the branches of the Oconee." This was the primary reason settlers gravitated to the Coastal area of Georgia and the Piedmont before coming to the hills and mountains of Northeast Georgia. Those areas had better farming land, and most settlers were looking for good farming conditions.

Georgia's First Lotteries: Pay If You Take It

Every night when you turn on television, you hear about Georgia's legalized lotteries. What they are doing is telling you who won, knowing full well most of the people who put their money down have already lost.

Well, Georgia's first lotteries were different. Back in the early 1800's, when treaties were being signed with the Indians, and Georgia was being opened up for settlement, the State of Georgia decided the fairest way to distribute the land was to hold a Land Lottery. The first Georgia Land Lottery set a precedent. Any resident of Georgia – and you had to be a resident of Georgia to participate - could put his name in the lottery. At that time, the registration was in Milledgeville, then Georgia's state capital, so more people from middle Georgia registered than from other parts of the state.

If your name was drawn, it was for a specific piece of land. Rich bottom land, great. A rocky mountain side, tough. The fee was the same for each: $18. But unlike today's lottery, if you didn't want your prize, you didn't have to take it, and you didn't have to pay. Some paid and took their land. Some paid and then sold it. If you didn't win, or if you didn't accept your winnings, you didn't pay money to the lottery.

✲ ✲ ✲

1820-1830: Hall County's Population Doubled

With the Census Bureau's announcement of official population numbers for the year 2000, there continues to be a great deal of conversation about how fast Hall County is growing. But if you figure by percentages, this county has grown faster at some times in its history, and in some decades has actually seen its population decline dramatically.

In 1820, for instance, only two years after Hall County was incorporated, the census showed a population of 5,086. Ten years later, in 1830, the census showed Hall County had 11,748. What happened, of course, was that Gold had been discovered in North Georgia, and Gainesville was the transportation and supply center for the Gold Rush. It was a boom town, but that didn't last. By 1840, as the intensity of the Gold Rush subsided, Hall County's population had shrunk from a peak of about 12,000 and the census reported only 7,875 people ... a loss of more than 30 percent. Hall County grew slowly after that, and it wasn't until after the War Between the States that it again reached the 12,000 level. In the 1880s and 1890s, Hall County grew steadily, and in the census of 1900 (100 years ago), Hall County topped a population of 20,000.

✲ ✲ ✲

Memories of Gainesville in the 1830's

It was in 1888 that William Park, then editor of the *Sandersville Herald* and the *Georgian*, came to Gainesville for a Press Association meeting, and recorded some of his memories of growing up in Hall County.

"In those olden days, the Hon. Mark A. Cooper lived here, and went to the Indian War as an officer in 1836. I well remember the muster and parading of the militia, when volunteers were called for, and executive orders were read by Maj. Reuben Thornton. ... During this campaign, Maj. Cooper was shot in the hand. ..."

Another memory from Mr. Park, "The old Methodist Church was also a place filled with pleasant memories. I had often heard my father speak of himself and others buying the old wooden Court House that in 1833 stood on the square, and moving it down to the present site for a Methodist Church building."

And a memory of the Gainesville square in the 1830's: "Disastrous fires and the tooth of time have made many changes in a half century. The old Mansion House kept by Maj. Reuben Thornton has been supplanted by the splendid Arlington (Hotel), and the elegant Hudson (Hotel) now replaces the old hotel kept in the long ago by Ripley and then by Sledge. ... (and) The James Law Building has given way to Stringer's Opera."

✲ ✲ ✲

Georgia Cracker Came From Frontier Wagoners

You don't hear the term "Georgia Cracker" much any more, but there was a time in the early history of our state when that was our most popular nickname. It was kept alive after our frontier days (after the 1800s, let's say) by the old Atlanta Crackers, Atlanta's baseball team before we went Big League and inherited the Braves name from Milwaukee.

The term Cracker came from the great frontier wagon drivers. Cities along the coast got their supplies by ship, but inland towns had to rely on freight wagons ... monstrous things usually pulled by at least six and often more horses. John Lambert, an Englishman, described the wagoners this way in 1814, "These wagoners are familiarly called crackers (from the cracking of their whips, I suppose) ... The wagoner constantly rides on one of the shaft horses, and with a long whip guides the leaders. ..."

Georgia's whip-cracking wagoners were among the best at navigating the treacherous frontier roads, and in time all Georgians came to be called "Georgia Crackers."

✲ ✲ ✲

The Old Federal Road and Flowery Branch

It was 1805, and there was a good deal of excitement in the area that would soon become Southern Hall County, the area that includes Flowery Branch. The United States Government had negotiated and finalized a treaty with the Cherokee Indian Nation to build a road through their territory, and the jumping off place into Indian country was in the vicinity of Flowery Branch.

Actually, the route that the Federal Road would traverse was not new. It was an old Indian trading route called the "Middle Cherokee Path," and it went from the gateway in Augusta to Athens, then to Flowery

Branch, and into the mountainous Cherokee Country, and then on to Ross Landing ...the site of Rossville, adjacent to Chattanooga. It was one of the trails identified by Hemperly in his book, *Historic Indian Trails of Georgia.*

The Old Federal Road was considered tremendously important, for it opened up "over the mountain" America to Charleston and Savannah, the all-season seaports of the American South, and thus to the markets of the world.

Not only could white traders now travel that route without being attacked by Indians, but the Army would clear it for wagons.

✲ ✲ ✲

Young's Tavern Preceded The Falcons

It has always intrigued me how certain locations, even specific small pieces of land, show up in history time and again but for different reasons. For instance, I rode by the Atlanta Falcons' complex the other day, and it struck me how proud I am of this year's Falcon football team and how pleased I am that their headquarters is located right here in Hall County. It hasn't been many years ago that I was at an event in which one of our major industries chose nearby land to locate the Wrigley plant. Both made history of a different sort.

And then I spotted the small cemetery right across the road from the entrance to the Falcon's complex, and it struck me: this was the location of Young's Tavern, and its history goes back at least to 1800, maybe further. Young's Tavern was a well-known stopping-place in those days. Land to the west of that spot was officially Cherokee Indian country. The first road to officially cross that Indian territory on the way to Rossville (now Chattanooga) was the Old Federal Road, which started at the curve near where one enters the Wrigley plant. The road opened in 1805, and Young's Tavern was sort of the jumping-off place.

Robert Young, the son of a Revolutionary soldier, had a 1,200 acre farm here and was a leading pioneer citizen. But he was primarily known for the 12-room log home called Young's Tavern, where frontier travelers on the Federal Road frequently stopped for lodging. It is known that Andrew Jackson ... fondly known as Old Hickory ... stayed there at times, and it is recorded that Jackson, along with his staff and two companies of militia, spent a night there on their way to the Seminole campaign in 1818.

I personally think it is appropriate that the Falcons are writing a whole new chapter in the history of that hallowed ground, and I've got an idea that Robert Young and Andrew Jackson and Chief Vann and a bunch of others would be proud that the history and the heritage is being continued.

✲ ✲ ✲

Census of the Cherokees

The year was 1835, and a special census was underway in North Georgia. It was in late October of that year that it became apparent Cherokee Indians would be required to remove themselves from North Georgia, and move west of the Mississippi River.

Anticipating this, Major Benjamin F. Currey, Superintendent of Cherokee immigration, appointed two census takers to enumerate the Cherokees scattered through the eleven mountain counties created in 1832-33 from the Cherokee Nation surveys. These census takers made house calls throughout the frontier area, taking an interpreter with them, and the amazing thing is ... they finished the census in about three months, mostly in winter, traveling on horseback. Reportedly, the census was thorough and accurate.

The census enumerators asked some rather personal questions, too, for the count was divided between full-blood and mixed-blood Cherokees. However, anyone with Indian blood would be required to go to Oklahoma.

It has always amazed me how ACCURATE land surveyors, map-makers, and census takers were in frontier America. They were good.

✲ ✲ ✲

Cherokee Nation Split on Indian Removal Treaty

The year was 1830, and there was a restlessness among the Cherokee Indians in North Georgia. Two rival parties had developed among the tribe, divided on the issue of leaving to make way for the westward migration of Europeans entering the area,

The National Party, which wanted to stay in Georgia, was headed by Principal Chief John Ross, an eighth-blood Cherokee who had become a major planter. The Pro-Treaty Party was headed by Major Ridge, the full-blood speaker of the Cherokee Council.

Andrew Jackson was in Washington and Wilson Lumpkin was governor of Georgia. Both insisted the Cherokees had agreed to move west and should do so. In Washington, some representatives from other parts of the U. S. took the side of Ross, while, for the most part, Southerners supported Ridge. When a vote came in Congress, the Indian Removal Bill barely passed, but once passed, it became obvious that all Cherokees would be required to leave Georgia. It was a time of division among the Cherokees, with those following Ross wanting to stay and those following Ridge agreeing to go. It was Ridge who signed the treaty with the United States.

✲ ✲ ✲

When Tracing Ancestors, Be Prepared For Surprises

For those of you who are into genealogy - that is, tracing your ancestors - let me suggest you read an article in the current edition of the magazine, *The North Georgia Journal*. The name of the article is "Grandpa Was an Outlaw," written by Anne Dismukes Amerson, and it tells the story of one Jeff Anderson who was the leader of a notorious band of outlaws that terrorized Lumpkin County during the U. S. Civil War.

It seems the Anderson family knew their outlaw ancestor left Georgia for Texas and never married and never returned to these parts. But those of you who are researching your ancestors know there is no greater challenge in the world than one of your own in the missing column. And there is no greater surprise than to find one of your ancestors was a somewhat unsavory character and ended up in your own backyard.

It seems Jimmy Anderson, who is the postmaster at Dahlonega and carries the same last name as Jeff Anderson the outlaw, was contacted one day by Bill Smyth, a grandson of Thomas Jefferson Anderson. Smyth had good reason to believe Jeff Anderson, the outlaw, might be the same as his Thomas Jefferson Anderson. But then there were some doubts. I won't tell you where it ends up. You go read the story.

But I will tell you this "North Georgia Journal" article is two stories in one. First, it is a fascinating glimpse of

Northeast Georgia during the Civil War and of the happenings on the home front. And second, it provides a delightful glimpse of the tangled web people often get trapped in when hunting information about their forebears.

✲ ✲ ✲

Riding A Wagon To Cleveland in 1867

John Muir, the conservationist, was walking a road near Yonah Mountain in 1867 and described his fellow travelers: "Traveled in the wake of three poor but merry mountaineers - an old woman, a young woman, and a young man – who sat, leaned, and lay in the box of a shackly wagon that seemed to be held together by spiritualism, and was kept in agitation by a very large and a very small mule.

In going down hill, the looseness of the harness and the joints of the wagon allowed the mules to back nearly out of site beneath the box, and the three who occupied it were slid against the front boards in a heap over the mules' ears. Before they could unravel their limbs from this unmannerly and impolite disorder, a new ridge in the road frequently tilted them with a swish and a bump against the boards in a mixing that was still more grotesque.

"I expected to see man, women, and mules mingled in piebald ruin at the bottom of some rocky hollow, but they seemed to have confidence in the back board and front board of the wagon box. So they continued to slide comfortably up and down, from end to end, in slippery obedience to the law of gravitation, as the grades demanded. ... The old lady, through all the vicissitudes of the transportation, held a boquet of French Marigolds."

☆ ☆ ☆

The Welcome Mat Is Out – 1888

In 1888, Gainesville produced a brochure (actually a 60-page booklet) urging people to come to Northeast Georgia. From its preface, "The object of this pamphlet is to present the attractions of Gainesville and the country tributary to it to all seeking homes, to tourists seeking pleasure, to invalids seeking health, and to men of enterprise seeking new fields for investment. (This brochure) is published by the citizens of Gainesville, who hereby extend to all comers 'a cordial welcome'".

"The score of counties comprising Northeast Georgia are raised on a plateau considerably above the remainder of the State, with an average elevation of from 1,200 to 2,000 feet above tide-water." It speaks of the area's "perfect climate, inspiring scenery, and curative mineral waters." The brochure goes beyond merely welcoming newcomers – it flatly states that they are wanted. "No portion of the State for the past few years has been more noted for its enterprise or for the steady influx of population. And yet it is but a virgin field – full of opportunities for all who come – with the comforts of an old country and all the inspiring possibilities of a new."

That was Gainesville, promoting all of Northeast Georgia in 1888.

✲ ✲ ✲

William Jennings Bryan Comes to Gainesville

The year was 1899, and Gainesville was holding a Chautauqua - of those cultural events in which noted people came and spoke ... and one of the headliners this particular year was the famed orator William Jennings Bryan. Bryan had run for President on the Democratic ticket in 1896 and had lost, but he was highly popular in Democrat-controlled North Georgia.

The local paper described his arrival this way, "As Mr. Bryan alighted from the train the band struck up a lively air and as he was escorted to the carriage with Governor Candler the great crowd almost yelled itself hoarse. The procession of carriages was soon formed and Mr. Bryan was driven up Main Street, around the public square, out Washington Street to the Seminary where he was assigned a room at Yonah Hall..."

And when he spoke, the paper stated: "There was such a gathering of the people as seldom comes together in this delightful mountain town ... . From every direction the people came .... He was applauded and cheered, and cheered and applauded."

✲ ✲ ✲

Famous People Have Visited Hall County

It's interesting to note the famous political leaders who have visited Hall County through the years, and every now and then I run across a surprise ... someone I had no idea ever came our way.

Most of us have heard that President Andrew Jackson spent time in South Hall County, at Young's Tavern, which was located adjacent to the present-day Atlanta Falcons complex. And most are aware that President Woodrow Wilson lived in Gainesville a while, practiced law here, and that one of his daughters was born here. And in more recent times, Gainesville has hosted Presidents Franklin D. Roosevelt, Lyndon B. Johnson, Jimmy Carter, and George Bush; and candidates Bob Dole and Phil Gramm.

But I ran into another one the other day in the book *The History of Hall County*. It is from a 1904 news clipping, and here's what it says:

"Mrs. James A. Garfield, widow of President Garfield, arrived in Gainesville Tuesday afternoon from Washington City to be the guest for a few days of her cousin, Capt. A. Rudolph, on Green Street. ... Mrs. Garfield is 72 years of age, but does not look more than 50. She is pleasant socially, bright and interesting intellectually, and maintains an unusual interest in matters political."

✲ ✲ ✲

Promotion By Outside "Friends in High Places." Gainesville and all Northeast Georgia have always had "friends in high places" who spoke favorably of the region.

In 1829, one Adiel Sherwood wrote a travel book, published in Philadelphia, called the *Gazetteer of the State of Georgia*. The author spoke highly of Clarkesville, Clayton and Gainesville, and said "there is no purer water, nor any healthier climate on the globe. In the months of August, September & October, the bilious fever obtains in the lower and middle sections of the state."

In 1878, the Piedmont Air-Line Railroad published a 36-page *Guide To Health and Pleasure Resorts on the Piedmont Air Line Route – More especially Summer Resorts of North-East Georgia*, and in it promoted Gainesville as the railroad center of mountainous Northeast Georgia. It predicted that Gainesville "is destined to become the leading summer resort of the South, as it is in the very center of all the great healing springs, and Gold Region. And is the most convenient point from which to reach them."

✲ ✲ ✲

CHAPTER 3 - Making a Living And "Makin' Do"

Banker Paul Seals almost always got a laugh when he pronounced, "Times are hard and money is scarce." But in many ways that could be an economic history of Northeast Georgia. It was an area of small farmers and inventive small businesses. Most every body worked hard and "made do" with what they had. But don't feel sorry for them, for they did not feel sorry for themselves.

The book *Northeast Georgia: A History* paints the picture: In the 1950s, a colorful speaker, then a highly successful executive with a major Atlanta corporation, spoke of his "growing up days" this way:

"I grew up in an unpainted old house in the mountains. A swept yard. All of us kids worked long, hard hours. I can remember getting up before dawn, and we kids would slide in on the old benches on either side of our eatin' table, and we would close our eyes while our father gave the blessing ... and gave the blessing .... and gave the blessing.

And as soon as he said "A Men" we lifted our eyes and looked across that scrubbed old table, and there wasn't anything there but (and he would always pause here) fried eggs and scrambled eggs, country ham and hot sausage, a big bowl of white-eye gravy, a platter piled high with cat-head biscuits, real butter, blackberry jam, and blackstrap sorghum. And did I mention two pitchers of milk and a bowl of grits?"

The same book reports on one farmer's cash income from cotton. "On Nov. 21, 1900, J. W. Williams took two bales of cotton to merchants Hodges, Camp and Arnold, of Winder, Georgia. The first bale weighed 455 pounds and the company paid 10 and 5/8 cents per pound for a total of $48.34. The second bale weighed 480 pounds, and they paid 10 and 3/4 cents per pound for a total of $51.60. Total cash paid to Mr. Williams was $99.94. It is likely this sum was Mr. Williams' total income from cotton for that season, and also likely that cotton was his major cash crop."

Small mountain farmers didn't need much cash. They produced their own food: salt-cured ham; canned vegetables (in jars), fruits, jellies, jams; milk, and eggs. Honey and chestnuts were there for the taking. Hunting was more for food than recreation, and the deer provided not only meat but buckskins. Many made their own soap, and some medications (I. e., ginseng) were harvested from the land.

When they did need to buy something, it (compared to 2000) cost very little. In 1892:

Shoeing one mule – 75 cents
Pair of plow handles – 45 cents
One harrow - $2.50
One pair shoes - $1.10
One pair socks – 10 cents
One bottle SSS tonic – 10 cents
One bottle castor oil – 10 cents
One pair Sunday pants - $2.50

Mama's egg money took care of most weekly needs. She made most of her clothes. Bolt cloth was very affordable, and often the sacks holding feed were in very usable print cloth. Thread was 5-cents per spool. Torn clothing was patched, and leather patches were usually sewn on the elbows of coats. In this economy, they could "make do," and $100 went a long way.

Northeast Georgia farmers struggled with small acreages, often on steep hillsides, poor soil, unpredictable weather, the boll weevil, and low cotton prices until the late 1930s, when some local business entrepreneurs, led by Jesse Jewell, moved farm chickens and "mama's egg money" up to commercial chicken farming, creating a major new source of cash income. Farming was the dominant economic engine in Northeast Georgia, so most families depended on their land to "make a living."

Making a living in Northeast Georgia became significantly harder in the 1930s, not so much because of the stock market crash, but because of a near "perfect storm" of disasters.

First, there was the decline of tourism in Clarkesville, Mount Airy, Gainesville, and other area towns. The summer people had created jobs and provided a ready market for fruits, vegetables, eggs, milk, and meat. The coming of the automobile took people to new summer resorts, as well as competitive mountain locations. The discovery that the mosquito was the culprit that spread the "bilious fever" opened up Florida and other coastal areas, even before the great depression.

The chestnut blight was possibly the greatest disaster ever to hit the Georgia mountains, killing 100 percent of the remaining big trees in the 1920s and 1930s, and closing the huge sawmill complex in Helen, Georgia. The boll weevil devastated cotton crops and took down many in-town businesses associated with it.

And to add insult to injury, in 1936 a massive tornado obliterated Gainesville, the banking, retail and distribution center of the area.

Many historians say that in adversity the true culture and character of a region comes forth. If that is true, then the 1930s marked one of the finest hours for Georgia's mountain region. They proved, time and again, that they were survivors.

Northeast Georgia became known as a region with hard-working people who lived frugally, but proudly. They were people who had no use for loafers, slavery, labor unions, or revenuers. They would instinctively help one another. They were self-sufficient and proudly independent.

Industry eventually came into Northeast Georgia, and discovered a work ethic second to none. Workers hired by the cotton mills, leather factories, and other factories gained a reputation for giving a full day's work for a dollar's pay. Not only that, they were smart enough to quickly learn new skills, were always on time, and were intensely loyal to the company they worked for.

It was in the 1970s that a long-time employee of a poultry-processing plant was being honored on his 10th year without missing a day's work. He was asked why he worked so hard. "It ain't just a job, and it sure ain't the money," he said. "I try to do a good job because I got a glory."

That sums up the whole thing, I thought at the time. The work ethic of the people of Northeast Georgia is strong because they've got a glory.

BRING ON THE JOBS

Business leaders of this region have never been bashful about seeking new industry from outside. Many small cities, especially in areas where one or two large industries dominated and strong labor unions were strong, opposed brining in new industries. A new employer might take workers from existing industry and disrupt the status quo. Not so in Northeast Georgia.

The Gainesville promotional booklet of 1888 had a section entitled "Business Opportunities". Included were these statements: "In manufactures, experience has demonstrated what success may be achieved in the lines already engaged in. The ground is far from covered, and enterprises of similar character here would yield certain remuneration to all willing to invest capital and labor in those directions." The brochure continued, even by listing "what we need." At that time, Gainesville was a resort town and had a number of hotels. Even so, this promotional piece said, "The hotel business is by no means overdone. The increasing number of summer and winter guests will require more accommodations."

During the 1930s and 1940s, the mountain region became known as "unfriendly" to labor unions which were gaining a strong following in the industrial Northeast. After World War II, Congressman Phil Landrum, who represented the Ninth District of Georgia (the mountain district), introduced the Landrum-Griffin bill in Congress, a bill requiring labor unions to give open access to their internal records, a bill bitterly opposed by labor union bosses. It was a highly popular move among the voters of Landrum's home district.

The more rugged areas did not get many manufacturing jobs. Potential workers were scattered. Railroads were non-existent. Georgia's massive sawmill in Helen, which had its own railroad to Gainesville, produced jobs in both the sawmill and in the field where lumber was being cut. Some low-mountain towns got cotton mills. Leather working factories were active. Some industrial labor was needed, but not much.

✲ ✲ ✲

Waking Up With The Chickens

The *North Georgia Journal* has a delightful story entitled "Waking Up With The Chickens". It starts out this way, "When I was a youngster growing up in the mountains of North Georgia in the 1930s, chickens were everywhere. They pecked around the yard, scratched under the front porch, and roosted in the trees. They chased flying bugs – and even chased each other if one of them had a juicy worm that another coveted."

The story goes on to talk about Rhode Island Reds, Plymouth Rocks, Barred Rocks and Dominickers. It talks about the delicacy reserved for Sunday dinner, but also explains wringing a chicken's neck. And it resurrects that lost piece of chicken, at least lost in modern times, the pulley bone.

The article talks about why ... here in the mountains of Northeast Georgia anyway ... brown eggs were considered superior to white eggs. The author says in this *North Georgia Journal* article that this is just a sampling of the knowledge he gained as a child of the mountains.

And the author of this article about our own Northeast Georgia mountains? His name is Zell Miller, and you will recognize him as a former Georgia Governor and United States Senator.

(Note: The *North Georgia Journal* is now the magazine called *Georgia Backroads.)*

☆ ☆ ☆

Food Was Important on New Year's Day

The question was logical, coming from a sixth-grade boy: "What did ya'll do on New Year's Day back in them olden days?" I can't remember when there was no Rose Bowl, and I think I can remember the other members of the Big Four: Rose, Sugar, Cotton and Orange. I can remember listening to some Bowl games on the radio. Television changed all that. It allows football fans to watch some pretty good games, but mostly it pays college football teams some big-time money to do their thing.

Anyway, what did people do on New Year's Day before TV started broadcasting umpteen zillion bowl games? First of all, it seems to me my folks went back to work, and didn't we go back to school almost immediately after Christmas? Our parents let us stay up till midnight New Year's Eve, and at midnight we shot all the fireworks we could afford.

The big event was the New Years day meal. Some families had it at dinner (which was noontime when I was a kid). Others ate at suppertime. But it was a monster, and you needed to eat the right things to make sure you had a good year. There was pork roast, with a raisin sauce. Collards – the more you ate the more dollar bills you would get during the year. And, of course, there was chow-chow to go on the greens. Black-eyed peas, cooked with fatback, assured you plenty of pocket change. Some folks had hoppin'-john, too. Did I mention cornbread? That wasn't all, but that was enough for a day or so. It was a family meal and a family event. At our house, we always started the year off together.

✲ ✲ ✲

Shirley McDonald Writes About Mrs. Babe Ruth

There are a number of fascinating North Georgia stories about old-time big league baseball, and about some of the characters who grew up here and went on to world fame. But the more I learn about Babe Ruth's wife, who was born in White County, near Cleveland, and grew up in Gainesville, the more intriguing her story becomes.

The reason this comes to mind is because Shirley McDonald, the White County historian, wrote a piece for the News-Telegraph recently, and she added a good bit of new information ... new to me, anyway ... about the family and the house on Asbestos Road where Clara Merritt was born.

For those of you who have no idea what I am talking about, Babe Ruth, the baseball legend, married Clara Merritt ... the same Clara Merritt who was born in a white house on Asbestos Road, a few miles North of Clevland. While she was still a baby, her parents moved to Gainesville, and here she grew up.

Obviously a beautiful young lady, she married a young lawyer from Athens, who was killed at an early age, and at that point Clara went to New York where she became an artist's model and ended up as a member of the famed Ziegfield Follies. It was while she was in the Follies that she met and married Babe Ruth. The more I learn about this native of Northeast Georgia, the more fascinating the story becomes.

✲ ✲ ✲

Chickens Oust Cotton As Number One Crop

It was 1949, and the lead story in the *Gainesville Eagle* was about the economy in Northeast Georgia, and specifically about Hall County. One of the things about news writing in those days: it was colorful. Listen to this ...

"The fuzzy down of the baby chick has all but ousted the fleecy lock of the cotton boll from its pedestal as chief money crop of Hall County." The story went on to say that the cash value of frying chickens the previous year had been about $750,000 while the income from cotton totaled $745,000.

The total income from cotton, however, reflected some of the government programs that had been instituted, even though the eroding land and the boll weevil were taking their toll on cotton farming in mountainous Northeast Georgia. Of the cotton farmer's income in Hall County, $450,000 of the $745,000 came from lint; $90,000 came from cottonseed. Government subsidy money amounted to $75,000, and another government program, this one for soil conservation, provided the cotton farmers with $130,000 in income. It was good reporting, as well as good writing.

✲ ✲ ✲

Rebuilding Northeast Georgia With Poultry Litter

One of our Georgia papers had a story a while back on poultry litter, and although the details of the story point out that the litter is not causing any significant problems, the implications of the story made you think otherwise. How else could you evaluate a story with a headline called "The Big Stink" that does not have one word about odor?

Maybe some of the younger environmental enthusiasts in our midst ought to go back to the point when the poultry industry was beginning, when our red clay hills were deeply eroded gullies, when the Chattahoochee River was red with silt.

Then came poultry, and the litter went back on the land, and the land became green. I have a professor friend who insists that bringing grain into Georgia from the Midwest, feeding it to chickens, and putting the natural by-product on the land is – and I quote him – "the largest transfer of soil fertility in history."

I personally think we should thank our poultry farmers for making North Georgia a green land that does not pump tons of silt into our lake ... instead of charging farmers with sullying our waters.

✲ ✲ ✲

Too Thick To Navigate, Too Thin To Cultivate

It was 1942 in Hall County, and one of our best-known poems then ... as now ... was the "Song of the Chattahoochee." You know: "Out of the hills of Habersham. Down through the valleys of Hall..." But the Chattahoochee River had a problem a half-century ago, before the Buford Dam backed up its waters ... during the time when the majestic river literally "rushed amain to meet the plain."

In the era when cotton was king in southern farming, not only did local farmers grow cotton on the rich bottom land, but also on the red clay hills, and the hills and mountains were ripe candidates for erosion, and erode they did. The County Agent in Gainesville 50 years ago was named Leland Rew, and he pointed to the muddy red waters, saying the Chattahoochee River was "too thick to navigate and too thin to cultivate."

It was the coming of the poultry industry that put the blue back in the waters of the Chattahoochee. This wasn't from the chickens themselves, but from their litter, the natural fertilizer that allowed the once fallow hills to turn green with grass and trees. I'll always be grateful to the chicken folks for erasing the wounded red hills and thick muddy water of 50 years ago, and repainting them a verdant green.

☆ ☆ ☆

Pasture Replaces Eroded Land

It was 1949, and there was a county-wide move afoot in Hall County to replace worn-out cotton fields with pasture land. The poultry business was taking hold, and whereas cotton depleted the soil and left it bare and open to heavy erosion, poultry litter applied to pastures built and enriched the land and kept the silt out of our streams and lakes.

So it was an important event when Otis Cato ... one of Hall County's leading farmers ... spoke to the local Rotary Club to encourage them to help with the promotion of pasture planting. Mr. Cato was introduced by T. O. Galloway, the District Conservationist, who noted that 75 percent of Hall County's topsoil had been lost through soil erosion from hill-country cotton farming.

Cato reported that about 5,000 new acres had been planted in pastureland during 1949, and they were shooting for 10,000 acres the next year. Said Mr. Cato: "I hope cotton raising will become just a hobby for farmers. We owe future generations good soil."

Here 50 years later it strikes me that we owe the poultry industry, and especially people like Otis Cato and T. O. Galloway, a debt of gratitude. We have inherited a green and beautiful, rebuilt land.

✲ ✲ ✲

Working Folks Make America Work

I don't understand why, but it seems to me that in America we are promoting every cause that pops up except the cause of the working folks – and I think it is high time we back off and say, "Hey, it is the working folks who make this place work, who make it great."

It is the working folks who have precious little time for politics or posturing because they are doing productive work. It is the working folks who obey the law, raise their children to be moral and productive citizens, try to scrape together enough money to make a down payment on a house and to send their kids to college.

They are leaders among the families who are active in the church and the Parent-Teacher-Organizations and the Scouts. They worry that their government is not hearing them, and that it is taking too much of their money and not always using it well, but they don't whine and claim they should be getting more of the gravy.

Working folks are what make America work ... and it seems to me every now and then we ought to recognize that fact. ... And I'm glad I am in position to do so today.

☆ ☆ ☆

Fighting Pests Like Boll Weevils

It was just after World War II, and it was beginning to look like Hall County was facing some economic hard times. Earlier that year, it seemed certain the area would experience a record cotton crop. There had been an excellent season, with plenty of rain at the right time. But then came a record horde of boll weevils, and it looked like pure disaster for local farmers.

The new daily paper had a story about research at the University of Georgia ...written by a young reporter named Bill Miller. Whereas the old standby for killing boll weevils had been calcium arsenate, two new poisons were being used in South Georgia with more success than the old one: benzene hexachloride and toxaphene. For those who wanted to plant cotton next year, the new poisons were recommended, but farmers would do well to order early for there was a growing demand, and the new chemicals would be scarce.

Meantime, more and more local farmers ... tired of disappointing crops and hardscrabble times ... were switching form cotton to chickens.

* * *

Price Supports For Cotton Not Working Well

It was 50 years ago, and local cotton farmers were concerned about the government support program. You see, the federal government had taken tight control on most farm crops in exchange for providing farmers with a guaranteed base price for their products.

Cotton farmers, for instance, were guaranteed they would get so much per pound for their cotton, no matter what the market was. It worked this way: the government would buy the cotton from farmers and pool it for sale. If the government got MORE money when they sold the pooled cotton than they had paid the farmer, they would then pay the farmer the difference. If, however, the government got LESS than they had paid the farmer, then the farmer got to keep what he had received, and taxpayer money was used to pay the difference.

What the farmers were concerned about was that the government had taken two-thirds of the previous year's cotton, and that glut of product was bound to force the price of cotton down. After all, government control and price supports for farmers were supposed to guarantee income for farmers, especially small family farmers. In 1950, Hall County's small farmers were concerned that program wasn't working very well.

What Living Was Like In Times Gone By

One of the most pleasant things that has happened in my search for local history has come from the things various people have shared with me. For instance, Gene Shadburn has loaned me a copy of a family history called "Roots and Branches: The Ancestors and Descendants of the Taylor and Cantrell Families of Dawson County, Georgia." And Laurie Freeman sent me a copy of the book her mother wrote, "Fanning The Embers" ... a delightful set of memories in which Lois Lynch Hulsey recalls what it was like in Habersham and White Counties in the 1930s. Then the other day, V. J. Strickland sent me some information about his boyhood and a photocopy of his Georgia School Patrol certificate that had the signature of the governor at the time, one Herman E. Talmadge.

You see, finding so-called "hard history" is not all that difficult - things like when Hall County was formed or Gainesville chartered; or when the railroad came through the area. There are records about these things; minutes of meetings, newspaper stories, legal documents. What is difficult to learn is how people survived on the frontier, how they looked, and how they lived, what they thought about, and how they felt.

One can get a clue about these things from family histories and letters, even from old maps. For instance, one of the stories in Gene Shadburn's book tells about William Henry Taylor at the end of the Civil War. He had fought in Gordon's Division and was at Appamatox when the war ended. He walked home, and it took him three months. The family didn't know if he was dead or alive until one day someone yelled from down at the creek to bring some soap and clothes. It was a tender time. William Henry Taylor was alive, and home from the war.

Land Under Lake Lanier Acquired in 1954

It was the spring of 1954, and the Corps of Engineers was getting ready to buy the land for what would become known as Lake Lanier. Ground had been broken for Buford Dam itself in 1950, but now the time had come to buy the land to be covered by the water.

Under federal laws of eminent domain, the government can acquire private land for public use. It was going to work this way: if you owned land needed for Lake Lanier, the Corps of Engineers would send an appraiser to determine a fair price, and that is what they would offer you. If you said "no," they condemned your property and offered to pay that same price. If you still didn't want to sell, you had to go to court. It wasn't a matter of whether or not the government got your land; it was how much they would pay you. Usually, for good bottom land you got $25 to $50 per acre.

Anyway, the first person to sign a deal with the Corps of Engineers was 81-year-old Henry Shadburn, of the Young Deer Creek area in Forsyth County. He received a check for $4,100 ... that is $4,100 for his homeplace, his out-buildings, and 100 acres of land. Before Lake Lanier filled up in 1957, the government used this system to acquire 56,000 acres of North Georgia land.

Ralph McGill Attends White County Ladino Clover Festival

I ran across a story the other day, among some yellowed old news clippings of mine, about White County's second Ladino Clover Festival, held in Cleveland in 1949.

Ralph McGill, the editor of the *Atlanta Constitution*, was the keynoter, and a number of the state's top agriculturists, conservationists, and foresters were there. James P. Davidson, editor of the *Cleveland Courier*, was master of ceremonies, and Gus York, of the Soil Conservation Service, was a major player in the occasion.

They were promoting animal agriculture and Ladino Clover because row-crop farming, and especially cotton, had caused mountainous White County to bleed red with erosion. Between that and severe timber cutting, compounded by the Chestnut blight, White County was a devastated land. But the idea of the festival was that with Ladino Clover covering the fallow fields, and animals rather than row-crow agriculture, North Georgia could once again be lush and green. "Today North Georgia is on the way to becoming a little Switzerland," McGill said. "It will take time." If you will forgive me some nostalgia, the young reporter assigned by the Constitution to cover the event ... and primarily to be a driver for Ralph McGill, was one Gordon Sawyer. ...

✲ ✲ ✲

CHAPTER 4 — God Fearin' Farmers and Hell Raisin' Gold Diggers

The adventuresome people who flooded into the mountains and established small farms, 1800 to 1828, were hard-working, freedom-loving, God-fearing family folks. They left the Indians alone, and for the most part the Indians left them alone.

In 1803 Georgia passed a Land Act to minimize speculation, and two lotteries directly affected the former Indian territory. But even before the first lottery in 1820, a land rush into the mountains ensued. The word was out: farm land was available in Northeast Georgia. Land was being cleared; homes established; churches built.

Then in 1828 a local resident named Ben Parks crossed the Chattahoochee River just west of Gainesville, and went deer hunting in the former Indian territory. He kicked what he thought at first was merely a colorful rock that turned out to be a Gold nugget about the size of an egg yolk. Once back in town he proudly showed his friends his new find. Word spread like wildfire, and all hell broke loose in the formerly quiet and peaceful valleys of the lower Blue Ridge Mountains.

GOLD ! In what is now Lumpkin County, Georgia.

Recorded history now shows Gold was almost simultaneously discovered in present day White County by a Negro servant of one Major Logan, of Loudsville. The site was on Duke's Creek. An earlier Gold find had occurred in North Carolina. So why didn't these Gold finds create the excitement of Auraria and Dahlonega? Could it be because Gainesville had contact with metropolitan newspapers and spread the word faster? Probably.

However, the word got out; for the next two years the Gold country of Northeast Georgia was a lawless and chaotic frontier.

Georgia Governor Gilmore, trying to explain the problem he suddenly had on his hands, wrote this impression of the "twenty-niners, "Many thousands of idle, profligate people flooded into it (Northeast Georgia) from every point of the compass, whose pent up vicious propensities, when loosed from the restraints of law and public opinion, made them like the evil one in his worst mood. After wading all day in the Etowah and Chattahoochee Rivers, picking up particles of Gold, they collected around lightwood knot fires, at night, and played ... at cards, dice, push pin, and other games of chance for their day's findings. Numerous whiskey carts supplied the appropriate aliment for their employments. Hundreds of combatants were sometimes seen at fisticuffs, swearing, striking and gouging as frontier men only can do these things."

If you think Governor Gilmore might have been exaggerating just a bit, consider this: The Georgia Department of Natural Resources, in a 1960 publication, quoted an 1831 newspaper article about the Gold rush thusly, "I can hardly conceive of a more unmoral community than exists around these mines: drunkenness, gambling, fighting, lewdness, and every other vice exists here to an awful extent. Many of the men, by working three days in the week, make several dollars, and then devote the remaining four to every species of vice." Many were foreigners, and one newspaper correspondent said 13 languages could be found among them.

This, then, was the blend of white men who first established the culture of the Northeast Georgia mountains: God fearing, hard-working farmers, seeking longterm family success, and Hell-raising Gold diggers hoping to immediately strike it rich, either by striking a rich vein of Gold, or else winning at high stakes gambling.

As decades went by, and Gold mining became an industry with expensive equipment and hired labor, most of the rowdiest elements of the Gold rush moved on, many to the California Gold rush of 1849. The culture of Northeast Georgia mellowed, keeping some of the best traits, as well as some of the worst, from both those who sought success farming the land, and those who sought instant wealth from Gold.

✲ ✲ ✲

The Saga of "Boney Tank"

The blend of a "crazy good" and a "crazy bad" person is seldom found in one individual, although there often is a fine line between the two. And being a "folk hero" is seldom a complimentary term, although it often is what most "crazy" citizens would like to be called. In all of my research about the historic people of the Georgia mountains, I have only found one man who could be described as a character, crazy good, crazy bad, and folk hero ... all at the same time.

His name was Napoleon Bonaparte Tankersley, and they called him "Boney Tank."

Listen to this: His mother was a rebellious Cherokee Indian maiden who was pregnant, ran away from the Trail of Tears, and hid in a cave. The father was suspected to be a reporter for the *New York World*, who was covering the frontier for the New York paper, and writing especially about the Cherokee as they left their native land and went to Oklahoma. What happened to him no one knows, for his articles apparently were never published.

Boney Tank was born in that cave with a twin brother named Augustus Henry "Tip" Tankersley. His mother later paired up with a gold miner named James Lawrence, and they threw both Boney Tank and his twin brother out to fend for themselves at a very tender age. (How is that for a beginning?)

Somehow, Boney Tank's official name got changed to "Charles and Bonaparte Tankersley." The "And" became part of the name, and his presence was often mistaken for two people. He grew up in Lumpkin, County, Georgia, in the heart of Gold country. Auraria was his hometown, if he had one.

When the Civil War threatened, he immediately volunteered for the Confederate Army, even though his home area had no slaves, and there were practically no major political disagreements with the North. He became a member of Company K, Seventh Georgia Confederate Infantry, as Charles N. Tank.

Boney Tank was in the first major battle of the Civil War, fought at Manassas on July 21, 1861 (Confederate purists call it the Battle of Bull Run).

That first battle at Manassas was expected to be a major victory for the Union. After all, the United States had a standing army, trained and ready to go to war, and the South did not. Daily newspapers were the new rage ... the new means of immediate communications at the time ... and for weeks the front page headlines predicted the Confederate Army would be obliterated (one of their favorite words) at Manassas, and the rebellion would be over.

So certain were the people of the North that Manassas would be a pushover victory that the press had reporters embedded with Union troops on the front lines, and several thousand civilians had traveled to Manassas and found spots on hilltops to watch the slaughter.

The Confederates had some troops there, but were still putting their army together. General James Longstreet had just signed on with the Confederate Army. He had been in the Manassas area only three weeks, and went into battle wearing civilian clothes.

The people of the South were concerned that the Northern press might be right. There was a great anxiousness, even fear, that this ragtag, untrained, poorly armed Confederate force might be crushed, and that the war would be over before it ever got started. So, when the news came announcing a total victory for the South at Manassas, the people of the South were jubilant.

Boney Tank had fought aggressively in the Battle of Manassas at the creek called Bull Run, where the Union army attacked and were repelled n the first major battle of the Civil War. He immediately gained a reputation as a fearless fighter on the battlefield, but he had been hit by a Yankee Minnie ball, shattering the bone in one leg. He was taken to Atlanta to recuperate.

As one of the first Confederate casualties from the first major battle of the Civil War ... a battle that was a huge Southern victory ... Boney Tank was hailed as a hero, and became an instant celebrity. He obviously enjoyed his celebrity status, although he later was reported as saying: "they durn near killed me with kindness; all them parties and stuff."

Possibly more important was the fact newspaper writers found he would always give them a colorful interview. Even New York editors, who had reporters in the

South covering that side of the war, could not resist running a story about him now and then when other news was slow.

Boney Tank rejoined the Confederate Army, this time with Company D of the First (Galt's) Division. Then he showed up in the cavalry Company G of Cobb's Legion, the Fulton Dragoons. (How appropriate. Confederate cavalrymen in the Civil War had somewhat the same "live in fame or go down in flame" image as did World War II fighter pilots). He was wounded again in the same leg, and would limp the rest of his life, a standing reminder of his exploits in battle. Later in life he wore his hat at a jaunty angle, covering one eye, and some stories said he had lost an eye in battle. That is probably more colorful than factual.

In the census of 1870 one Napoleon Tankersley shows up as the "liquor dealer of Auroria (GA)." He had a wife named Melissa "Eliza" Lowe Tankersley, and there were two children in the household. His brother, "Tip" Tankersley accused Boney Tank of stealing his wife.

Three years later, in 1873, Boney Tank went to court for "moonshining," was convicted and served time in jail. Being a "moonshiner", and standing up to revenuers, actually added to his growing status as a folk hero in mountainous Northeast Georgia.

After his stint in prison he showed up as "an agent for the sales of cotton, whiskey and Gold mines." It should be remembered that he could neither read nor write, but it became obvious he could think fast, and talk convincingly.

Next we find Boney in court, charged with "salting" and selling a Gold mine to a "Yankee" investor. "Salting" was a practice in which Gold particles would be panned from a stream, mixed with a few nuggets, loaded into a shotgun and blasted into the walls of a mine. An assayer would be called in to collect the evidence of Gold, and thus declare the mine to be much "richer" than it really was. The sale of the mine would be valued on the Assayer's estimate. Another time, Boney Tank appeared in court charged with selling "another one-eyed man" a mule with its tongue cut out.

Boney Tank's exploits caught the attention of some great writers in an era when newspapers loved a colorful story because that would sell "penny newspapers" to the masses. An 1896 story in a Gainesville paper described him as "cool, serene and imperturbable." Of his appearance it says: "He still wears his hat cocked to the left side, over his absent eye, chews his tobacco on the same side, and has the same fascinating presence." Of the impression he had on a person it said: "When you talk with him you feel you are with a genius of his kind – that there is only one of him in the wide universe and you have found him." The *New York World* said in one story that he was "a Napoleon without a Waterloo." The New York writer said he was "a giant, ruling his domain by his powerful fists, taking on any bully or any contender in Auraria." It claimed he was "the man who was never whipped."

Boney Tank, however, said he did lose one fight. It seems a flour salesman from Augusta came in the

Auraria general store, and Boney let him know nobody sold anything there until he had an okay from Bonaparte Tankersley. The way one got that approval was to fight Boney. Now the salesman was a scrawny little guy, but before Boney Tank knew what had happened he found himself head down in a half-full barrel of flour, being rolled out the front door and off the porch. The "unconquerable" Boney Tank had met his match. Boney Tank would laugh telling the story, and the two became fast friends. (At least, that is how the story goes.)

Among his homefolks in Auraria (also known as Nuckolsville for the Nuckols family), it appears Boney Tank was a respected citizen and a real folk hero. His neighbors listened to him at election time, and candidates endorsed by him always won the Auraria "box."

His family considered him a "good father" for his and Eliza's seven children. Although he was not "converted" until he was on his death bed, he apparently saw to it that his family attended church regularly.

Napoleon Bonaparte Tankersley, aka Boney Tank, died April 23, 1908, and is buried in the Baptist cemetery in Auraria, Georgia.

His obituary in The New York Times said this:

"RULED COUNTY WITH HIS FISTS

Napoleon Bonaparte Tankersley of

Knucklesville Died Full of Years.

GAINESVILLE, Ga., April 26 (1908) – Napoleon Bonaparte Tankersley, better known as "Bony Tank", and for many years the undisputed physical king of North

Georgia, is dead at his home in Knucklesville, Lumpkin County, Ga., aged eighty.

For many years "Bony Tank's" chief occupation was whipping people. He was a giant physically, and in his youth read a history of Napoleon Bonaparte, for whom he was named. After reading the history, Tankersley said he must live up to the fighting record of the man for whom he was named, and began a career of fighting.

Knucklesville became famous as a battleground. No man ever passed through there without either fighting "Bony Tank" or running. Pistols and knives were not used in the Knucklesville fights, only the bare knuckles. No man was allowed to settle in Lumpkin County without fighting "Bony Tank". Bony never met his waterloo, although scores of men were imported from other counties to fight him.

His sword was law, and his knuckles gospel for North Georgia. Militant as he was, he was also a devout Methodist, and never missed church. He reared a large family of sons and daughters, who are highly respected."

☆ ☆ ☆

Hernando de Soto, First European in Georgia

The year was 1539, and the Spanish explorer Hernando de Soto was looking for Gold in Georgia. He had landed with 600 soldiers at Tampa Bay and then turned north. When he got to present-day southwest Georgia, he marched his troops northward toward the Savannah

River ... now the border between Georgia and South Carolina. There is great debate among historians about what route DeSoto took in crossing Georgia. Some insist he came through the Gainesville area and went on to Nacoochee Valley, but most say he took another route.

It seems certain, however, that while traveling, he sent out scouting parties, and if so, then one of the primary Indian trails likely explored was along the Eastern divide. Gainesville is located square on this divide, from which water to the east flows to the Atlantic Ocean and west to the Gulf of Mexico. It was a primary North-South Indian trading trail, well marked, and it seems logical that if the Spaniards came into this part of Georgia at all, they likely came right through Gainesville.

The thought struck me: wouldn't it be ironic if (almost 500 years ago) the FIRST European to set foot in Hall County was Hispanic?

* * *

First Southern Gold Found in the Carolinas

Because the Dahlonega Gold discovery was so dominant, and perhaps later because the U. S. Mint was located in Dahlonega, some modern-day reporters imply North Georgia marked the first Gold discovery in the United States – and it seems to be we should correct that impression. After all, so far as I know, even the most avid local Gold historians will agree the first authenticated discovery of Gold in the South took place in 1799 in what is now Cabarrus County, North Carolina, and then in Mecklenburg County, where Charlotte is located. The find triggered a Gold Rush, and that area remained a Gold mining area until the California Gold Rush of 1848.

The first Gold discovery in Georgia is generally believed to have been in 1826, in Villa Rica. The name Villa Ricca means City of Riches.

All that takes absolutely nothing away from the Gold heritage of Northeast Georgia, and especially Lumpkin County. Gold was discovered in that county in 1828, and the same year, there was a find in White County. We have ample Gold history in this area; it's okay if we weren't first.

✲ ✲ ✲

Locating Gold In Hall County

To mention Gold does not create great excitement in Hall County any more, unless you are mentioning the fact that Gainesville has one of the largest jewelry stores in the South. But there was a time when Gold mining was a part of Hall County's economy, and if someone mentioned a new Gold "find," things got lively. Most evidence of Gold craziness is gone now. Even Gainesville's Gold Street is gone, done away with by the construction of and around the Northeast Medical Center.

The other day, I was down at the state Capitol and went by to see the Coast and Geodetic Survey folks to ask if they have anything on Gold in Hall County, and they did. It is old data, granted, but they show 10 places in Hall County where Gold was found in a quantity large enough to be recorded. Most of the records go back to the late 1800s, but there on the map is the location as identified by an Au (the symbol for Gold) in the records: On property owned by Longstreet, Will Stephens, John Harrington, G. A. Elrod, and Big Joe Mine, Merck, Hubert Peck, A. W. Bell, Joseph Roberts, the Mammoth Mine, and on the O'Shields property.

Okay all you Gold Bugs ... come on home. There's Gold in them thar hills of Hall.

✲ ✲ ✲

Gainesville Gets First Private Mint in U. S.

The year was 1830, and there was a shortage of hard currency in the land. Here in North Georgia, gold miners found it hard to trade in Gold dust, for although merchants and bankers took it, there was always some loss and a constant concern about its purity. So ... an enterprising young jeweler from Milledgeville, the capital city of Georgia, came to Gainesville and established what is believed to be the first privately owned mint in the United States. He turned out $2.50, $5, and $10 God coins that were said to not only be fair, but to actually contain more Gold than the face value.

Templeton Reid's shop was believed to have been located on West Washington Street, between Grove and Maple Streets ... probably in the present parking lot area adjacent to the Gym of '36. Reid left Gainesville after about six months, moving close to another Gold area, Rutherford County, North Carolina. He later moved back to Milledgeville, and then to Columbus, where he died in 1851.

His coins have become rare collector's items, and if you can find one of Templeton Reid's Gold pieces, it is ... today ... literally worth a mint.

✲ ✲ ✲

Dahlonega Gold Coins Displayed in Atlanta

The American Numismatic Association held its 110th Anniversary Convention at the Cobb Galleria Convention Center the other day. This annual meeting is said to be the largest assembly of coin dealers and collectors in the world, and the value of the exhibits there was well over one Billion dollars ... that's Billion with a B,

What got my attention, however, was the announcement that they had a display valued at eight million dollars of United States Gold coins minted in Dahlonega between 1831 and 1861. It struck me as very appropriate that gold coins minted in Georgia would be one of the highlights of this meeting, since the convention is being held in Georgia this year.

Gold was first discovered in Georgia in 1828, and the first find is generally credited to Ben Parks while hunting for deer in what is now Lumpkin County. About the same time, there was a discovery in White County too ... up near Helen.

Not long afterwards, the U. S. Government established a mint in Dahlonega, which operated until it was shut down by the Civil War. The foundation of the old mint structure is now the main building at North Georgia College and State University, and the coins minted there are now some of the most valuable collector coins in the world. It's good to have them back home in Georgia.

✲ ✲ ✲

An 1830 View of a Frontier Town

Gainesville was a frontier town in the early 1830s, but it was already a trading center, and with the Gold Rush nearby, it had some of the characteristics of a boom town. The rough and tumble prospectors weren't the only ones to show up in this town, and and certainly not the only ones to raise a ruckus now and then.

As one writer described 1830 Gainesville, "The Cherokee Indians were yet in the land, and they often made visits to the town to see the sights and to trade, bringing Gold, moccasins, bead work, and chestnuts to exchange for blankets and other things they needed and fancied.

The white settlers, from the river bottoms and the mountain land around Gainesville, often came to town on Saturday, and large numbers came on Court Week. Generally, it was peaceful, but every now and then, things got out of hand. A description, from another old document, tells it this way, "...men, with loud shouts and challenges swore they were the best man in (Hall) County, and stripping to the waist, drew rings on the ground, and leaping like wildcats into the arena, dared their foes to the contest of physical strength and combat."

That was downtown Gainesville, about 1830.

✲ ✲ ✲

The Queen City of The Mountains: 1913

Cheryl Vandiver loaned me a book the other day, a 1913 City Directory of Gainesville, Georgia, and I thought you might be interested in how that document described Gainesville, the Queen City of the Mountains, in 1913.

"The altitude of the city is 1,253 feet; population about 10,000, including suburbs. As a BUSINESS POST Gainesville is pronounced one of the most solid, safe and progressive cities of its size in the South. Gainesville affords cheap power, intelligent labor, raw material of various kinds and transportation facilities which make it a logical point for MANUFACTURING INTERESTS. The combination of mountain and valley scenery, pure water, invigorating air and an ideal year-round climate, brings Gainesville into prominence as a CITY OF HEALTH. Gainesville believes in EDUCATION and the promotion of morals and has a system of public schools looked upon as a model. For higher education, Brenau College Conservatory for young ladies and Riverside Military Academy for boys offer the best of opportunities. The city owns the water-works system and is encircled with a sewerage system. The principal streets are curbed and sidewalks tiled. The business district is paved. In public buildings this city rivals many of the larger cities of the South. The hotel accommodations are good and the power plants on the Chatahoochee and Chestatee Rivers furnish light and power in abundance, all these giving Gainesville every MODERN CONVENIENCE."

That was Gainesville Georgia, in 1913.

A South Carolinian Visits Gold Country

(From a letter written by GS about 1980 to a friend from South Carolina who wanted a recommendation for a one-day tour of Georgia's Gold Country near Dahlonega)

Start on the Dahlonega square, and go to the Dahlonega Courthouse Gold Museum. "Formerly the Lumpkin County Court House, now the oldest public building in North Georgia, constructed in 1836. It houses exhibits and relics of the area's Gold Rush days."

Look for historic markers. **Findley Ridge** – Georgia 60 on the South edge of Dahlonega. **Consolidated Gold Mines** – Georgia 52 in Dahlonega.

And, since you went to Clemson, you should send your IPTAY pledge to repay us Georgians for what you took from the **Calhoun Gold Mine.** The historical marker says: "Famous Calhoun Gold Mine where it is said vein gold was first discovered in Georgia by white men. In 1828, while deer hunting, Benjamin Parks, of Dahlonega, accidentally found quartz gold in pockets of lodes. His find was so rich in gold that it was yellow like the yolk of an egg. Shortly after discovery, this mine was sold to U. S. Senator John C. Calhoun, of South Carolina. It was operated by Thomas G. Clemson, son-in-law of Calhoun, and some of the gold was used to found Clemson College, S. C.." This marker is located on GA 60, 3.7 miles south of Dahlonega.

If you have time you should also go to **Auraria.** The historic marker there reads: "Auraria (Gold), in 1832 the scene of Georgia's first Gold rush, was named by John C. Calhoun, owner of a nearby mine worked by Calhoun slaves. Auraria and Dahlonega were the two real Gold towns in the U. S. before 1849. Between 1829 and 1839 about $20,000,000 in gold was mined in Georgia's Cherokee country."

"From Auraria in 1858 the 'Russell boys', led by Green Russell, went west and established another Auraria, near the mouth of Cherry Creek that later became Denver, Colo. Green Russell uncovered a fabulous lode called Russell Gulch near which was built Central City, Colorado, 'richest square mile on earth'".

By the way, the Smith House is a great place to eat, especially if you are hungry.

✲ ✲ ✲

President Monroe Acquires Swampy Florida

The year was 1821, and Gainesville, Georgia had just officially become the county seat for Hall County. To the people in the English-settled port cities of the American east coast, Gainesville was a frontier town, the jumping off point into Indian country.

But the hot debate in Washington, D. C. was not about the frontier in the southern mountains; it was about whether or not the United States should acquire Florida from Spain. At that time Spain was busy with wars in Europe, and didn't want to spend money or commit troops to Florida, even though the upstart Americans were threatening. President James Monroe was proposing we buy Florida from Spain, but not everybody felt Florida was worth having.

John Randolph figured anything south of Georgia was worthless, and made this passionate plea on the floor of the House of Representatives: "Florida, sir, is not worth buying. It is a land of swamps, of quagmires, of frogs and alligators and mosquitoes! A man, sir, would not immigrate into Florida ... no, not from Hell itself."

President Monroe prevailed, and the U. S. acquired Florida from the Spaniards ... just about the time Hall County was being carved from Indian country, and Gainesville became its county seat.

☆ ☆ ☆

CHAPTER 5 – Creative Capitalism, Mountain Style

The South generally, and Northeast Georgia specifically, was not included in the industrialization of America ... the creation of steel mills and automobile manufacturing and similar industries in the North and upper Mid-West. Thus, industrial jobs were scarce in these mountains. The land was poor, and the fields small, so farming did not reach the large-scale production found in the plantation areas of the South.

So it was that the hard-working people of Appalachia learned, first, to create their own jobs by creating new businesses, large and small, or by bringing new industries in from outside, usually the North.

Early on, these mountain folk developed an "entrepreneurial attitude". The people living in the mountain area of Georgia were an independent lot, conservative to use today's terminology, and had an innate desire to be their own boss. They were also totally unafraid to take financial risks. Some say: what did they have to lose? But there was more to it than that ... much more.

Investment money was scarce locally. Banks did not come into being in the area until the 1880's, and this money was not available for risky business ventures. There were myriad reasons a person should not try to start a new venture, but the fact was somebody was always starting something. Some succeeded; many did not.

Look at some of the economic engines that drove the economy of Northeast Georgia.

First and foremost was farming. Agriculture was the dominant business in the entire South, and cotton was the cash crop. To be free and to own land was a measure of success for most people who first settled America. It was a way of life ... a culture, if you will.

Gold was unique to the Georgia mountains, and once the "free Gold" (that which could be panned from streams) played out, Gold mining required large capital for equipment. This is one industry that drew a good bit of outside capital, but generally this was not true investment capital. It was gambling, but it brought in infusion of money into the area just the same. The Gold arena brought forth some of the most creative of the creative capitalists.

Another economic engine presented itself in the ingenuity of Cherokee Chief Vann, an innovator. There's a difference between an inventor and an innovator. An inventor creates something entirely new; an innovator takes something that exists and makes something new from it. Inns existed alongside well-traveled frontier roads in the late 1700's, but Chief Vann put a string of them – one day's travel apart – along the Federal Road through Cherokee territory from Flowery Branch to Ross Landing at Chattanooga. Not only were the travelers assured of a safe place to stay, they could pay at the first stop and eliminate the risk of being robbed along the way.

The Morse Brothers had been in the lumber business in upstate New York, and saw great possibilities in the failing lumber mill in Helen, Georgia. They acquired it in 1917, and became the largest lumber mill in the United States. But that was just the beginning. That enterprise spawned a host of other businesses: a railroad to Gainesville; narrow gauge railroads into the mountains; independent timber businesses to supply hardwood logs; a major tanbark business; and other ancillary operations.

All this red clay was bound to be good for something, and thus a brick industry grew up in the late 1800's and early 1900's. Pottery clay was found in the area and it didn't take long for a family-centered pottery industry to develop.

Dr. H. J. Pearce was an innovator and an entrepreneur in education. He started Brenau College. He was also instrumental in starting Riverside Military Academy. He sold that to another entrepreneur in education, Gen. Sandy Beaver, who also acquired a winter campus for Riverside Military Academy in Florida.

Dr. Crawford Long, who pioneered the use of anesthesia, and Dr. James Henry Downey, who invented a "machine" to hold broken bones in place while they healed, were innovators (and good characters) in the field of medicine.

Chickens and eggs had been a small part of farming from year one, but during the depression of the 1930's Jesse Jewell devised a way to produce and market chickens as meat, and as America moved into World War II an entirely new industry was being born. Jesse Jewell was an innovator and a real character ... maybe a little bit on the Crazy (but good) side.

THE POINT TO BE MADE IS THIS: mountainous Northeast Georgia had very few jobs created by large industry, the kind found in the steel mills of Pittsburgh, or the automobile companies in Detroit.

Thus, part of the culture of Northeast Georgia is this bent for entrepreneurship, or a desire to be one's own boss, and the need to create jobs where none exist. Call it whatever you like, CREATIVE CAPITALISM is an attitude and a solid part of the culture of Northeast Georgia.

Jesse Jewell and the Broiler Business

(This was written as the Preface for Homer Myers' book entitled "Pass The Chicken Please: the Life and Times of Jesse Jewell)

The year was 1950: a business friend was talking; *"Jesse was promoting a community project, which wasn't unusual. He hadn't mentioned money yet, but we knew that was coming. The Corps of Engineers was building Buford Dam, and the new lake was going to cover Gainesville's nine-hole golf course. Jesse figured the city could get enough from the Corps to at least buy the land for a new 18-hole course, and we could get it designed by some famous golf course builder. We could sell off lots between the golf course and the lake for enough to finish the golf course and build a Country Club. Gainesvillians needed to go ahead and get the land (and here came the kicker) and you won't have to put up any cash. All you will have to do will be sign a note till Gainesville gets the cash. He already had a spot picked out where some farms were available, and here we were in his Lincoln going to see it. He took us all the way out of town, across the Chattahoochee (River) and up a dirt road. We got out and walked a ways and came to an open spot where we could see the bottom land along the river. There Jesse stops and waves his arms and says, :'Look at that. When the dam is finished, water will cover this whole area up to about right there, and the first fairway will go out that ridge, and the club-house will go down there...' He was on a roll, but all I could see was scrub oaks and red clay, and all I could feel was the chiggers chewing on my legs."*

Jesse Jewell could see things others could not see. In the 1930's for a farm to have a few chickens meant egg production. Farmers bought their favorite baby chicks in the Springtime, and they came in boxes delivered by the mailman. They kept the hens for egg production, and sold (or ate) the young roosters as "Spring Fryers." The laying flock ate corn produced on the farm and the eggs (sold on Saturday when the family went to town) provided "Mama's egg money." All across America in the 1930's it was common knowledge there was no way a living could be made from growing and selling frying chickens. Spring fryers were, and always would be, a tasty by-product of egg production.

Jesse Jewell, looking for a better way to make a living, saw something different. Looking from the consumer's side he saw that people liked fried chicken, and he figured if they could get fryers the year 'round, they would buy them. Not only that, more people were moving into cities and those super stores were being developed. Hadn't he already been selling fryers in Miami?

The demand for chicken meat grew rapidly in World War II, especially in the military, and Jewell developed a system for producing more chickens the year around. It came to be called "vertical integration" and it turned out "pan ready" frying chicken.

As Homer Myers describes in this book the early "broiler business" in Northeast Georgia was lively, often controversial, and ready-made for the sales ability and drive of Jesse Jewell. All were welcome to join in, and a lot of people other than Jesse became a part of its development.

But it seems fair to say it was Jesse Jewell, more than most, who saw that this fledgling industry had the potential for providing chicken meat to housewives all across America. He could see it as a major competitor for beef and pork, and the salesman in his soul led him to carry out that vision. There was a large selling job to be done, and at the end of World War II he began to tackle it in the American marketplace as well as at home. Jesse Jewell could see this new industry producing "the tastiest, healthiest meat in the world" and it would come from Gainesville, Georgia, "the garden spot of the universe." He was never bashful when talking about his product or his hometown.

At the end of World War II the older poultry areas – the "egg basket of America" in the Midwest, New England, other areas, expected the new "broiler industry" to wither and return to its "proper place" as a by-product of the egg industry.

When the old Midwest-dominated poultry organizations failed to get excited about the possibilities of the new broiler industry, Jesse was involved in starting the Southeastern Poultry and Egg Association. He traveled widely, selling this new organization, and he became its second president. He packaged and branded his own chicken, hired an advertising agency, and used a newly popular television to reach the customer. He traveled the Eastern United States selling chain stores and meat markets on his products, and enticing food editors to print new recipes using chicken.

He sold his new friends in the broiler industry on the idea of a national advertising campaign for broilers, convincing them that as the market grew, the industry could grow and prosper. That was the start of the National Broiler Council, and Jesse Jewell was its first president. He bought a company airplane and spent both time and money promoting to the marketplace and to the industry itself. His enthusiasm for the opportunities offered by the American free-market system spilled over into the wider business community, and he became president of the Georgia State Chamber of Commerce and a board member of the U.S. Chamber of Commerce. And back home, much to the consternation of some Georgia poultrymen, he invited one-and-all, from anywhere, to visit his company and see how J. D. Jewell, Inc. got the job done.

In 1970, as research was being done for the book *The Agribusiness Poultry Industry: A History of Its Development*, a survey was sent to a large number of recognized poultry leaders and educators and one line made this request: "Please list the 10 men you feel contributed most to the development of the modern agribusiness poultry industry." More than 200 names were mentioned, representing all phases of the industry and all areas of the country, but only one name totally dominated the returns. That name was Jesse Jewell.

Always enthusiastic, Jesse Jewell worked hard to lay a foundation for the modern agribusiness poultry industry, and in so doing he became somewhat of a legend, known and respected all over America.

But what was he like, really? What was it like to live and work with this legend? And who were the people around him who cheered him on, and who operated the company while Jesse built an industry? Homer Myers has interviewed more than 40 people who knew Jesse Jewell personally, and knew the industry he launched. From those interviews, and extensive research, Homer has created this very readable and personal biography of Jesse Jewell. In so doing, Homer has done a great service for the poultry industry and especially those of us who knew, or knew of, Jesse Jewell.

Gordon Sawyer
Gainesville, Georgia
2008

P.S. – *There is a point on Gainesville's Robert Trent Jones designed golf course where you can see the cool blue of Lake Lanier beyond long, green fairways. It is a public golf course, open to one and all. Stately homes surround the course, and at the end of the peninsula stands the Chattahoochee Country Club. Across the Chattahoochee River, back in downtown Gainesville, on Jesse Jewell Boulevard, just across from the place where the Jewell office once stood, stands a tall white marble statue with a chicken on top.*

Vann's Tavern on the Old Federal Road

The year was 1805, and the Cherokee nation had just agreed to allow the Americans to build a new road across its land in North Georgia. Called the Federal

Road, it connected Augusta with today's Chattanooga (then Ross' Landing), and the new road entered Indian country just North of the village of Flowery Branch.

There was an enterprising Indian chief named James Vann who saw an opportunity in all this, so he built a string of taverns along the Federal Road ... possibly the first motel chain in Georgia. As a part of that chain, he built Vann's Tavern in Hall County near the Chattahoochee River where old Oscarville was located. Not only was Vann's Tavern an important stopping place on the old Federal Road, but Vann also had a ferry nearby, later known as Winn's Ferry. Eventually the land was acquired by the Boyd family, who sold it to the government when Lake Lanier was formed.

Vann's Tavern was saved from the waters of the lake, and moved log-by-log to New Echota, the Old Cherokee capital, which has been reconstructed near Calhoun. There it stands, and if you like you can visit this bit of Hall County history ... now over 200 years old.

✲ ✲ ✲

Developer "Duke" Williams Created Downtown Gainesville

We have had a lot of conversation recently about our developers, but let me tell you: in my judgment, Hall County has never had a developer to match our first one, Duke Williams. Duke" was from Greene County (his real name was Wilson Williams, by the way) and he drew lot 148 in Hall County's Ninth District in the Land Lottery. In case you are wondering, Lot 148 is present-day downtown Gainesville. You know, the square, Washington, Bradford, Spring, Main Streets. But a lot other people drew Hall County land, too, so how come Gainesville was built on Lot 148?

Well, Old Duke was a far-sighted, enterprising type, and he got a surveyor, one Timothy Terrell, to survey a town on lot 148 in 1821, and he deeded 50 acres to Hall County (I mean he GAVE it to them) to be used for public buildings and other public uses. Duke promoted that and advertised that as the center of Hall County. The town's public square is where "Old Joe" now stands. Lot one was where the Hunt Tower is located. He divided up lots and sold them to businesses so they could be in the center of this blossoming, new frontier town. Developer Duke Williams is long since dead, of course, but he should be proud of what he wrought.

✲ ✲ ✲

Put The Post Office In A Tavern?

The situation we have at the Gainesville Post Office ... in which much of the available parking space is being filled by Post Office employees, creating a traffic nightmare and leaving postal customers unable to get to their boxes ... came to mind the other day while I was digging out some old Gainesville history.

It goes this way: Gainesville's Lot 3, which is located about where the current Georgia Mountain Center parking deck's entrance is, was originally established by Duke Williams, who founded downtown Gainesville. In 1822, Old Duke sold it to Simon White, an Indian trader. Then it was acquired by one Stephen Reed who promptly sold it to Wiley Harben. Now, Wiley Harben opened a Tavern on that lot, and shortly thereafter (in 1823). And guess what? Wiley Harben was appointed Gainesville's first Postmaster, and he maintained this city's first Post Office in his tavern.

Now, let me ask you something: would you rather have to go to a tavern to get your mail, as happened in 1823, or would you prefer to pay for a box and then not be able to park you car to get your mail, because Post Office employees have filled all the parking spaces? I reckon that's what the government calls progress.

☆ ☆ ☆

Electric Power Comes To Gainesville

The year was 1897, and the exclusive national business publication, The Manufacturers Record, had a report about Gainesville, Georgia. Here's what it had to say: "The Gainesville and Chattahoochee Power and Manufacturing Company was formally organized in Baltimore on Feb. 6. The following officers were elected: S. C. Dunlap, President; T. P. Ivy, vice president; J. T. Dunlap, secretary. The directors are: S. C. Dunlap,

T. P. Ivy, J. W. Smith, J. W. Taylor, C. C. Sanders and Z. T. Castleberry."

The Manufacturers Record went on to say the company was being formed "for the purpose of developing 3,000 horsepower near Gainesville, Georgia ...:" They were talking about a 3,000 horsepower electric power generator, and that was big in those days.

The report said the corporation had secured 755 acres adjacent to Gainesville and planned to build a dam across the Chattahoochee River. The power company would supply electricity for a franchise lighting system, an electric street railway, city lighting and pumping stations, a cotton mill, and other industry.

Can you imagine how exciting that was in North Georgia in 1897: electricity was coming to Gainesville, Georgia?

✲ ✲ ✲

Daily Hack Service: Gainesville to Dahlonega

The year was 1878, and Mr. L. Q. Meaders was advertising his Daily Mail Stage Line in the published schedule of the Piedmont Air-Line Railroad ... you know, the railroad from Charlotte to Atlanta that comes through Gainesville. Mr. Meaders noted that he ran the line year round "... between Gainesville and Dahlonega, running each way every day, Sundays excepted. Hacks will leave both places early every morning, carrying passengers either way; and for the accommodation of the travelling public, I have purchased additional and improved vehicles, and now have the MOST COMFORTABLE HACKS to be found in North Georgia. ..."

His advertisement continues: "Will have none but sober and attentive drivers, gentle teams, [and comfortable hacks]. Special care taken of ladies and children who are traveling alone. Satisfaction guaranteed."

Reading that old ad made me wonder: if you wanted to travel on public conveyance from Gainesville to Dahlonega nowadays, how would you do that?

✲ ✲ ✲

Longstreet Hotel History Comes to Light

A little chunk of Gainesville's history came to light the other day when an official Georgia Historical marker was dedicated. It marks the location of General James Longstreet's famous old Piedmont Hotel ... well, not all of the old Hotel, but the remains of one wing. It's an important wing, though, for that is the wing where one of President Woodrow Wilson's daughters was born ... right here in Gainesville.

The remnant of the old hotel has been in disrepair for many years. Nobody knew, and probably nobody cared, about its historic past. But after its importance was discovered, it was acquired by the Longstreet Society, and they have set out to restore it and to make it a museum.

There are some surprises, too, as the Gainesville history of Longstreet comes to light. He was a Republican when being a Republican in the South was not acceptable. He espoused the vote for Negroes. He became very unpopular in the South. But he made history as one of the best Generals the Confederates had. And he made his mark here in Gainesville. He is history worth preserving, and I commend the Longstreet Society for their efforts.

The Industry Is Gone But Asbestos Road Lives On

I was driving down through White County the other day, still above Cleveland, and here was this road marker: Asbestos Road. It brought to mind a bit of the economic background of Northeast Georgia that I ran across while researching the history of the mountain section of our great state. Northeast Georgia is rich with all kinds of metals and minerals. There's Gold, of course. But there is also iron and copper, and all kinds of rocks. And among the rocks in North Georgia, you will find asbestos. Asbestos exists widely in nature. The rocks on which San Francisco stands are mostly asbestos, I am told, and certainly we had (maybe I should say have) an abundant supply of asbestos in White and Habersham Counties, and probably in much of the rest of this area, too. Part of this region's economy in the early 1900s rested on asbestos mining, and on a series of small asbestos processing businesses which provided employment for local people.

But then, here in America, asbestos has been demonized, and many trial lawyers have made immense fortunes suing companies, claiming their clients had been injured or killed by exposure to asbestos in one form or another. America's top asbestos producer, Johns Manville, was forced into bankruptcy in 1982. Then came a long string of major American corporations that were wiped out by large jury awards: names like Armstrong, Babcock and Wilcox, Pittsburgh Corning, W. R. Grace, Federal-Mogul. Asbestos litigation has pushed at least 54 major corporations into bankruptcy ... taking out the companies and all the jobs they offered. For many, asbestos was a small part of their product line. Early in 2001, a Manhattan jury awarded $53-milliuon to the estate of a deceased auto mechanic who allegedly died from exposure to asbestos in brake linings. Now, our courts have a decision to make. If courts continue to award money at that level ($53-million for every mechanic who ever worked on asbestos brake linings), the American automobile industry will be wiped out.

Asbestos as an industry left Northeast Georgia a long time ago. About all that is left is the name of a road in White county, and the signs that identify it.

✲ ✲ ✲

Gainesville Businesses (City Directory) in 1882

In digging out the history of this area, I keep bumping into references to, and quotes from, an 1882 City Director of Gainesville. If ANYBODY knows where a copy of this old book is, how about letting me know. Anyway, one quote attributed to that Directory outlines the businesses and industries in town. It reports on three colleges. It lists the street railroad; various railroads to other cities; and hack lines (one hack line went three times a week to Augusta, called the metropolis of the state). There were two tanneries and a thriving leather industry, and the widely known carriage and wagon factory of G. W. Walker.

There were some businesses you would expect in 1882: R. J. Holland and Son Merchandise Store; Jno. A Webb, dealer in stoves and tinware; W. P. Smith's livery stable on Oak Street. There were some businesses one might NOT expect in a frontier town in 1882, also: Early Rogers had an Art Gallery on the square; Miss Lizzie A. Woodward was a "fashionable dressmaker" on Athens Street; James A. Findley had wines, liquors, and a "first class pool table". There were hotels and saloons. W. S. Cox was the town undertaker, and he had "... hearse and carriages furnished when desired." That was Gainesville's business community in 1882. ...

✲ ✲ ✲

A Leather Business Boosts Hall County

The year was 1969, and Hall County was celebrating its Sesquicentennial. In case sesquicentennial is not a familiar word to you, as with me, apparently it meant Hall County was 150 years old.

Anyway, in 1969, Hall County was still nationally recognized for fine leather goods. Some of the finest and most ornate saddles in America were made here along with other leather items like bridles, harness, halters, and belts. For the sesquicentennial celebration, the Waterproof Leather Company ... that is, Bailey and Son ... of Flowery Branch commented this way: "Only the best is good enough for our customer and only the best is good enough for the people of Gainesville and Hall County, for they deserve it," the Flowery Branch company said in an advertisement. "They have created for themselves a prosperous, dynamic, and growing community ... by hard work, perseverance, and proper planning."

Things change, and America's leather industry withered, but in the year of Hall County's sesquicentennial, it was still a vital part of this area's economy.

✲ ✲ ✲

Saddles From Buford and Gainesville

It was 1950, and one of Gainesville's major industries was a saddle factory. Actually, it was the last in a long and distinguished line of saddle and harness manufacturing plants that graced the North Georgia area. The massive Bona Allen plant in Buford had been the kingpin ... one of the largest leather working plants in the United States, if not the largest. There was a plant in Demorest that did nothing but make saddle trees. Several smaller leather-working plants had been located in Gainesville, but the one remaining fifty years ago was Wofford Leather Company.

The saddle and harness market had begun to decline in the early 1900s with the advent of the automobile. And as electric motors became smaller and more portable, the huge leather belts that once ran industrial plants began to disappear. But there was a market for two kinds of saddles: the first was the standard, lower-priced saddle with very little, if any, fancy leather work. And the other market was for fancy saddles ... the kind that had scrollwork and was literally leather art. These saddles also often had silver trim, which was a work of art too. Sears Roebuck sold both kinds of saddles, and most of Sears' saddles were produced in Gainesville, Georgia. Fifty years ago.

✲ ✲ ✲

Georgia Shoe Company Reorganizes

It was 1949, and Georgia Shoe Company was expanding and reorganizing. Georgia Shoe Company had its headquarters in Flowery Branch, but it also had plants in some nearby locations like Buford. What the company was doing, according to the announcement by S. L. Perling, the company's General manager, was to reorganize production and shipping for greater production and more efficiency.

The Flowery Branch plant would expand and would produce the company's main line, which was work shoes. Other plants would specialize in hunting and fishing shoes, engineers boots, and other specialized shoes. The company would continue to make Army-type and paratrooper boots, but with the war over, they would make up less of the total output. Shipping and warehousing would be in the old Bona Allen building in Buford.

Georgia Shoe Company was one of Hall County's major industries at the end of World War II, and it was going through big changes as it made the transition from an all-out war effort to the new peacetime economy.

An Era of Home Delivery

It was the late 1940s, and local citizens were bemoaning the fact you couldn't get home delivery like you once could. You could still get a house call from your doctor, but they were encouraging you to either go to their office or the hospital. Milk delivery wasn't as dependable as it once was, but ice delivery was still regular and on time.

Another service local citizens were missing was bread delivery. It seems a Mr. C. F. Gunter once operated a bakery where the old Royal Theater stood fifty years ago. Now, if you don't know where that is ... it is next to the present location of the Collegiate Grill (which, by the way, started 50 years ago). It seems Mr. Gunter had regular deliveries of bread and cakes throughout the residential section of the town. You could buy six tokens from him for a quarter, and each token was good for a loaf of bread delivered to your home.

It wasn't just the home delivery that made his products so appealing, though. It was the fact that the loaves of bread were hot and right out of the oven ... and somehow, bread just wasn't as good after it had cooled off. Home delivery, from bread to babies, was beginning to decline, and Gainesville's citizens missed the service.

The Chicken Business: Economic Growth for Hall County

The eonomy is on the rebound with gusto, and Hall County is one of these fortunate communities that has a well-balanced job base ... if we will take care of what we have. There is always a reason to seek new industries, like hi-tech, and we should do that aggressively. But it is important also that we take care of the industries we have, so we can protect the jobs people now have in this community and keep growing.

The reason this comes to mind is that economists are predicting 2004 will be a good year for the chicken business, and possibly as much as one-third of Hall County's economy is dependent on that industry if you include both chickens and eggs. And it is important that the chicken business make a good profit so they can invest in development and marketing of some new products. There is both short-term and long-term reason for the industry to go after a bigger chunk of the meat market right now.

Short term, there is good reason to believe chickens and eggs can gain a bigger chunk of the high protein food market. That has to do with a low volume of meat in the pipeline, and the fact the chicken business can fill the void and gain market share. That is short term, but it is in our favor.

Long term, the chicken and egg businesses are in good position because there is growing interest in high protein diets. There is a good bit of research showing people are healthier if they eat a high protein diet, and consumers are reacting by eating ... among other things ... chicken and eggs. But there's more to it than that.

Let's go back 20 years. Twenty years ago, if you bought a chicken in a meat market, it was a whole bird with giblets stuffed inside in a waxed-paper wrap. Now only 11 percent of chickens are sold whole, 41 percent are sold as pre-cut chicken parts ...you know, breast meat, or drumsticks or thighs. But 48 percent of the chicken meat marketed right now is what they call "further processed". You get it as chicken nuggets, or chicken tenders, and beyond that as chicken tetrazini or other ready-to-heat-and-eat products.

But, if the chicken business is to expand its markets in this field, it has to make some high-risk investments and that means it needs some money from profits. That's the way business works. If ... the economists' predictions come true, and the poultry folks invest as I predict they will, I'll bet you they will create more new high-paying jobs in Hall County the next three years than all the rest of the economy combined.

Jesse Jewell And The Broiler Business

World War II had ended, and the broiler business was catching fire in Northeast Georgia. Actually, chickens had furnished farm spending money for this area since the late 1800s, and had started rapid expansion in the late 1930s and during World War II. But now it was moving out of the farm sideline category, and becoming a real business ... even an industry.

Early in the year, Gainesville's Jesse Jewell had been elected President of the Southeastern Poultry and Egg Association at a convention held in Atlanta. Southeastern had been formed only two years before, with 75 members, and now they had 5,000 members across the South, with a majority from North Georgia. More than 500 people attended the 1949 poultry convention.

To support this rapidly growing industry, a State Poultry Laboratory was opened on Main Street in cooperation with the Georgia Poultry Improvement Assocdfiation ... a facility described as a "pathological poultry laboratory." There was a certain boom-town atmosphere about the chicken business in Gainesville at that time. A lot of people obviously were making money, and a lot of others wanted in. It was exciting.

☼ ☼ ☼

The Wall Street Journal Reports On The Broiler Boom

It was 1949, and the talk of the town was the national publicity Gainesville had just received because of the newly-evolving broiler business. It had all come about because the Wall Street Journal had written a major story entitled "Gold Mine in the Hen House" ... a story that featured Gainesville and the rapid growth of the broiler business.

But it wasn't just the Wall Street Journal. Newspapers all over the United States picked up that story, and friends and relatives were calling people in Gainesville to comment on the news.

The Wall Street Journal reported that in the early 1930s Georgia had produced and sold some 35-million frying chickens. By 1939, the state had produced 106-million fryers. Then in 1948, Georgia produced 351-million broilers ... and almost all of them were being produced and processed in Northeast Georgia, mostly from Gainesville to Cumming to Canton. The Wall Street Journal reported that Gainesville, "once financially desperate," had moved into third place in per capita income in Georgia, and that most of this could be attributed to the development of the poultry business. It was a great business success story, and it seems fair to say it helped put Gainesville on the national map.

✲ ✲ ✲

The Daily Broiler Market Report

It was 1949, and the state of Georgia had a nationally-recognized price-reporting system for frying chickens, so it was natural almost everybody in Northeast Georgia ... growers, feed dealers, hatcherymen, processors, and also local merchants and business folks ... was glued to the radio every morning to see how things were going in the broiler busijness. Here's the way it sounded one Tuesday early in 1949:

"The poultry market is weak and unsettled. Prices are unchanged to one cent lower. Offerings of birds 2 ½ to 3 pounds were fully ample to in excess of moderate demand. The supply of heavier weights was adequate but not pressing. Prices paid FOB farm for fryers, all sizes, picked up early Monday morning ranged as follows: New Hampshire Reds and White crosses 27 ½ to 30 cents with a few picked up at 31 cents in cases where some processors bought exclusively from other growers. Barred Rock crosses were at 26 ½ to 28 cents."

It was a time when the feed dealer and the grower took the risk, and if the market was high, they made good money ... sometimes unbelievable money ... and if demand went down, the market went down, and they lost their shirts.

✲ ✲ ✲

Local Newsrooms Move To Atlanta

It was late January 1962, and Gainesville was almost a deserted town. The big Southeastern Poultry and Egg Convention was underway in Atlanta, and in those days probably half the people attending were from Hall, Forsyth and Cherokee counties ... well, you'd better add the poultrymen from Habersham, Dawson, and Lumpkin counties, too.

The people left behind in Northeast Georgia were keeping up with the convention, though, for both WDUN and WGGA were set up right in the middle of the convention floor, and personalities like Jim Hartley would buttonhole local folks as they walked by ... and you wouldn't believe some of the conversations that went on, right on the air, for part of the activities included the hospitality rooms that opened up in the hotels each night.

John Yarbrough, editor of the *Poultry Times*, the Gainesville-based trade newspaper headquartered with the *Daily Times*, was busy gathering tidbits for a column called "Cap'n Chick." And trade association executives like Harold Ford and Abit Massey were hard at work with the programs and speakers. It was a watershed time for the rapidly integrating poultry industry. Poultry processing was becoming more automated, and the industry was beginning to focus on new products and modern marketing. There were even a couple of Georgia-based advertising agencies present: Crawford and Porter, of Atlanta, and the new outfit on the block, Sawyer Advertising from Gainesville.

✲ ✲ ✲

Jesse Jewell Pioneers Consumer Advertising For Broilers

It was mid-century. WDUN was a new radio station in Gainesville, competing with WGGA and "Mrs. Smithgall's son Charlie." TV stations in Atlanta were becoming the rage for advertisers, and were beginning to push into listening audiences of long-time 50,000 watt powerhouses like WSB radio. But no matter who you were listening to, or looking at, Gainesville, Georgia was making its mark in the consumer advertising world. The reason was because Jewell sales manager, Theron Brown, working through Harry Crawford, of Crawford and Porter Advertising Agency in Atlanta, was covering the entire state with a new singing jingle that some people can still hum 50 years later. It went like this:

Jesse Jewell, frozen fresh chicken.
Jesse Jewell, sure is great.
Jesse Jewell, frozen fresh chicken.
The finest tasting chicken, you ever ate.

The jingle was recorded, of course, but the voices that told the rest of the story came on live. There was Ray Moore, a talented young announcer at WSB-TV, and in Gainesville, who else but WGGA's Jim Hartley, whose wife was secretary to Jewell Company's Charles Thurmond.

Hall County Returns To Auto Manufacturing

A number of manufacturers of automotive components have located in Hall County in recent years - modern plants making well-engineered precision parts that go into vehicles ... everything from ball bearings, to small electric motors, to transmissions, to wheels. These are new plants, using new technology, but Gainesville has a long history with the transportation industry; all the way back into the horse and buggy days.

Northeast Georgia developed early as a leather center, making harness and saddles. Gainesville Spoke and Handle Company made singletrees, doubletrees, and whiffletrees, the wooden bars which hitched a horse's harness to the wagon or plow to be pulled (or pushed).

The G. W. Walker company was one of Gainesville's largest industries in the late 1800s, making carriages, buggies, wagons, trucks, drays, and delivery wagons. But it appears Bagwell and Gower Manufacturing Company was the only one to make products for both the horse and buggy era and the new automobile period. Bagwell and Gower was a widely-known maker of buggies, carts, and wagons. But there can also be found references to this company making and selling phaetons ... that's p-h-a-e-t-o-n-s ... and a phaeton in that day and time was generally a touring car.

1930: One Telephone Line: One Call

I had an opportunity the other day to visit the BellSouth Test Laboratories in Atlanta, and the young guy explaining the technology to us noted that once upon a time it took one telephone wire to connect two people so they could communicate. Your wire went to the telephone office, and the operator patched your wire to the wire of whomever you wanted to talk with, and ... bingo ... you could talk with each other.

When I got back home, I dug out the photo history of Gainesville, and there's a picture of a telephone pole in front of the old Court House (the brick one that was destroyed by the tornado of 1936) that has six crossbars on it, and it looks like there were 10 wires per crossbar. There's another picture in front of the old Presbyterian Church, showing one of those 60-wire poles, but in addition there is another pole with at least 20 wires on it.

Anyway, about 1930, it took one more maze of wires to connect people in downtown Gainesville.

There's another picture in the photo history of Gainesville's first "modern" switchboard, which was installed here in 1918. If you look closely, you can see places for 17 operators, and that shows only one side of the room. That switchboard was in operation in our town until a few years after World War II.

Along the way, our BellSouth Lab guy reported, new technology was developed that allowed 24 voice messages per wire ... then 673 ... then more than 2000. And now they can transmit 516,000 messages over one strand of fiber optic cable about the size of a human hair. All that in my lifetime. Amazing.

☆ ☆ ☆

Bloomers in Clayton: Circa 1920

I've been reading a book entitled *Sketches of Rabun County History,* and one of the fascinating economic events was the beginning of the boys and girls camps in the mountains of Northeast Georgia. The book was written by one Lillian Smith, and it tells you a whole lot about our own corner of the state of Georgia about 1920.

Let's quote from the book. "The coming of the children to Rabun County caused a minor revolution in 'manners' in our county. For these children, and their elders, came in their new 'camp clothes' and in those early days, after the first World War, this meant 'bloomers' for the girls and their counselors. To a community accustomed to old conservative ways this onslaught of the new was like a loud noise piercing our morals!

Letters poured in to camp directors written by civic groups politely requesting the campers to wear stockings rolled up above the knees when they came to town, and for years, onlookers were treated to the captivating sight of a hundred girls stopping at the edge of town, carefully pulling up long black stockings above forbidden knees before entering what was then our unpaved streets."

The culture, she was a'changing, circa 1920.

Gainesville Data: Late 1940s

It was the late 1940s, and the Chamber of Commerce was sending out information about Gainesville and Hall County. ... Hall County had a population of about 42,000, and Gainesville was close to 14,000. Both had grown more than 20 % in the previous 10 years, and Gainesville, with a growth rate of 26.8 %, was listed as one of the fastest growing small cities in America.

There were three banks with $13.8-million in resources, and one Building and Loan with $2.2-million. The information stated the city had 18 white churches and eight Negro churches, and twelve civic groups.

The city had a police force of 16 people. There were three cruisers equipped with two-way radio, and the patrolmen were uniformed. Hall County had a Sheriff and three deputies. They were also equipped with two patrol cars with two-way radio, and they provided police protection outside the city. In addition, eight Georgia State Highway Patrolmen with four patrol cars were stationed in Gainesville, and they covered most of Northeast Georgia.

That was Gainesville, 50 years ago.

✲ ✲ ✲

Aviation Comes To Gainesville #1

Gainesville has always been involved in aviation, despite the fact airports need a lot of flat land, a scarcity in this area. Flying was hardly underway in the early 1900s when a landing strip was established where today's Athens Street crosses the railroad, then known as the brickyard area. Barnstorming airplanes would come to town and, for a fee, take people for a ride. Then, in the early 1920s, Gainesville bought about 12 acres at the site of the present-day Lee Gilmer Memorial Airport. Gainesville Mill donated some more land, and it was made level enough for the airplanes of that time.

In the mid-1920s, Congress got involved, and formed an air transportation committee. Among routes being proposed was one from Washington to Atlanta, and a plan was under consideration calling for emergency landing fields every 10 miles and stopover air fields every 60 to 100 miles. Gainesville's Chamber of Commerce, then headed by Sidney O. Smith, jumped all over that plan. Henry Estes, a Gainesville merchant, was dispatched to Washington to testify, seeking designation of Gainesville as the first Atlanta to Washington stopover airport, and to seek airmail service. We didn't get the stopover designation, but we got the beginnings of a great small-city airport.

☆ ☆ ☆

Aviation Comes to Gainesville #2

Dean Parks made the first solo flight in Hall County on July 5, 1929, and was the pioneer aviator who first laid out the present Gainesville airport. Flying had caught the fancy of America in the 1930s, and the local Chamber of Commerce insisted that a good airport would help Gainesville attract new industry, as well as help solidify its position as the trade center of Northeast Georgia.

When World War II came, the U. S. Navy took over the Gainesville airport and made it a training facility with emphasis on teaching pilots instrument flying. The Navy expanded and improved the facility. What had been a good airport prior to the war was returned to the city in 1947 as an excellent airport capable even of handling most commercial airplanes.

Gainesville renewed its effort to get commercial airline service for this city, but as one old-timer explains: "We were just a notch too close to Atlanta for them to take off there, land here, and make it pay." Several attempts were made to establish commuter service to Atlanta and nearby airports, but that hasn't worked, either. Gainesville's enchantment with flying, though, may be coming out about right, for this city has one of the most desirable private aircraft airports in the South.

☆ ☆ ☆

Picking The Pockets of "City Folks"

"Where did you get the money to buy your sawmill equipment?" I asked. "You just said the biggest problem mountain folks had starting a business was getting what we now call investment capital."

"Well, it was city folks that helped us get started", he replied. "We learned to pick their pockets legal like. It wasn't bad. They loved it." Except for the Gold era, picking the pockets of city folks, mostly Atlantans, started when city people first got touring cars. "I lived near Clermont as a kid," he continued. "City folks would put together a long string of cars ... a caravan. They'd all put on their 'dusters' and goggles, get in those open cars and here they'd come. You could see them coming a mile away from that big cloud of dust."

"We put up a sign: Free Water, Both Kinds." "Okay," I said. "I'll bite. What do you mean, both kinds?" It turned out the local folks would have buckets of cool spring water for their city guests to drink, and creek water for car radiators, some of them already belching steam.

"But how did you make money?" I asked. "I'm getting to that," he says. "You would be amazed what those folks would buy. Worn out plow handles. Chicken coops, if they'd been washed out. Boiled peanuts made the most money for me, especially if you boiled them in beer. It didn't take much beer. Just a splash, and you could smell those peanuts for days. There was some nice stuff, too, like handmade quilts. They came through twice a year, spring and fall."

"That's how I got together enough money to buy my first loggin' saw," he remembered proudly. "Picking the pockets of city folks. They loved it, too. We wore sort of worn-out bib overalls, and they were certain they had met some real hicks. They might have been right in that."

Dean Jones: A Farm Leader and A Farmer's Farmer

We don't pay much attention to agriculture in Hall County any more, even though this county is, primarily because of income from the poultry industry, still one of the leading agricultural counties in Georgia. But if we look at the history of this region, we will quickly recall that it wasn't too long ago that farming was the leading economic engine here, and that we had some statewide, even nationwide, leaders among our local farmers.

The reason this comes to mind, of course, is that our long-time friend, Dean Jones, died the other day, and with his passing, we probably saw the end of an era. Dean lived near Flowery Branch, and I still tend to think of him as a dairy farmer, even though he had moved out of that and into the paint horse business years ago. His home and farm sat squarely in the path of South Hall County's growth, and even though he had come to accept that growth, he remained a farmer, and a farm leader, to the end. He was active in the Hall County Farm Bureau, and served for several years as its president. He represented our area on the statewide Board of Directors of the Georgia Farm Bureau for as long as I can remember, and that goes back a ways. His obituary says he was a national director of the American Paint Horse Association, a fact I did not know, but I am not at all surprised.

Dean Jones was a leader among farmers at a time when farming dominated the economy of this region, and he remained a farmer, and a farm leader, to the end. Dean was a real farmer, not a hobby farmer who made a living in other ways. Real farmers in our county are now getting sparse as we become an urban area and the price of land goes up and taxes go up with it. But I hope we all remember our history well enough to understand what Dean Jones did for farmers here, and for that matter, what he did for all of us who live in Hall County.

✲ ✲ ✲

The Poultry Capital of The World?

Gainesville is often referred to as the Poultry Capital of the World. That may be stretching it a bit, but not much. There's even a monument to the chicken in downtown Gainesville. From poultry processing plants in Gainesville, Murrayville, Pendergrass, Habersham County, and other nearby communities, more than TEN MILLION CHICKENS A WEEK go to market throughout America and around the world. Add to that the "further processing plants" (those that convert whole chickens to chicken tenders, nuggets, frozen recipe dishes, etc.), and one begins to get an idea of the scope of the chicken-based food business in this area.

But there is more: the hatcheries and feed mills, the manufacturing plants that make the automated processing equipment, soybean processors like Cargill, and even the poultry industry's national trade newspaper. Despite its high level of automation, the poultry industry is the largest employer in this region. In the world of agriculture, commercial poultry and egg production is Georgia's largest farm income producer, outranking cotton, soybeans, even timber.

And yet, except for the multitude of trucks rolling along major highways, the average citizen sees very little of this local economic giant. There is a reason. Poultry is part of the food business, and one of the top priorities is to keep the final product absolutely free of all diseases and bacterial contamination. Thus farms are usually located off the main highways. Hatcheries are kept at an aseptic level comparable to a hospital operating room. Workers at poultry plants wear hair nets and clothing similar to nurses in an emergency room. Poultry operations are not unfriendly; they just don't want people wandering through. And they certainly don't want to introduce any type of contamination. So, they are generally out of sight and unavailable for public tours.

There is a side benefit to this "quiet" industry. Prior to the 1940's farmers tried to grow cotton on these red clay hills, and soil erosion almost destroyed the land. The Chattahoochee River ran so red with clay that one county agent said it was "too thick to navigate and too thin to cultivate." As local farmers shifted to poultry in the last half of the 20th century, farmers applied poultry litter to the land and then planted pastures or pine trees. Much of the green one sees in this area today can be credited to the poultry industry ... both green as in the environment, and green as in dollars.

☆ ☆ ☆

CHAPTER 6 – Religion and Morals: The Dedicated Good Guys and Their Errant Children

Every culture throughout the world rests on a foundation of basic beliefs. Most are, or at least began, as a religion. Some seek to convert the whole world to their beliefs (Christianity and Islam) while others take a live-and-let-live attitude.

The people who settled Northeast Georgia came with a strong desire for religious freedom. They had come from countries in which either the church (usually Catholic) or the King, dictated to them what to believe and how to worship, This desire for religious freedom, as well as political freedom, was a major factor in their support of democracy. America's early settlers did not trust, or care to be subservient to, an all-powerful church or an all-powerful government. And they certainly did not want to live in a culture in which church and state combined power and were one and the same.

And yet, not every one agreed upon, let alone abided by, the basic tenets of the religion around them.

So, the question is posed: what was the moral and ethical foundation for the culture of Northeast Georgia from the earliest settlers through the end of World War II?

✲ ✲ ✲

PROTESTANT CHRISTIANITY AND THE CULTURE OF THE MOUNTAINS

It seems fair to say the foundation for the culture of Northeast Georgia was Protestant Christianity. The earliest preachers were totally dedicated in their calling to bring the Good News to the people on the frontier. While there were very early Presbyterians and Lutherans, followed by Episcopalians from English coastal colonies, it was the Methodists and Baptists who led the way in developing churches in mountainous, sparsely-populated Northeast Georgia.

The earliest church services were usually held in homes or business buildings. As preachers of the various denominations arrived, church buildings were built. Some historians say the construction of a church building marked the front edge of civilization. Missionary activities toward the Indians were apparently not as energetic as in Northwest Georgia.

Congregations grew as the population increased, and churches were located in central communities so they could easily be reached by wagon. County seat towns tended to grow larger, and thus had the largest churches.

Then came the Civil War, and denominations ended up with churches that were either northern or southern – Presbyterians, Methodists, Baptists ... all of them. Although slaves were relatively rare in the Georgia mountains (as compared with coastal Georgia) most churches built prior to the Civil War had "slave balconies," a feature exclusive in Southern churches (and later, a great location for the church choirs).

The late 1800s and early 1900s marked another "Great Awakening" period in the South. Church membership grew, and across the region, new churches were built, most of them brick or stone, with stained glass windows and a similar architectural style. Circa 1900, Gainesville saw new sanctuaries for each of the three major denominations – Baptist, Methodist, and Presbyterian. Each built large, new buildings only one block apart. All were located on Green Street, near the town square. All were located on the trolley route, easily accessible by residents and resort visitors alike.

"Demon rum" was the common enemy ... or to use the more formal term, "spirituous liquors." The WCTU – Women's Christian Temperance Union – was the driving force both nationally and locally, and the movement brought forth a large number of women who were, as one preacher said, quite willing to "raise a ruckus." In the South, at that time, genteel women simply did not speak out at county commission meetings, or other public events at any time. But the WCTU brought forth a leadership style that was considered a bit on the crazy side (but a GOOD Crazy, mind you).

Demorest, Georgia deserves special mention at this point. Founded as a religious community with a rigid moral code, Demorest brought in dedicated Christians from all over the United States. The moral tone of the community was described thusly:

"Society here is cultured and moral. The people have come from all parts of the United States, actuated by a common purpose to build a model city. Saloons, gambling houses, and other low places of resort are forever prohibited, not only by public sentiment but by an uncontestable clause in the title deed of every foot of ground."

Not all prohibitionists were women, either. One summer resident who owned land in Demorest was J. M. Fletcher of Nashua, New Hampshire. He was owner of a large manufacturing business and a poet. This was part of a poem he penned for the Demorest Pioneer Club in 1895:

From North and South, from far and near,
    Cometh our little band.
Each one a hardy pioneer
    To brave this mountain land.
As if by inspiration moved
    We sought this Southern soil
To prove the principles we loved
    By hard and honest toil.
The days when we were pioneers
    In Demorest of old
Are tempered with the smiles and tears

And sacred let us hold
The scenes and seasons that we planned
Together as we wrought
And here in Dixie's sunny land
For prohibition fought.

Although all denominations in Northeast Georgia were not as rigid as in Demorest, they came close. The moral and ethical underpinning of the culture of the mountains was Protestant Christianity ...as preached by the preachers of the late 1800s and early 1900s.

✲ ✲ ✲

WHITE LIGHTNIN', FAST CARS, AND OTHER ILLICIT (But Socially Acceptable) ACTIVITIES

The making of moonshine whiskey was not only an illicit activity that had an impact on the business and culture of Northeast Georgia - in most of the region, making GOOD whiskey was a respected profession.

As a summer resort region, well-to-do summer people came from muggy, hot coastal areas and were willing to pay good money for items or activities not normally accepted by the people who lived in the mountains.

From the 2001 book, *NORTHEAST GEORGIA: A History*: "During the period from 1880 to 1919, there developed an amazing mountain institution, a rather highly respected, but illegal industry. Many known moonshiners were involved in politics, were leaders in their communities, and officers in their churches."

A number of local enterprises, mostly located in Gainesville, found good business among the moonshiners – all very legal, even though they knew full well what their customers were doing was illegal. Grocery wholesalers sold sugar and Mason or Ball jars. Automobile dealers sold the "day trippers" cars and parts. Banks made them loans. And local lawyers handled their case when they were caught. The moonshiners were an important economic engine of the local economy.

But it was the STOCK CARS that got a life of their own. A spinoff from the moonshine/bootlegger business, stock car racing has become a sport followed by literally millions of Americans from coast to coast. The narrow, curvy mountain road drivers who delivered white lightning to Atlanta and other cities, usually driving a 1939 Ford coupe fitted with a "souped up" motor and heavyweight springs, enjoyed racing with one another almost as much as they delighted in outrunning a Deputy Sheriff.

When Southern stock car racing was new and neither well reported on nor well respected, Dawson County, Georgia, "day trippers" gained a reputation for being the best-of-the-best high speed drivers. They often raced each other on dirt tracks, but it was when a raced was started in Daytona, Florida, that the winners were crowned. Half of the "race track" was on a state highway, and the return half was on the sandy beach. The Daytona race was not organized; it just happened. Word got around that "they" would be racing at Daytona on such-and-such a day, and the informally formed world of stock car racing simply showed up.

And did they run. Cars burned rubber into the highway, then skidded onto the beach, spinning wheels and throwing sand in a huge spray. It didn't take long before spectators adopted their own favorite driver, and they would get a favored spot on the raceway, and cheer as their guy went by. When the race was over, the party started. It wasn't just an event; it was THE event. And anybody who was anybody in stock car racing did not want to miss it.

In the early days, five Dawson County drivers won the Daytona at least 10 times. There was Gober Sosebee, who officially won at Daytona three times, and would have won it a fourth time if he hadn't been disqualified. Toward the end of one race, instead of stopping to refuel, one of Gober's pit crew jumped in the car with a five gallon can of gas, leaned out the window, and refueled on the run. What kept the car from blowing sky high only God knows, and if it had blown, it would certainly have killed Gober, his pit crewman, a couple of other cars on the track and no one knows how many spectators. Gober came in first, but they took the trophy away from him, and a new rule was added to the mostly unruly Daytona. Would you call that crazy? Not Gober.

There was Loyd Seay, who was killed at 21, not from a car crash but from a gunshot during an argument over sugar for the family's still. Roy Hall won Daytona once, as did Bernard G. Long. And way before modern day women's rights came to be politically correct, Carleen Rouse became the first woman to take the Daytona trophy. It would be years later before Bill Elliott, awesome Bill from Dawsonville, became another Dawson County King of Daytona.

At this juncture, it appears stock car racing might well receive what moonshine whiskey never has ... national respectability.

In addition to moonshining and stock car racing, there were other activities that became an accepted part of the mountain culture. There were "private clubs" in which a person could buy a membership for as little as one dollar, and under the private club law, the "club" could sell liquor, have slot machines, and even high-stakes poker nights. In the summer resort era, Gainesville even had a red light district.

This legal-illegal Northeast Georgia culture appears often in the history of the mountains, and looks suspiciously like the era in which God Fearin' farmers and Hell Raisin' Gold diggers struggled to see whose culture prevailed.

✲ ✲ ✲

THE LOVE-HATE RELATIONSHIP BETWEEN THE PREACHERS AND THE MOONSHINERS

From the earliest days in frontier America, and especially in Appalachia, there was a love-hate relationship between churches and moonshiners. Some of this split-personality culture came to the Georgia mountains with the arrival of the early Scotch-Irish Presbyterians. The Scotchmen who migrated first to Ulster, in Ireland, and then to America, had some Calvinist beliefs that were somewhat rigid, and generally served them well in the rugged wilderness of mountain land. They were hard working, frugal and fiercely independent. They were good traders, and became the first to explore the Appalachians, trading all kinds of things to Indians in exchange for deer hides – buckskins. The Scotch-Irish Presbyterians generally took their religion seriously, but they also were proud of their ability to make good whiskey ...a skill that obviously did not conflict with their religious beliefs.

Thus developed a culture in which Preachers (teaching Elders in the Presbyterian Church) harangued their flock never to imbibe beyond a temperate level in spirituous liquors, while the laymen (ruling Elders) were very often manufacturing corn whiskey by the gallon. It was simply part of the accepted culture at the time on the American frontier. And although this culture may have started with Presbyterians, it quickly infected all denominations.

During the Civil War, the federal government imposed a licensing tax on the manufacture of whiskey, and after the war it was actively enforced in Northeast Georgia as well as in other states. There was already growing resentment in the mountains against the federal government because of Reconstruction and occupation, but when the "Revenuers" became more and more active, the moonshiners pushed back, and the North Georgia "Moonshine War" of 1876-77 was underway. Shots were fired at some Revenuers, so President Ulysses S. Grant sent in the troops, supposedly to protect the federal revenue agents. The memory of the Civil War was fresh on Southerners' minds. And the appearance of Union soldiers was not well received. Shots were fired at the 2nd United States Infantry, but the Union Army prevailed – again. Some mountain families had sided with the Union during the Civil War, but now even that group recoiled at "the Yankee invasion of the Georgia mountains."

In time, the Georgia Whiskey Rebellion subsided, and the Revenuers returned to their enforcement of the laws. Robert Scott Davis, in his study of the North Georgia Moonshine War of 1876-77 said: "By 1876, cases involving the prosecution of revenue law violators virtually monopolized the docket of the Federal District Court in Atlanta, Georgia."

Meantime, the mainline churches were becoming more powerful throughout the mountain area, and campground meetings drew thousands to hear prominent preachers. The church-goers and the moonshiners had learned to live together in peace, and in some cases were the same people.

During the period 1880 to 1919 (plus or minus a few years), when the mountain area of Georgia was a summer resort region, saloons were legal in most towns where the "summer people" gathered. There were two types. One type of saloon served drinks at a low price, usually serving untaxed moonshine whiskey. The more posh bars served "call brands," almost always recognized brands on which taxes had been paid.

In 1919, the 18th amendment to the U. S. Constitution was passed, an act that prohibited the manufacture and sale of "spirituous liquors." It was a gold mine for moonshiners. Then in 1933, the 21st amendment nullified the 18th. Prohibition ended, and the sale of legal, tax paid whiskey returned to Georgia so long as a city or county voted it in.

Leading into World War II, most of Northeast Georgia was "dry" – that is, whiskey could not be sold legally inside the county line. Thus, most Gainesville residents bought their whiskey in Arcade, a roadside village just west of Athens, or at "that discount store" in North Atlanta. And, in a pinch, non-tax paid whiskey could be found in a Gainesville suburb called Sandy Flat.

Every time some government, city or county, made noises about legalizing the sale of whiskey within its boundary, the preachers and moonshiners would combine forces to kill the bill – the preachers and the Women's Christian Temperance Union in honest opposition to Demon Rum, and the moonshiners to keep out competition from legal whiskey.

✲ ✲ ✲

Chattahoochee Missionary Baptist Association Is Formed

The year was 1826, and a meeting of North Georgia Baptist Churches had been called, to be held at Hopewell Church in Hall County. It was at this meeting that the Chattachoochee Missionary Baptist Association was formed. The churches represented were: Hopewell, Wahoo, Mt. Salem, Tesnatee, Yellow Creek, Dewberry, Flat Creek, Mossy Creek, and Chestatee.

The five oldest churches in the Baptist Association were said to be Hopewell, 1807; Flat Creek, 1818; Harmony, 1824; Yellow Creek, 1825; and Sardis, 1825.

At the time the Chattahoochee Association was formed, Indians still roamed the land, and all churches were scattered and relatively small. The average size of the churches in that original Baptist association was 37 members. Hall County was on the American frontier in 1826, in the edge of the mountains, but new settlers were coming in a solid stream ... and two years after the Chattahoochee Baptist Association was formed, Gold was discovered, and the population boom began.

✲ ✲ ✲

1914: Mossy Creek Campground Drew 5,000 People

I rode by the Mossy Creek campground not long ago, and it reminded me I had seen something about a Mossy

Creek Camp Meeting recently when I was doing some research in an old newspaper. So I started the search and finally found it in the *Gainesville Eagle* of July 30, 1914.

There was an announcement that the Mossy Creek Camp Meeting "will convene on the 12th of August and run until the 17th. "Dr. S. R. Belk was to be the primary speaker, and it was noted that he would preach twice a day. Rev. W. M. Barnett and Rev. M. B. Whitaker were to help with the meeting. August was the time for camp meetings during that era, and for a reason. Crops were "laid by," and harvest was not yet started. It was warm, and fresh food was plentiful. Many families came early to tidy up the campgrounds and get their tents ready. A lot of courtin' took place among the young people.

Dr. Belk was busy in the fall of 1914. He also preached at the Lebanon Camp meeting, and there was an announcement about the Murrayville High School opening for September 18. Boarding students needed to get their reservations in, according to an announcement by ... guess who? ... S. R. Belk, Presiding Elder, Gainesville District.

A lot of people went by train to the Mossy Creek meeting, and the old Gainesville Northwestern Railroad would stop right near the campground to let people off or pick them up. A news story later said more than 5,000 people went to the Mossy Creek meeting that year. (1914 was a good year.)

✲ ✲ ✲

First Methodist Church Established in 1834

It was Hall County's Sesquicentennial in 1969, and the Rev. Parks Segars was giving a report on the beginning of Gainesville's First Methodist Church. "Col. Ephraim M. Johnson can be called the 'Father of Gainesville Methodism'," the Segars report said, "for it was under his leadership – after a suggestion by a Presbyterian, Mr. McWharten – that a congregation was started ... meeting at the Presbyterian Church. In a borrowed house, with a local preacher, belonging to no circuit or district, and with fifteen members, Brother J. W. Glenn organized the First Methodist Church in Gainesville." Eventually, the Rev. W. Calverhouse became the first preacher.

The report goes on to say: "... the old Gainesville Court house, a frame building, was sold; Colonel Johnson bought it for $150. Presbyterians, Baptists, and Gainesville citizens who were not related directly with any church, and neighbors from the country roundabout, assisted the Methodists in moving the old Courthouse to a lot at the corner of South Bradford and Church Streets. "And thus it was, in 1834, that the First Methodist Church was officially established in Gainesville."

✲ ✲ ✲

Dewberry Church Number One and Number Two

Out of Hall County comes a story, probably well-massaged by time, of why there is a Dewberry Church number one and a Dewberry Church number two. Some 80 years ago, the original Dewberry Church developed a schism over the subject of predestination. The argument threatened to split the congregation. It set cousin against cousin, family against family. Every Wednesday night, prayer meeting was rent with debate.

At a crisis point, each side retreated, and a reconciliation ensued. To celebrate the peace, the congregants held a mammoth dinner on the grounds. That afternoon, the churchyard was filled with tables made of two-by-ten boards laid across saw horses and covered with the linen from a dozen closets. The boards sagged under their burden of fried chicken, roast beef, baked ham, candied yams, mashed potatoes, creamed corn, collard greens, green salad, fresh tomatoes, and innumerable pies and cakes and cookies.

The two faction leaders, warmed by their renewed fellowship, sat at a picnic table. Unable to contain a final thrust, one said: "You see this chicken leg I am holding? I don't want to start any old arguments, but just to prove a point, I want to say that I am predestined to eat this chicken leg." The other older man reached over, knocked the drumstick from his hand and onto the ground. A large dog picked it up and ran off with it.

What happened next is not necessary to describe. But now in the hills there is a Dewberrry number one and a Dewberry number two. Neither seems any more fixed on predestination than most of the other churches in the neighborhood.

(Unpublished. Written by Sylvan Meyer, editor of the *Gainesville Daily Times* when this was written in 1984. He won a Nieman Fellowship to Harvard, then became editor of the daily newspaper in Miami.)

✲ ✲ ✲

North and South Presbyterians Merge

It was mid-century, and some of our local Presbyterian men were in Atlanta for a three-day conference. At the time, it was said to be the largest conference of its type ever held in the United States ... purely a men's conference aimed at strengthening men as Christians. There were 5,700 delegates from all over the South, and the meeting made headlines in the local papers.

But the big news from that meeting was a growing interest in reuniting the Northern and Southern Presbyterian Churches. You see, during the War Between The States ... way back in the 1860's ... the Presbyterians had split into a Northern Presbyterian Church and a Southern Church. And here in 1949, the men of the church (although not a ruling body) were calling for reunification.

As with most things in church government, reunification of the Presbyterian church did not come immediately. In fact, it came somewhat slowly, but in time it did come. At mid-century, we were just beginning to think about ending a lot of things left over from the Civil War.

✲ ✲ ✲

A Backward Collar Preacher On a Bicycle

Pat McGeachy was in town the other day, speaking at a church meeting. For those of you who don't remember Pat McGeachy, he was pastor of the First Presbyterian Church not long after World War II. Those were days when we expected certain things of our pastors, whatever the denomination ... things you didn't mess with. They were expected to wear dark suits, drive unassuming cars, not get involved in politics, never attend a cocktail party. Their wives were to cook a lot, sing in the choir, and work with the children. You know the job description.

Into this culture came one Daniel Patrick McGeachy, the son of a noted Presbyterian minister in Decatur, but a young man with his own ideas. He wore a backward collar, which we thought was reserved for Catholics and, maybe, Episcopalians. Since he lived only a couple of blocks from the church, he decided it would be more efficient to ride a bicycle to and from the church ... which he did. But the primary thing that took some getting used to was the fact he played a guitar. It was great for young people's meetings, but then one day he accompanied the choir with it.

Anyway, Pat said he didn't think people would mind him riding the bicycle around town ... so long as he didn't look like he was enjoying it.

✲ ✲ ✲

Competition For Church Parking Spaces

It was 1950, and there was a parking problem downtown. No, it wasn't the kind you are thinking about, where the merchants were concerned about parking near their front doors on the square. This parking problem had to do with the churches on Sunday morning.

You see, three of Gainesville's major churches were located on Green Street, right near the Square: First Baptist where Regions Bank now has its headquarters; First Presbyterian one block away, where the little gazebo is at the back of the SunTrust building; and First Methodist was one block further out, the only one of the three church buildings which is still standing. Green Street had to handle all the traffic from that side of town ... I mean ALL of it. There was no E. E. Butler and no bypass. Gainesville was growing. The churches were growing. Church attendance was growing. And traffic was growing. To compound the problem, long-time church members wanted to park right at the front door, just as they had always done.

They eventually solved the problem. First Baptist moved further north on Green Street; First Presbyterian moved to Enota Drive; and First Methodist moved all the way across the lake. But at mid-century, it was about as easy to walk to church as it was to find a parking place near one.

✲ ✲ ✲

The Ten Commandments and Our Judeo-Christian Base

It seems to me the debate we're going through about the Ten Commandments is much more involved, and important, than the surface discussion about separation of church and state. A lot of people, I suspect, are pleased that we are pushing the debate over in the church/state corner, and would like to keep it there. But the fact is this debate is about what we accept as America's moral foundation, and whether or not Protestant Christians will be allowed to remain an active influence in our American democracy.

We seem to forget that the moral foundation on which Western Civilization, and especially American democracy, is built, is the Judeo-Christian tradition. We find all kinds of references to this idea among the writings and speeches of our founding fathers. We track the evolution of democratic government across Greece, to Rome, to the Protestant Reformation on mainland Europe, and especially to Scotland and England.

And always you will find a common set of Christian values that will allow the radical idea of government by-the-people ... democracy if you will ... to work successfully. Almost all historians will agree that without this moral underpinning, democracy will fall apart.

✲ ✲ ✲

Church and State: A Political View

One of the interesting debates of our time is: what should be the relationship between church and state? Because our founding fathers did not want government controlling the church, they wrote separation of church and state into the constitution. And, because of the power of the Roman Catholic Church, and the continuing scrap between the British King and the church at that time, they didn't want the church running government, either.

America's liberal media goes ballistic every time conservative church members get involved in politics, which they do, and accuse Republicans of all kinds of dire things because Christians are a major force in their party. But those same newspapers are complimentary when church members who lean liberal organize for political action.

I personally think it is right that the organized church not be allowed to run our government, and that our government should not run the organized church. But I also think it is great that the people who go to church on Sunday, and to work on Monday, are active in politics. If they can't take us the right direction, who can?

✲ ✲ ✲

When Football Games Started With a Prayer

It was 1949, and football season was getting underway. There was the usual excitement prior to the game. The cheerleaders had practiced their gyrations, and the marching bands not only had done their practicing of the music, but also had practiced their formations on the football field. There was a doctor on the sidelines, a volunteer by the way. And some parents were set to miss the kickoff because they were getting ready for the after-game dance. Football season was an exciting time fifty years ago, and part of the reason was because it involved so many people in addition to the football team.

There was one other person to be involved, too. You see, at that time, football games were opened with prayer, and one of the decisions that had to be made was who would be invited to give that opening prayer. Everything would stop, and there would be a hush from the crowd, and over the public address system would come a prayer ... usually asking for good sportsmanship, and imploring the Almighty that no one would be hurt. At the Georgia and Georgia Tech games, the prayer would be followed with the raising of the flag and the national anthem. As quaint as it may sound, fifty years ago we could pray at public gatherings like football games.

✲ ✲ ✲

Blue Laws and Closing on Wednesday

World War II was over, but the "Blue Laws" were still in effect. You don't remember the Blue Laws? Well, retail establishments were to be closed on Sundays, EXCEPT for those that might be needed by customers in an emergency ... and it was that little loophole that created the problem.

Certainly, drug stores fit the emergency criteria. If somebody got sick, they needed medicine. But what about food stores if a family accidentally ran out of milk? And filling stations (you know: the place where people got gasoline for their car): did they fit the emergency group, especially if someone needed to go to the hospital? And there was this troubling trend of stores that wanted to stay open Sundays just to sell goods to people. And some stores were staying open later and later during the week.

But not all merchants were in agreement with the longer hours. Early in 1949, sixy-four downtown Gainesville businesses agreed to close on Wednesday afternoons during the summer. They closed, too, every Wednesday afternoon till September ... just before school started.

☼ ☼ ☼

1903: A Historic Hall County Dry Vote

Hall County has always had a love-hate relationship with whiskey. During the late 1800s, when Gainesville was a major mountain resort town and wealthy people from the coast spent their summers here, it seemed natural that Gainesville had bars and served drinks with meals. Then, at the turn of the century 100 years ago, a major movement began in America to do away with alcohol completely ... and it caught on here.

So in 1903 the entire county had a vote on whether it would be wet or dry. A prohibition campaign committee was formed, and energetically and vocally, it went to work. Here's how the local newspaper reported the results: "The drink demon was vanquished in a day. It only took the prohibitionists from 6:38 am to 6:38 pm to do the work, and for four years more we are free from bar rooms, and the indications are that this city and county will never have them again." A total of 2013 people voted in that 1903 election and of that number 1,766 voted "dry" and 247 voted "wet." This, of course, had nothing to do with moonshining or bootlegging ... that was another issue. This overwhelming vote did away with legal whiskey and bar rooms.

✲ ✲ ✲

Police Raid A Downtown "Still"

It was 1950, and the Gainesville Police department was busy. You see, Gainesville was a dry town, but they had been having some problems lately with alcohol ... you know, drinkin' and drunk drivin' ... things like that. So the Gainesville police department was cracking down.

At 9:15 on a Tuesday morning, police staged a raid on a house at 738 North Bradford Street, less than eight blocks from the downtown square. But this was not just an illicit whiskey seller; this was an active still. According to the report: "A 35-gallon capacity copper whiskey still and approximately 250 gallons of corn mash were captured. Apparently, the still had been tucked in the brick walls of what had once been a basement furnace.

The raid was led by Police Chief Bill Bagwell with the support of Captain Hoyt Henry, Officer Frank Strickland, and Officer Bill Murphy ... certainly some of the most respected officers ever to serve Gainesville.

Said Chief Bagwell: "We are turning up the heat on bootleggers ... This makes the eighth whiskey case in the city since Friday."

* * *

A Petition To Sell Beer and Wine

It was the early 1950s, and all Gainesville was in a dither. There was an unconfirmed rumor going 'round town that somebody was about to petition the city government for a license to sell beer and wine. All of Hall County was dry, and although it was well known that many locals made regular runs, either to Atlanta or to Arcade over near Athens, to get their supply of beer or whiskey, legalizing the sale of alcoholic beverages was somewhat frowned upon. The forbidden juice could, of course, be obtained locally in places like Sandy Flat ... but that was pretty risky, for it came from mountain stills and didn't have Federal tax stamps, and good people could get in trouble if caught with that.

Anyway, it was Springtime, and a group of forty local citizens showed up at the City Commission meeting with a petition in hand opposing the local sale of beer and wine. Beyond the forty who attended the meeting, their petition had 978 names on it, objecting to the rumored request for a license, and asking that the city stay dry. The petition drive had been headed by the Gainesville Ministerial Association, and the powerful Womens Christian Temperance Union. It would be be several years before ANYTHING with alcohol was legalized in Gainesville.

Lumpkin Mooneshine Has A Problem

It was the late 1940s, and the Dahlonega Nugget (known at the time for its tart, tongue-in-cheek commentary) was upset with the deer hunters. It wasn't deer HUNTING that bothered the Nugget, it was the large number of deer hunters from outside the county descending on them. The local newspaper figured the problem was being caused by high-powered rifles and smokeless powder, newly available to city folks.

Shooting deer was okay, but all these hunters were causing a real problem with one of Lumpkin County's leading industries.

To quote from the Nugget: "The deer season has been a stimulating influence on the retail moonshine business, but it has hurt the distilling industry. ... A fellow's factory just isn't safe from detection with so many hunters roaming the woods."

✲ ✲ ✲

A Spirited Discussion Between Houses of Ill Repute

There was a time when Gainesville had some ... shall we say ... disreputable things going on, and the amazing thing is that the local papers of the day not only knew about it but reported the facts in full. For instance, try this quote: "The home of the Bales women, in the northern suburbs of the city, has for a long time been a place of resort for a great many of the boys and young men of this town." It goes on to say: "Often are the times that the police have raided this establishment, presided over by Sallie Bales, mother of the two charmers, Hattie and Lula."

Anyway ... on one occasion, the Bales and two young men were charged with "rasing cain" in a disorderly manner. The city court fined each of the men two dollars and Hattie two dollars, but when they got to Lula, she claimed she was being discriminated against, and she asked the Mayor's Court, "... why it was that the authorities were everlastingly making war upon them and never did anything towards obliterating that cess-pool of vice known as the Richmond house." When she had finished her say, the court fined Lula three dollars, about which the paper said: "But she had had her say, and we suppose she was wiling to pay a dollar more for that privilege."

CHAPTER 7 – Reading, Writing, and Common Sense

Not everyone was well educated in early frontier Georgia, but there is ample evidence that an education was a high priority among the early backwoods settlers ... and a very high priority among the dedicated clergy who delivered the Word of God to the mountains.

The early Foxfire books, collections of long-ago memories of mountain characters recorded by students as part of English classes in Rabun County present a stream of memories about education received in the crude, one-room school houses of the mountains.

Matt Gedney, in his book *Living on the Unicoi Road* reports on an interview with 80-ish Laura Abernathy Cannon. Laura was born in 1909, and lived on the Unicoi Road above Helen. Laura Cannon got more education than her father, and attended three different schools. The first was a "one room affair" on Loudsville Road, about two miles from her home. Second was the "new school in Helen." And finally the Nacoochee Institute, a

Presbyterian school once located where the Valleys of Nacoochee and Sautee meet.

In the direct notes from Laura's interview, a picture is painted of her father's education and her school experience. Speaking of her father: "He got his education by working, what little education he had. He never went to school a day in his life. Now my mother did. They had a little one room schoolhouse and one book, Webster's Speller, I think they called it. She went; she had a little education, but he didn't. But they was a Mrs. Dean that was a school teacher, and she had a son the same age as my father, and she taught him. Because the schools were so far between, you'd have to go for miles to get to a school house. The little school I went to was just one little room and a big ole stove in the middle of the room, with a sand box around it on account of fire, to keep fire down. (We) had just old benches. You just sat on an old bench and didn't have a desk."

Laura and the others walked to school. "Started in July," she said, "and we'd go through July and August, and then we would stop. After everything was 'gathered in,' the hard part of winter we went to school and then when it was time to go to farming again, we'd have to drop out of school. Altogether, we only went seven months. Everybody had to work."

In the late 1800's and early 1900's, higher level educational institutions began to blossom all across the mountains, most of them created under the auspices of churches.

Brenau College was founded in Gainesville in 1878 with Baptist influence. Young Harris College came into being in 1886, in Young Harris with Methodist support. Piedmont College began operations in 1897, in Demorest, with first Methodist and later Congregational support. All of them featured hard work, weekly chapel, and disciplined academics.

After the Civil War, the U. S. Mint building in Dahlonega stood empty, and with prodding from Congressman William Pearce Price and others, it was given to the State of Georgia "for educational purposes" and reopened in 1873 as the North Georgia Agricultural College. Then in 1875, Senator John B. Gordon persuaded Congress to make it a military college.

✲ ✲ ✲

Preparatory schools were also being formed. The Rabun Gap School took in its first class in 1903, and 50 miles away, the Nacoochee Institute was formed under the auspices of the Presbyterian Synod of Georgia. Both schools had devastating fires in 1926, and were merged at the Rabun Gap location. The Rabun Gap-Nacoochee School received "powerful" support from Ernest and Robert Woodruff of Coca Cola, and later from the Rockefellers.

Riverside Military Academy was chartered in 1906, in Gainesville, and under the leadership of General Sandy Beaver, gained international recognition. The Tallulah Falls School was founded in 1909 with financial support from the Georgia Federation of Women's Clubs.

As transportation improved, the schools of Northeast Georgia changed. Neighborhood schools became larger with more grades, but then there were rural schools and city schools ... and the city schools had advantages. Being larger, with students located nearby, the city schools offered more subjects and activities like football teams.

It would be after World War II, when the great movement for "consolidated schools" came front and center, that schools in the more rural mountain counties were perceived to provide an education on a par with their city cousins.

And it would be after World War II before integrated schools would come about in Georgia ... schools which had an enrollment of both white and black (and now Hispanic) students.

There is no doubt about it - education, like religion, is a major factor in determining the CULTURE of an area. But how is education to be measured? Is the region with the highest test scores a more desirable culture than one in which student scores are lower, but parents give their children a drive to succeed? Is an area better off to have a large population of "elite" people, or a large population of people with "common sense"?

EDUCATION MOUNTAIN STYLE. A SEQUEL

I did my first in-depth research about mountain schools while working on my 2001 book *NORTHEAST GEORGIA: A History*. I looked at the highly successful people who had attended these small schools in Northeast Georgia, people who had achieved great success in many fields, and decided there must have been something special about these old schools. They were not founded to create scholars; they were operated to prepare people for a better life. They were created by educators who considered it their calling to educate people so they could read the family Bible; so they could make a better living; and, yes, so they would be better citizens in a democracy.

The schools endured because the independent, cash-poor, hard-scrabbled mountain parents denied themselves to come up with the money – or more often something to trade – to pay a good teacher.

These schools proved their effectiveness with the successful lives of their graduates, who in turn gave of themselves so the next generation would be educated.

How did I come to the conclusion that 20th century schools of the Georgia mountains were so special?

A personal story, if I may.

It was Spring, 1949, and I was the youngest, greenest reporter on the staff of the Atlanta Constitution, so I was routinely assigned the stories the "real" reporters did not want. Every now and then, I would get a story that had front-page possibilities, and I figured this new assignment to cover an event way up in the mountains had possibilities because a staff photographer had been assigned to go with me. I got a staff car with a full tank of gas for the weekend, and out-of-pocket expenses. It was the best deal I had seen since I got out of the Navy.

So it was on May 29, 1949, that I drove to Young Harris, Georgia, to cover the dedication of a new church at some mountain college. That was about all I knew about the assignment, except that Bishop Arthur J. Moore was on the program, and that alone said it was newsworthy.

We left early that sunny Sunday morning, arriving in Young Harris a couple of hours before starting time to get the basic information, to be sure the names were spelled right (in those days to misspell a name was a firing offense), to determine who should be interviewed and included in the pictures, and to get the "flavor" of the event. The news was that 600 alumni of this small college were involved; that the church building was dedicated to the late Dr. Joseph Astor Sharp, a longtime president of Young Harris College; and that the $150,000 building had been paid for by dedicated alumni ... an amazing amount for a large university at that time, let alone a small mountain college. Not only were graduates of this school financially successful, I surmised, they were also generous, and had a high regard for the education they received there.

The story that ran in the Monday morning edition was not nearly as long as I had originally written, but it carried four photographs and got a good play in the news.

For a long time after that I kept hearing the haunting verse from the Robert W. Service poem, *The Spell of the Yukon,* that goes like this:

There are hardships that nobody reckons;
There are valleys unpeopled and still;

There's a land – oh, it beckons and beckons,
And I want to go back – and I will.

That was when I first got interested in the history of Georgia's mountains ... that and some prodding I got from Ralph McGill after driving him to give a talk at a Ladino Clover festival in Cleveland, Georgia (but that is another mountain story).

✲ ✲ ✲

In Georgia, things were changing rapidly for education at all levels immediately following World War II. Elementary and high schools, many of which still provided only 11 years of education, added the 12th year. Elementary, middle, and high schools became larger consolidated schools, and the small community schools were closed.

A foundation was laid in the first half of the 20th century by a mountain CULTURE that insisted having good educational opportunities was important ... along with Christian values, common sense, frugality and a driving work ethic.

✲ ✲ ✲

In 1907, Education Started With Self-Reliance

We're in the graduation season, and it reminded me of that little book I came across some time back that had been given to a teenager in the year 1907. The title of the book is *Self Reliance*, and it was written by Ralph Waldo Emerson.

Most people seek conformity, Emerson says, while those who would achieve greatness will strive for self-reliance. Let's quote Emerson, "The objection to conforming to usages that have become dead to you, is that it scatters your force. It loses your time and blurs the impression of your character. ...But do your (own) thing, and I shall know you. Do your work, and you shall reinforce yourself."

Emerson continues: "I hope in these days we have heard the last of conformity and consistency. ... Every true man is a cause, a country, and an age. A man Caesar is born, and for ages after, we have a Roman empire. Christ is born, and millions of minds grow and cleave to his genius. ... An institution is the lengthened shadow of one man..."

Emerson says in the conclusion of his essay: "It is only as a man puts off from himself all external support, and stands alone, that I see him to be strong and to prevail."

What intrigued me most about that little book was that, in the year 1907, we were teaching our teenagers to be self-reliant – to stand on their own.

Gainesville High Holds First Graduation

The first graduation from Gainesville High School after the city schools were established was held on June 12, 1894, and even though only seven young men and six young women received diplomas, it was quite an event.

One of the graduates, looking back on that graduation many years later, had this to say about it:

"The curriculum at the time was very thorough and complete for high school. We went far into the classics, completing Sallust and Horace in Latin; trigonometry and part of analytical geometry in mathematics; and physics, chemistry, and history with a splendid course n English literature."

The examinations, graduates remembered, were very thorough. "Not only were we examined with written questions in each subject, but orally by the (entire) Board of Education." About the oral examination, one graduate remembered: "Well do I remember Colonel (C. C.) Sanders having me go to the blackboard and prove a proposition in trigonometry, before the board and visitors." It was well understood that if a student didn't know the material, that student didn't get a diploma. Several hundred people attended that first graduation, held in the magnificent Stringer Opera House.

Clyde Outz Named To Ag Educators' Hall of Fame

I hadn't seen Clyde Outz in a while, so I was delighted to read that he had been inducted as a charter member of the Georgia Agricultural Education Hall of Fame. And it was appropriate that he accepted the award at the Future Farmers of America Center over at Covington.

There was an era in America when vocational agriculture was pretty much the basic preparation for life for many of us. Not only did a student learn agronomy and animal science, he learned about business and public speaking and leadership. It was much, much more than mere classroom education, and it thrived on competition that went all the way to the national level. You've never experienced excitement until you have seen a youngster win a state or national award before a convention hall full of FFA blue jackets.

Clyde Outz started out at the old Clermont High School before he went off to World War II, and he came back to finish up at North Hall High. In all, he taught agriculture 41 years. His students have been leaders in many areas, and have provided much of the core knowledge for the poultry industry. His FFA Chapter won tons of awards, so I think it is more than fitting that the award Clyde Outz received the other day put him in the Georgia Agricultural Hall of Fame.

✡ ✡ ✡

Celebrating 100 Years of Georgia 4-H Clubs

It was 100 years ago this year (2004) that the first 4-H clubs were formed in Georgia, and there probably is no accurate record of how many thousands of youngsters have come through this program. We think of 4-H as a program for rural youngsters, for farm kids, and that was its historic beginning, but today in Georgia, there are 190,000 4-H members. You will still find the bulk of its members from farm and rural backgrounds, but you will also find members from cities, too.

For those of you among the uninitiated, 4-H has a 4-leaf clover as its emblem, and the 4-H's stand for ... well, how many of you can recite the meaning of 4-H? The 4-H's stand for Head, Heart, Hands, and Health, and the pledge says: "I pledge my head to clearer thinking; my heart to greater loyalty; my hands to larger service; and my health to better living ... for my club, my community, my country, and my world."

4-H clubs were the beginning point for many of Georgia's leaders through the years, training youngsters to be better farmers, that is true, but also instilling in them qualities of leadership. For many farm youngsters, the route to adult success led right through their 4-H Club, followed by active participation in FFA – Future Farmers of America. And for many 4-H members in Georgia, the path to success almost always had one major point of influence: the Rock Eagle 4-H Center.

So ... for 100 years, Georgia 4-H has taught young people the value of working to improve their communities, their country, and themselves. It's a great program, and I for one, hope it will go forward another 100 years.

✲ ✲ ✲

Ross Apperson and the Declaration of Independence

They had an estate sale the other day on Candler Street, about a block off Green Street, and it was almost as much a history lesson about Gainesville as an event to dispose of family belongings. Ross Apperson was known in Gainesville as a fine teacher and a unique character, and his wife – who died several years ago – was known as a driving force in the United Daughters of the Confederacy.

As could be expected, the old home was crowded with a combination of fine antiques and stuff. Most of the people were there for antiques. I was there to look at the historic stuff, and I was not disappointed. Much to my wife Jean's consternation, I came out with 15 books and a bunch of memorabilia from long-gone local businesses.

But I came out with a bunch of memories, too ... memories of my own and from other people who had known the man. There was one memory that stood our, however. Ross Apperson was a dramatic sort of a guy, and he was often called on to recite that great story about what happened to the Americans who signed the Declaration of Independence. It always brought goose bumps; and for some, tears. You didn't just hear American history; you lived it. There was no way one could hear that dramatic presentation without being proud of our American heritage, and determined to preserve it. It struck me that this is a pretty good memory to leave behind.

✲ ✲ ✲

400 Visitors In Town For A Chautauqua

The year was 1897, and Gainesville was planning a Chautauqua ... you know, one of those events in which you bring in a group of noted speakers and entertainers, and it goes on several days. They were expecting 400 teachers and visitors to be in town all week. Said one observer at the time: "...it is going to be bigger, better and more brilliant than anybody anticipated. ... Profs Van Hoose and Pearce say that people (even) call them up over the phone and want tickets."

The program was to highlight General Gordon, who would deliver his ... let's quote here: "... would deliver his great lecture on 'The Last Days of the Confederacy,' which has charmed audiences all over the United States." Sam Jones would give three lectures, and Charles Underhill, the famous elocutionist, was to give, as they said, "one of his great entertainments." Between lectures, the New York Male Quartette Club was to be in town all week. There was another drawing card. Drs. Van Hoose and Pearce and their local college were completing a new auditorium. Said the local paper: "The splendid auditorium will soon be entirely finished, ... and Gainesville will have an assembly room of which Atlanta might be proud."

The Chautauqua was a big event in Gainesville ... in 1897.

✲ ✲ ✲

Teaching the Virtues

The other day I stumbled into a brief review of an education book called *Teaching The Virtues*, and the review had some thoughts that make me want to find the book and read it.

First, the author says, "schools should have behaviour codes that insist on basic civility, decency, kindness, honesty, and fairness. What a revolutionary thought."

Too often, she says, "college students studying ethics courses deal mostly with government social policy, and are debating social issues like abortion, euthanasia, capital punishment, DNA research and such, while they learn almost nothing about decency, honesty, personal responsibility, or honor."

The author further says, "we need to reaffirm a moral vocabulary that declares it is wrong to be cruel, to steal, to lie, to abuse children, or to parent children you do not support; and that it is morally objectionable to gamble away a family's resources, or refuse to take responsibility for one's obligations; and if you commit these offenses, there is no one to blame but yourself."

Sounds like common sense to me.

✲ ✲ ✲

Discipline in Georgia Schools Circa 1871

The year was 1871, and the State of Georgia decided teachers were not only responsible for the education of children but also their discipline. As a part of the discipline "training," students had to memorize a rhyme:

"For study each pupil is furnished a seat; he must keep it in order and perfectly neat; his books and his desk, which what appertains; he must notice and care for, with similar pains; and the floor close about him must also be kept ... as free from all litter as when it was swept.

Suspension or even expulsion from school ... may follow persistent breaches of rule ... disobedience stubborn, repeatedly shown ... disorderly conduct or quarrel alone ... or truancy, too, or indolent waste ... profanity's words or language waste ..." ...

You've got the picture. The students had to memorize that, and live by it, and if they didn't (in 1871), the teacher was encouraged to give them a thorough whipping.

Out of this system, we are reminded, came senators and governors, respected preachers, and successful business leaders, along with doctors and lawyers ... for not only did these students gain an education; they also learned personal discipline.

✲ ✲ ✲

Yes Ma'am. No Ma'am. And Sit Up Straight.

It was mid-century in Gainesville, and if you were a student and addressed your teacher, you said "yes, sir" or "yes Ma'am" ... usually "yes, Ma'am" because there were more women teachers than men.

The reason this came to mind is that some time back the State of Louisiana mandated that the students in that state go back to some 50-year-ago Southern customs ... and among them was a requirement that the students in that state's schools address their teachers as, guess what: "Yes, sir" or "Yes, Ma'am." The Governor and the Legislators figured it this way: If students are better behaved, they will learn more. And if they miss out on learning respect at home, they will at least be exposed to it at school. The Louisiana law requiring students to be polite, the politicians say, also bypasses all the folderol about separation of church and state.

I was telling all this to Bimbo Brewer here in Gainesville, and he said they were missing one thing that he used to hear from his teacher here in Gainesville. "What's that?" I asked. "Well," he said, "she used to give me what for, and would end up saying 'and sit up straight." Fifty years ago in Gainesville, you addressed your teachers as "Yes, sir" and "Yes, Ma'am," and when she said "sit up straight," you snapped to.

✲ ✲ ✲

Discipline At Gainesville High, Circa 1940

One of the issues that keeps bobbing up in Georgia nowadays is about discipline in our public schools. Not long ago, one of Gainesville's infamous coffee clubs got in a conversation about school discipline ... only this time they were remembering what discipline was like in Gainesville High School in the 1930s and 1940s. From local schools, you had people like Bub Dunlap, Sid Smith, Carl Lawson, John Burl Hulsey. There were others, but for the moment we were focusing on local schools. What had brought the subject up was a column Johnny Vandeman had written some time ago about a teacher who had maintained absolute order in her classes.

It was the era when C. J. Cheeves was Superintendent of Gainesville Schools, and he maintained his office in Gainesville High, which at the time was just off the square, where the Gym of '36 is now located.

Anyway, most teachers had their own method for keeping discipline in their classrooms, and for the most part, classes were orderly. But if some student got out of hand, and especially if a student did things that disturbed the other students in the classroom, the teacher sat the student on a stool in the hallway, just outside the classroom door.

Once an hour, Mr. Cheeves walked the hallways, and if a kid was sitting on a stool outside the classroom, everybody knew all hell was about to break loose. Absolutely no student wanted to push a teacher to the point where they were banished to a stool in the hallway. And certainly no student wanted to push C. J. Cheeves to the point where he called the parents and invited them to his office to have a discussion with their youngster.

As this group remembers it, we didn't have big problems with discipline in school in those days.

☼ ☼ ☼

The Classics of Western Civilization

There was a celebration at Columbia University a while back marking the 75th year of the school's famed core curriculum devoted to the classics of Democratic Western Civilization – you know, the works of Aristotle, Plato, Locke, Shakespeare, Milton, Jefferson ... the foundation of thought that has built the Western free world.

To that celebration, I say: "Hooray for Columbia." And the reason is simple. All across America, in the elite halls of universities, there is a strong attack on Western Thought as biased, outdated, racist. In other words, we have a big bunch of academics who insist that Western Thought is wrong because it comes from – to use their words – "dead white males."

The politically correct thing to do, these elite college types say, is to replace the classics of Democratic Western Thought with multiculturalism. In their eyes we should throw out our historic Western Thought, and replace it with gender studies, class thought, rituals of the Third World – you know, multiculturalism.

Well, before we unceremoniously throw out Western Thought, maybe we should remember that it is the foundation of the most successful form of democratic government ever devised by free men.

When Barefoot Was Better

The World War baby boom was beginning, and then as now, along about the first of June, school turned out, and the youngsters turned loose. There was a certain freedom about summer holidays. For most families, the mother was at home, and there were all kinds of neighborhood activities that just happened ... very little was really organized, it just happened.

But one thing was certain, and it was a freedom that came with the season, and that was going barefoot. When school turned out, kids took their shoes off, not only was it all right to do so, it was expected.

Il would be early in the season, along about June, so the feet were still a bit tender. You could see the youngsters walk gingerly on the gravel driveways, then turn loose with all the speed their legs could give them when they hit grassy areas. By the end of summer, the feet would be tough, and the young people could be as carefree running on gravel roads as on a freshly mown lawn. But here at early summer, the feet were still tender.

Every now and then, the children wore tennis shoes. They were always Keds, and they certainly weren't fancy, and they didn't cost much. I kind of feel sorry for today's kids, wearing those fancy, high priced, clunky-looking successors-to-tennis-shoes. Barefoot was better.

✲ ✲ ✲

GHS Plays First Game At City Park

The coming of football season brings to mind the fact that Gainesville High School had a rich pigskin history during the past century. Prior to 1916, the GHS football team practiced and played on a field located at the intersection of Broad and Spring streets – across Spring Street from the present-day front parking lot of the Northeast Georgia Medical Center.

The City Park field was graded, and the 1916 Gainesville High team was the first to play there. That team opened its season in Dahlonega, where they lost 26-6 playing the North Georgia Agricultural College. They beat Athens 20-6 in Athens, and then October 14, 1916, Gainesville defeated Athens 26-6 in what is said to be the first football game at City Park. They lost to Boys High, in Atlanta 33-6 and then lost 6-0 to Monroe A & M in a game that generated a bit of heated discussion. The coach at Monroe was one Hugh Bostick, a former University of Georgia star, and he substituted himself in the game in the fourth quarter and scored the winning touchdown. It was legal, though, and the score stood at 6-0. Oh, the final 1916 game was to be a return game with Boys High, but Gainesville didn't have enough money to make the trip, so it was cancelled.

✲ ✲ ✲

CHAPTER 8 - About Crazies (The Bad Kind)

There is a dark side to the culture of Georgia's mountains. As one journalist said: "The mountains are ready-made for unsavory characters. They can disappear fast, and become very hard to find, even if you want to."

Olin Jackson has compiled a whole book entitled *Moonshine, Murder & Mayhem in Georgia,* a collection of stories from his *North Georgia Journal* and *Georgia Backroads* magazines. In its 450 pages one can find ample evidence that Georgia's mountains at various times had a culture of violence and outlaws all its own.

The violence goes back to "pre-history" Indian wars when the Creeks and Cherokee fought for control of the mountains for deer hunting rights. From that history come names like War Hill and Blood Mountain.

Gold Rush characters had an unruly streak, and very often their unruly bent turned to violence as the whiskey carts sold their wares to those around campfires at night.

Long after coastal Georgia and South Carolina became civilized, with crime reasonably well under control, the frontier mountain area continued to have flare ups from the worst kind of crazies.

There were bank robberies and train robberies. There were the Indian deaths of Chief Vann and Stand Watie, and the hanging of Corn Tassel. There were notorious outlaws like John Murrell and Bill Miner. There were high stakes kidnappings, and unsolved murders. And always there was a running battle between moonshiners and revenuers.

☼ ☼ ☼

MURRELL'S GANG HEADQUARTERED IN HALL COUNTY, GEORGIA

If we held a vote to select the CRAZIEST of the law breaking crazies in North Georgia history, Murrell's gang would certainly be in the top five, and possibly be named as the Grand Champion crazy of them all.

John Murrell was born in middle Tennessee, the son of an itinerant preacher father and a mother who operated a tavern along the Natchez Trace, where he heard from travelers the exciting tales of horse stealing, robberies and looting. In that era, adventurous river roamers would acquire a barge in Louisville, fill it with goods, and float it down the Ohio River, and then the Mississippi, and sell the whole caboodle – barge and all – in New Orleans. They would then buy a horse, and with their money would traverse the Natchez Trace back to Louisville. They were prime targets for bandits all along the Trace.

Murrell started by stealing horses, but got caught and spent a year in jail in Tennessee ... reading law books, and studying the Bible. Once out of jail, he and his brother migrated to North Georgia where he was not known, where there were mountains for quick cover, and where there were a lot of covered bridges. His early trademark crime was to hide in the rafters of a covered bridge, drop down on the unsuspecting prey, rob them and steal their horses. If things didn't go well, Murrell did not hesitate to shoot his victim.

However, Murrell had loftier goals than individual robbery. Using the talents he had learned from his father, and knowledge of the Bible learned in jail, he would pose as a preacher and hold a community revival. His gang had grown, and as Murrell mesmerized his "congregation," his gang looted houses and stole horses.

Says Olin Jackson in his book: "John Murrell's boldness, ruthlessness, and lavish distribution of the spoils, attracted scores of followers. His operations, which extended over a number of states, included robbery of mails, banks, stores, the piracy of river boats, and slave kidnapping. Legend also attributes literally hundreds of murders to Murrell and his unholy gang. He was known to be active as far west as Texas and the mountains of Arkansas, but his headquarters was said to be the old "Bolding House," near Bolding Bridge, which spanned the Chestatee River between Hall and Forsyth County, on the edge of Northeast Georgia's mountains.

In time, the bridge burned, or was burned. When Lake Lanier was formed in the 1950's, the federal government acquired the house and destroyed it as the rising waters of the new lake covered the bottom land around it. However, the Bolding House, the foundations, and surrounding yard were destroyed by unknown persons who scoured the entire area, no doubt hoping to find loot hidden by Murrell.

John Murrell was captured in Tennessee in 1834, spent 10 years in prison, and died mysteriously shortly after he was released.

☆ ☆ ☆

THE LAST DAYS OF TRAIN ROBBER BILL MINER

One of the Wild West's most notorious outlaws ended his checkered career following a train robbery just north of Gainesville, Georgia. He was known in his lawless early days as Bill Miner, although his real name was George Anderson.

Born in Kentucky in 1843, he was one of the legendary bandits that made a career of robbing stage coaches and trains, and in his younger years was known for killing anyone who got in his way. His forays took place mostly in the far west, but he also was involved in train robberies in the mid-west, and as far afield as Canada.

Bill Miner had a reputation as a gentleman bandit, polite and gentle until crossed. He also had a reputation for breaking out of jails, and was often referred to as "the gray fox."

It was in the later years of his life, in 1911, that Miner and two accomplices robbed Southern Railway's train number 36 near the White Sulfur station, north of Gainesville. They stopped the train by waving a red lantern, often used to signal track problems, and the engineer dutifully stopped. The era of train robberies had pretty well gone by, and the idea of a train being robbed in Georgia seemed ridiculous.

Miner blew the train's safes with a charge of dynamite, but only one safe was blown open. The bandits took the loot from that one safe and left, missing a fortune in Gold in the other.

By the time word spread of a train robbery in North Georgia, it was big news, and the newspapers of the day made it the story of a lifetime. But to the consternation of local law enforcement agents, state lawmen, railroad officials, Pinkerton's, and the "general public," the "gray fox" had faded into the sunset. Search though they might, Bill Miner had simply evaporated.

It was a week later that the threesome was captured near Dahlonega, and the leader of the pack was identified as George Anderson, his real name. Only later would it come out that the train robber was the notorious Bill Miner.

Miner was tried and sent to a Georgia prison, and true to his reputation, he escaped. In time, he was captured and placed in a more secure lock up. And to the general public's delight, he escaped again.

Bill Miner was now in his 60's and not as spry as he had been years earlier, or he might have disappeared again. But, weakened by exposure in a swampy area, he was captured again, and this time he died in prison.

✲ ✲ ✲

The Ed Butt Murder Case In Union County

The Year was 1922, and the talk of all North Georgia was the Ed Butt murder case up in Union County. You see, Ed Butt had been tried for murder, found guilty, and sentenced to die. But his lawyer had appealed his case and asked for a new trial. Well ... while all that was pending, Ed Butt escaped from the Blairsville jail and went to Canada.

The local paper reported he then went to Oregon, and we quote the paper here: "... where he got sick of [his] job and wrote the Sheriff of Union County to come and get him stating he would rather be hanged in Georgia than live in Canada or Oregon." But when the Sheriff asked county officials for the money to bring him back, they sent word to the Sheriff: "he got out there, now if he wants back, let him pay his own way."

And guess what: a few weeks later in 1922, good old Ed Butt showed up at the Sheriff's office in Union County, still convinced he would rather be hanged in Georgia than live in the unbearably cold climate of Canada or the miserably wet climate of Oregon.

✲ ✲ ✲

Guy Rivers, the Wooley Place, and Lake Lanier

Some interesting things disappeared when Lake Lanier backed up, but probably nothing more fascinating than the 1830s home of one Margaret Wooley. It had been built at Wooley's Ford, on the Chestatee River, and was a regular stopping place for people on their way from Cherokee Indian country to Gainesville, the nearest trading post.

But the Wooley Place did not earn its place in history because of the family or the location, but as a frequent gathering place for one John Murrell, alias Guy Rivers. His was one of the most notorious outlaw gangs ever to operate in these parts, and it made its mark throughout the South. These were true desperadoes and were credited with murdering 32 people in Georgia alone, and 441 in all the Southern states. Why Guy Rivers returned regularly to the Wooley home no one knows, but rumor had it that bodies were buried in the basement and treasure hidden in the walls.

Guy Rivers was eventually captured and sent to prison in Nashville ... up in Tennessee ... and there he died, and took all of his secrets with him. But part of his legend, and any solution to the mysteries of the Wooley Place, can only be found deep under the waters of Lake Lanier.

☆ ☆ ☆

We Have Faced, And Defeated, Homeland Threats Before

We Americans never have been very good at remembering our own history. For instance, I was listening to a national TV reporter the other night, and he said: "This is the first time Americans have faced threats in their own homeland." Had he said it was the first time we had faced attacks "of this kind," I might have agreed. But he said, and meant, that this was the first time Americans had been threatened in America.

History says otherwise. The Europeans who settled our own Northeast Georgia in the late 1700s and early 1800s faced frequent brutal attacks. Go visit Fort Yargo. It is a state park, and it is close by. It is one of the small forts where frontier settlers gathered to ward off attacks by the Indians. There was fighting in Texas, and even though some would like to disown that state, it is American soil. Do I need to remind Georgians that the Civil War was fought entirely in our homeland (except for some naval battles)?

Or in recent history, people my age can tell you about ships sunk just outside the New York and Charleston harbors in World War II, and about catching teams of sabateurs in Florida, landed there by German submarines. Many of you will remember when the Soviet Union started unloading nuclear missiles in Communist Cuba, and President Kennedy faced them down. Even so, many Americans panicked, and I can today lead you to some bomb shelters that were built by concerned local citizens in Gainesville, Georgia.

The current attack on America is different, I agree. But it is not the first time we have faced, and defeated, threats to us on our own soil. We have handled them in the past, and we'll handle this one, too.

✲ ✲ ✲

Do You Have Information About Gainesville's Ghosts?

Okay, all you history buffs ... I need your help. I keep getting questions about the ghosts of Gainesville. You heard me right: ghosts.

The one I get the most questions about is the Library ghost. It seems there was once a cemetery on the land where the Hall County Library is located. Then a home was built either on that land or close by, and after that a hotel was built which eventually became the old Wheeler Hotel. The Kiwanis Club met there until the 1950s, and the best news stand in town was located there. The hotel building was torn down to make room for the library. Through all of these changes, a ghost is said to have been seen there now and then. The ghost was a young female, very pretty and friendly. There's got to be a story here, but that is about all have been able to dig up ... so to speak.

Then there is the Brenau ghost who, some say, resides in the rafters above the college's beautiful and famous

Pearce Auditorium. As could be expected, this one is a college girl.

Tales have been told about a ghost at the old house on the Chattahoochee where pre-Civil War outlaws hung out. But when Lake Lanier filled up, that house went under water, and the ghost hasn't been heard from lately. Anyway, if you have any information about Gainesville's ghosts, how about writing it down and sending it to me.

✲ ✲ ✲

CHAPTER 9 – Politics, Politicians, and Court Week

There's a truism in our American form of democracy that says "all politics is local."

In one sense, local politics is very serious, the heart of a system in which we-the-people decide how to live with each other, who will make the laws we live by, and who decides disputes in court.

In another sense, American history shows carrying out a democracy is often colorful, rambunctious, and sometimes even dangerous. It all begins at the county court house.

THE DEMOCRAT ONE-PARTY SOUTH

For 100 years following the Civil War, most of Georgia embraced the Democratic Party, and so did most of Northeast Georgia. Only a few mountain counties, right against the North Carolina line, admitted publicly that they had Republicans.

How this happened could be a book unto itself. Immediately after the Civil War, the so-called reconstruction period, the South was controlled by Washington

Republicans determined to punish the South for slavery, and especially for seceding from the Union.

Federal officials carrying out reconstruction policies in the South were very often former Union Army officers, and in Southern legend are referred to as "carpetbaggers" (because the high-class suitcases they carried were usually made of carpeting). When things got out of hand, Union troops were called in to restore order and punish the troublemakers.

In opposition, the Ku Klux Klan evolved, and was active in Northeast Georgia, although not nearly as pervasive as in other parts of the South. It was not a pretty period for Republicans or Democrats, or for that matter, America.

In Hall County, Confederate General James Longstreet was ostracized by many, and deemed a "scalawag" because he was openly a Republican and a friend of Ulysses S. Grant.

A Democrat political structure was created that "kept the Negroes in their place." With no Georgia Republican candidates running for office, the Democrat primary election became THE election. Only one race every four years gave Georgia voters the opportunity to vote for a Republican, and that was the race for President and Vice President of the United States in the General Election. Forget whether this was right or wrong; this was the way it was. And this held true until after World War II.

The Republican Party – what there was of it – was made up of three separate groups. First were the

Republicans who honestly believed in small government and fiscal conservatism. .Second came the "Post Office" Republicans, so-called because they hoped to get a federal job (i.e. Postmaster) if a Republican won the presidency (which usually happened at that time). And finally the Southern Republican Party contained a handful of powerful blacks whose families had been given Republican leadership recognition during reconstruction. They were recognized by national Republicans, and made the most of it.

At the end of World War II, if 10 people showed up for the annual official meeting of the Hall County Republican Party, it would have flabbergasted Republicans and Democrats alike. That had been the political culture of mountain Georgia, as well as the rest of the South, until a new generation of politically interested people came home from World War II.

ABOUT THREE MOUNTAIN GOVERNORS

To read the official biographies of North Georgia's historical politicians, one would think the area had been ruled by rather staid men who lived straight, uncontroversial lives. But when you look at "the rest of the story" one gets the impression that only colorful, controversial mountain characters (or more likely, crazies) were elected to office… which may say more about the voters of Northeast Georgia than about the officeholders.

Take the example of three governors with ties to the mountain area, all who served before 1900 ...

...Joseph Emerson Brown became governor in 1857, and served during the Civil War.

...James Milton Smith became governor in 1872 to fill the unexpired term of Republican governor Bullock, and then Smith was elected and served until 1877.

...Allen Daniel Candler was a Congressman, and then governor from 1898 to 1902.

✲ ✲ ✲

Joseph Emerson Brown – a quick biographical sketch. A lawyer and State Senator from Canton, Brown was elected Governor of Georgia as the Democratic compromise candidate in 1857. He was elected and served as Governor during the Civil War. A graduate of Yale University and a respected lawyer, he became Chief Justice of the Georgia Supreme Court under Republican rule during Reconstruction. Brown was elected a U. S. Senator from Georgia and served from 1880 to 1891.

Joseph Emerson Brown pops up in a lot of historic episodes, but almost always is mentioned when party-switching is in the news. Late in the 20th century, in the 1990's, when a number of Georgia Democrats were switching to Republican, Governor Brown's name came up in history as one of the first office holders to switch parties ... and more than once. There is a historic marker in mountainous Union County that tells the story.

Brown served as Governor of Georgia as a Democrat prior to, and during, the Civil War. He was a native of Union County, in far North Georgia ... a county named Union because its people supported the Union during that war. After the war ended Brown advocated submission to Reconstruction, and closer ties to the Union. He ran for the U. S. Senate as a Republican, and got beaten, but under Reconstruction was made Chief Justice of the Georgia Supreme Court, an appointment acceptable to the Republican majority in Washington.

After the state returned to home rule, Brown switched back to Democrat and won the race for U. S. Senate in 1880. Historic records say the marker is located in Union County because that is where Senator Brown grew up, right at the location of the old Woody Gap School. However, it is speculated the marker may be in Union County for another reason. Since the marker was authorized during the period when Georgia was solid one-party Democrat, Union County may have been the only county in Georgia that would admit to having had an elected Republican.

✲ ✲ ✲

James Milton Smith: a short biographical sketch. Originally a blacksmith in Twiggs County, Georgia, Smith studied law on his own and began his practice in Thomaston. When the Civil War erupted, he entered the Confederate Army as a Captain in the 13th Georgia Infantry, and rose to the rank of Colonel before being injured and leaving active duty. He served in the Confederate Congress until the war's end. After the war he became an active lawyer in Columbus. Smith was elected to the Georgia legislature, and became Speaker of the House in 1871. A year later he was named Governor, and was re-elected, serving as Governor until 1877.

Smith was a low-key character. He had only two years in state government to prepare for the governor's office, but obviously handled his sudden elevation very well. A Democrat, he was elected to the Georgia House in 1870, and became Speaker in 1871. In 1872 Reconstruction Governor Rufus Brown Bullock left the governor's office, and left Georgia, to escape a movement to impeach him. Smith stepped from Speaker to Governor. As head of the Democratic Party he was re-elected, and history credits him with bringing the state out of the Reconstruction era.

He is buried in Alta Vista Cemetery, in Gainesville, and that is a story unto itself. In 1880, Smith's wife – Hester Ann Brown Smith – died just north of Gainesville, at the White Sulfur Springs resort, after a long illness. She was buried in Alta Vista Cemetery. Probably all Governor Smith knew about Gainesville came from his visits to his wife at the White Sulfur Hotel, but he directed that he be buried with his first wife. Despite the fact he remarried, his wishes were carried out ... thus two governors are buried in Gainesville's historic cemetery.

✲ ✲ ✲

Allen Daniel Candler, a native of Lumpkin County, was born in 1834 and graduated from Mercer University. When the Civil War broke out, he enlisted in the Confederate Army as a private, and came out a Lt. Colonel, but not without receiving serious wounds.

He moved to Gainesville in 1870 and quickly became active in business and politics. He built a street railroad, and became president of the Gainesville, Jefferson, and Southern Railroad.

He served as Mayor of Gainesville before being elected a state representative in 1872. He was elected State Senator, and then in 1881 was elected Congressman from the Ninth District of Georgia … the mountain district … and served several terms.

After serving in Congress, Hall County's Allen Daniel Candler again focused his political interest on the State of Georgia, serving as Secretary of State and then Governor from 1898 to 1902. Before his death in 1910, he compiled the Colonial, Revolutionary and Confederate Records of Georgia. He is one of the two governors buried in Alta Vista Cemetery.

To read the above material from his official biography, one might think the good Governor was a staid, matter-of-fact, lawyer-like person. Not so.

Allen Daniel Candler was a character of the highest order … maybe a bit on the crazy side. He was a populist, a man of the people, a person who held high office but who enjoyed being a common man among common men. Not only was he colorful and popular, he was a highly effective governor. He was always popular with the newspapers of the time, for he never failed to "give them colorful copy" that they could "flower up."

Example: Harris Blackwood, a local scribe who is somewhat of a character in his own right, spoke one night at the monthly History Forum at the Northeast Georgia History Center at Brenau University, on the subject of Georgia politicians. A number of people likely came to hear Harris and get some laughs, and they were not disappointed. But the highlight of the talk featured Governor Candler. Harris did not simply report that the good governor had been wounded in the Civil War, he said Colonel Candler "got his eye shot out" and made the most of it. In his campaigns throughout Georgia, Governor Candler became known (with his own prompting) as "The one-eyed plowboy from Pigeon Roost" (that is NOT playboy. Plowboy) The Governor left a lot of humorous material to work with, but even Harris admitted he "may have embellished the story a bit."

Governor Candler was a true character ...maybe a bit on the Crazy side. But GOOD CRAZY, mind you, in the best political tradition of the Georgia mountains.

✲ ✲ ✲

Court Week: A Community Gathering

There were many frontier debates about the location of a "county seat" (or "County Site", as some old records show). In the earliest days, the primary purpose of a county seat was courts and the Court House ... the center of law and order. It was in the Court House that the official records were kept ... deeds to property; marriage licenses; births noted; wills recorded. The Sheriff's office was often in the Court House, and the County Commission usually met there. It was the center of government for the entire county, and, of course, it was "the seat of justice," the place where the Judge held court.

As civilization moved across the frontier, the Court House was usually the largest structure in town, and the Court House square was the center of town. Georgia's legislature attempted to locate county seats close enough so every rural citizen could reach the Court House in no more than one day's travel (thus 159 counties).

The designation as county seat insured it would also be the business center of the county, which brought on political infighting between early landowners and businessmen. To put it simply, the culture of the frontier recognized the county seat, with its Court House, as the most important community in the county.

So it was, when Court Week was declared by the sitting (or visiting) judge, it was the signal for every family in the county to go to town, and as they arrived, they parked their wagon (and later their Model T or Model A Ford) around the downtown square. Some came early to get a prized spot ... especially those bringing ginger beer or other goodies to sell. They loaded their wagons with a big basket of eggs, a few chickens in a cotton basket, Chestnuts, a jug of milk ... all to be sold or traded to merchants for "Mama's egg money." In winter, boys would bring small animal pelts from animals they had caught on their trap line.

Court week was when the militia drilled. Itinerant preachers placed their soap box on a busy corner, climbed on it, opened the Bible, and preached for hours at the top of their lungs (this continued into the 1950s),

The Courtroom was the main attraction. Some trials drew more spectators than others, but the people in town seemed to always know when a showcase trial was going on, and colorful lawyers addressing the jury always drew standing-room-only crowds. Almost everyone knew courtroom procedures, and to be drawn for a jury was a distinct honor. It meant you were a respected citizen, and not only that, jurors got paid (not much, but paid anyway).

Other events were taking place, too. In Gainesville, way out where Brenau College was located, horse races, buggy races, and other events were taking place. In fact, one street adjacent to the College was known as "Race Street." (Years later, the term "Race" would be misunderstood, and the street would be officially re-named Boulevard.) It was ideal for races: level, wide and with obvious start and stop lines. The best drivers, or riders, gained a following, and betting was lively.

A lot of "courting" went on during Court Week, too, and many married couples admitted meeting each other while "flirting" during Court Week.

Court Week was fun, but it also developed a great awareness, and grassroots respect, for the American judicial system.

Rural families came to know one another in their communities through church, community schools, and being neighborly. They broadened their circle of friends through politics and campground revivals. But Court Week was special.

✲ ✲ ✲

The Real Political Debate: Liberal vs. Conservative

The debate began a long time ago, but became real with the election of Franklin D. Roosevelt as President: do we want a government that is liberal or conservative?

Liberals believe in big, dominant government. Liberals believe government should help in planning and controlling our personal lives. Liberals believe we are a nation of hyphenated groups, and that each group must receive special privileges. Liberals believe government is responsible for jobs and the economy; and that the free-enterprise system cannot be trusted and should be tightly controlled. Liberals believe taxes should redistribute the wealth, and that high taxes must be levied for social programs. Liberals believe in a weak military, and that our foreign policy should focus on appeasement and sharing our wealth with other nations. Liberals believe in more government, and less personal freedom.

Conservatives believe in limited government. Conservatives insist government should provide us with a level playing field, and then, except in disasters, each person should stand on his or her own. Conservatives believe we are a nation in which every individual has equal rights, that there are no hyphenated Americans, and that the majority rules. Conservatives believe the road to personal achievement, as well as national greatness, can best be found in the competitive free-enterprise system. Conservatives believe money belongs to the people, not government, and that taxes should only cover basic governmental services. Conservatives believe in a strong military, and that other nations will respect us more for military strength than for appeasement and handouts. Conservatives believe in more personal freedom and less government control.

Liberal or conservative. That is what the REAL debate is about.

☆ ☆ ☆

Colorful Political Oratory and Language of the 1830s

There was a time in Georgia politics when anyone elected to office had to be a bodacious orator ... you know, bodacious as in remarkable or noteworthy. That was how politicians campaigned in the 1830s, by attending meetings and giving colorful talks: sometimes about things political, sometimes not.

If they considered their opponents biased, they accused them of thinking "obliquely." If an opponent was considered snobbish or better than the average person, they said he was persnickety. They rarely came right out and called an opponent a drunkard, but they did often say they appeared to be half-drunk. And if that didn't get a reaction from the crowd, they would charge their opponent was "subject to fits."

The politicians of the 1830s were colorful speakers, and wherever they went, they drew large crowds. Partly it was because people were interested in their government, and in the people who held office. There was a growing debate between two political factions about whether their government should give more power to the states or to the union, and feelings ran strong. But people also attended these political rallies because there wasn't much else to do, and this was great entertainment.

✲ ✲ ✲

About Whiskey: This Is My Stand

(A State Senator, running for re-election, was asked about his stand on a local option vote on whiskey)

Thank you for calling on me to discuss this controversial subject. I had not intended to discuss it at this particular time. However, I want you to know that I do not shun a controversy. I will be glad to give you my opinion on any subject, no matter how fraught with controversy it may be. Here is how I stand on the subject of WHISKEY.

If, when you say whiskey, you mean the Devil's brew; the poison scourge; the bloody monster that defiles innocence, dethrones reason, destroys the home, creates misery and poverty; yes, literally takes the bread out of the mouths of little children, then certainly I am against it with all of my power.

However ... if when you say whiskey, you mean the oil of conversation, the philosophic wine, the ale that is consumed when good fellows get together, that puts a song in their hearts, and laughter on their lips and the warm glow of contentment in their eyes; IF you mean Christmas cheer; if you mean that drink ... the sale of which pours into the treasuries untold millions of dollars, which are used to provide tender care for little crippled children, for our blind, our deaf, our pitiful aged and infirmed, and to build highways, hospitals and schools, then certainly I am in favor of it.

That is my stand on WHISKEY, and I will not equivocate or compromise one iota.

✲ ✲ ✲

Hayek's Book : *The Road To Serfdom*

The governments of the world were in turmoil in the 1930s. A socialist philosophy of government was gaining followers in some countries, and in others strong dictatorships were taking hold. The colonial empires were crumbling.

There was a growing popularity around the world of centralized planning by a strong federal government. In Britain, the Labour Party was pushing for detailed economic planning of agriculture and industry. And as Richard M. Ebeling reports: "For years before America's entry into the war, Franklin Roosevelt's New Deal had transformed the United States through a degree of government spending, taxing, regulation and redistribution.. ..." In many nations, ours included, the Soviet Union was often portrayed as the model socialist society "...freeing 'the masses' from poverty and exploitation."

It was into this worldwide political landscape, 60 years ago this month, that an economist named F. A. Hayek published a little book entitled *The Road to Serfdom*, and it had the subtitle, "A classic warning against the dangers to freedom inherent in social planning." That was 60 years ago, and Hayek was saying centralized, social planning by government would destroy freedom and would not work.

Hayek's theme was not popular in America with either the Roosevelt Democrats or the Rockefeller Republicans, and Hayek was considered a "right wing zealot" by some. But as the dangers to freedom he identified became reality in country after country, his writing gained credence. And in 1974 he was winner of the Nobel Prize for Economics.

Hayek became a foundation stone on which today's conservative movement is built, and his prediction that centralized social planning would fail is proving true. Said

Richard Ebeling, who is president of the Foundation for Economic Education, on the 60th anniversary of Hayek's book: "Hayek died on March 23, 1992, at the age of 92. In the 12 years since his passing, *The Road to Serfdom* has come to be seen as one of the greatest political contributions of the twentieth century."

✲ ✲ ✲

William Jennings Bryan: A Democrat?

Every now and then we get in a conversation about how the meaning of words change, and how the basic beliefs of political parties not only change but can even reverse through the years. Probably the one that pops up most often when someone is researching political history is the fact that a person with the beliefs we now call "conservative" would have been called a "classic liberal" 100 years ago. Or Southern Democrats were said to be "conservative" 40 years ago, and Up-East Republicans were known to be "liberal." Times change, and in many cases, the meaning of words change, too.

But I ran across a bit of history the other day that intrigued me. It came from a report of the Democratic National Convention from a little more than a century ago. From that convention, the great orator, William Jennings Bryan, was chosen as the Democratic candidate to face the Republicans' William McKinley, who won the 1897 election. Whether or not to adopt the gold standard was a big issue at that time, and Bryan became famous for his "Cross of Gold" oration. It was not just a speech, it was political oratory at its zenith.

Anyway, the Democrats proudly pointed out that their candidate was a man who, and I quote here: "... denies the right of any government to take from any man by means of taxation any money not needed for government expenses." And William Jennings Bryan went on top say that the government should not "...tax one man to enrich another."

According to today's definitions, that is just about as conservative as one can get. Which raises the question: If William Jennings Bryan were alive today, would he be a Republican? Things do change, don't they?

✲ ✲ ✲

John Wood and Hearings in Washington

It was 1949, and John Wood, the U. S. Representative from Georgia's Ninth Congressional District, was in a hot and high profile debate in Washington. It was front page in most of America's premiere newspapers and dominated national radio news. At the time, Wood was a prime mover in the House Un-American Activities Committee. He and 3 Democrats were opposed to reopening an investigation of the Alger Hiss/Whittaker Chambers controversy. While a State Department official, Hiss had been accused of delivering secrets to Chambers, who had been identified as a Communist spy.

Wanting to reopen the investigation were three Republicans and one Democrat. The group pushing for reopening was led by a young member of Congress from California named Richard M. Nixon. Wood and his three cohorts stood firm and were able to block the hearings, but Nixon gained national fame ... especially a year later when Hiss was found guilty and sentenced to prison.

America had just come out of a World War, and we were edgy about the world Communist movement, and our Congressman, John Wood, was right in the middle of it.

☆ ☆ ☆

When Political Losers Need to Wear A Gun

This is political season, and there are winners and losers, and always a lot of tall tales about characters of the past. The losers, of course, have the privilege of going down to Goat Rock. Been there, done that. But there's another one that always comes up after the primary elections that has to do with a losing candidate wearing a big six-shooter. Some say the story involved Jess Morgan after he lost a race for City Commission. Others say it had it had to do with a longtime Hall Countian who ran for Sheriff. Anyway, the story goes like this:

In the days when winning the Democrat primary was tantamount to election, we often had bushels of candidates running for various offices, and this particular year, there were 14 candidates for Sheriff. One, in particular, figured he could win easily because he could count more than 400 relatives in Hall County. There was no runoff election at the time; whoever got the most votes in the primary was the Democrat nominee. Since the Democrat party totally dominated, that person would be elected Sheriff.

Well, the election came, and our sure-thing candidate did NOT win. He lost. But the next morning after the election, he showed up at the Court House wearing the biggest, meanest looking .45 six-shooter imaginable. Whereupon the Court House gang reminded him: "What are you doing with that pistol on; you didn't win the Sheriff's race?"

"I know," he said, "but I figure anybody who has 400 relatives in Hall County and only got 22 votes NEEDS to wear a gun."

✲ ✲ ✲

How To Lose Votes in Hall County Elections

There's a basic political story that repeats itself every few years in Hall County, with a certain amount of truth to it, that goes something like this. This guy who was running for Sheriff walked into the country filling station at Quillians Corner. (Remember, this was in the 30s, when about the only thing in Quillians Corner was the old store.) A local farmer leaning on the counter took one look at the candidate and said: "There's no way in hell I would vote for you." Taken aback, the candidate asked: "May I ask why not?" "Because," the voter shot back, "you've got a button missing on your shirt."

You would think that kind of nonsensical political logic would go away, but not so. The other week, Dr. Ed Shannon walked into Jaemor Farms and collared Jimmy Echols and said: "Echols, I want you to know I'm never going to vote for you again, and what's more, I'm not going to vote for anybody in your family." Jimmy knew Shannon well enough to know he should leave it alone, but hoping to humor him, he said: "May I ask why not?" Whereupon Shannon answered (and I'll delete a few expletives here): "Because you quit turning out that homemade peach ice cream I like, that's why,"

✲ ✲ ✲

Changing Political Parties Not New

With all the hubbub about Zell Miller, and whether he is going to remain a Democrat or switch to a Republican, you would think this was the first time a Georgia mountain boy had ever pulled a stunt like that. But ... there's a historic marker up in Union County that will tell you differently.

Joseph Emerson Brown was practicing law in Canton when he became a State Senator. In 1857, he was elected Governor of Georgia as the Democratic compromise candidate. He was re-elected and served as Governor during the Civil War. After that war ended, Brown advocated submission to Reconstruction and closer ties with the Union, and he affiliated with the Republican Party.

Being a Republican wasn't all that unpopular in North Georgia, but the rest of the state was another matter. When he ran for the U. S. Senate in 1868, he got beat. A graduate of Yale and a respected lawyer, he then became Chief Justice of the Georgia Supreme Court. After the state returned to home rule, Joseph Emerson Brown switched back to the Democratic Party, was elected a U. S. Senator from Georgia, and served from 1880 to 1891.

And why is the historic marker in Union County? Because that is where Senator Brown grew up, right at the location of the old Woody Gap School. It MAY also be there because when that marker was installed, Georgia was solid one-party Democrat, and Union County was about the only place that would admit to having had an elected Republican.

(P. S. – Zell Miller remained a Democrat.)

✲ ✲ ✲

What About Georgia's FIRST Republican Governor?

A good bit has been said lately about the fact that it has been 130 years since Georgia had a Republican Governor. But practically nothing has been said about the term of Rufus B. Bullock or his interim Republican successor Benjamin F. Conley. Let's start with the end of the Civil War when Georgia, along with the rest of the South, was in political limbo and under the control of Union troops. To be readmitted to the Union as a state, Georgia had to have a constitutional convention. It had to annul secession and abolish slavery and several other things.

Rufus B. Bullock, a New Yorker who had moved to Augusta prior to the war, had served as an officer in the Confederate Army's Quartermaster Corps. Bullock accepted the outcome of the war, and thus was considered a "radical," but was named to the convention and had been an effective leader in the three-month-long effort that adopted Georgia's new constitution. Under reconstruction, the Union Army commander called for an election in 1868, and Republican Bullock faced Democrat John B. Gordon, a popular Confederate General. The election was chaotic. Former slaves had their first opportunity to vote, but Carpetbaggers and Scalawags got involved. There was a question which, if any, former Confederate soldiers could vote. It was a mess. When the ballots were counted, Republican Bullock beat Democrat Gordon 83,527 to 76,356.

In the Legislature, the House had 29 Negroes and the Senate three. The Legislature voted to throw them out, and Governor Bullock called the Union troops back in, and the Negro legislators were reinstated. But General Alfred Terry not only reinstated the Negroes, he also threw out 29 Democrats and replaced them with the 29 Republicans who had opposed them in the election of 1868.

✲ ✲ ✲

Truman Punishes Our Third Party Democrats

World War II was over, but a political war was brewing. President Truman was being tough on some Southern Congressmen who had supported Strom Thurmond of South Carolina. Yes, it was the same Strom Thurmond who later became a Senate Republican. He had bolted the Democratic Party and run as a Third Party candidate. Truman was holding up Postmaster nominations made by our Ninth District Congressman, John Wood, of Canton, because Wood had supported Thurmond.

Truman was, he openly admitted, rewarding the labor unions who had led to the Democratic Party victories, and any Congressman who expected his nominations for local offices to be approved by the President would have to vote to repeal the Taft-Hartley law. Our Congressman, in turn, shot back at the president, saying he would not "surrender to the labor bosses." So Truman was refusing to act on Wood's nominations for Postmaster, including Huram Hancock for Postmaster of Gainesville.

As 1949 ended, Conservative Southern Democrats ... including our own Congressman Wood and Senator Richard Russell ... were at war with the Liberal side of the Democratic Party.

✲ ✲ ✲

Madge Houser Fights For Her Home

Construction of Buford Dam was underway, and the government was condemning the land that would be covered by Lake Lanier. Some landowners simply took what the government offered, and moved on. Others challenged the offer and went to court. But there was one, her name was Madge Houser, who just plain didn't want to sell her homeplace. That was where she lived, and that was where she planned to continue living. It didn't impress her one whit that the government wanted to build this big dam, and that her place was right in the middle of it.

She didn't want these government people to come snooping around, surveying her property. And she didn't want people coming by to tell her how much they would pay her, either. So she would go the Grand Jury every time it met, and demand that the Solicitor do something about it. At one point, she said she had a twelve gauge shotgun, but I don't recall that she ever pulled it out. The government condemned her property and paid her. But she still refused to move, and the lake started backing up. The Courts eventually evicted her, but to a lot of us, she was a legend and a local hero. In my book, she is still the poster person of a determined American fighting for her rights.

✲ ✲ ✲

Gainesville Policeman Price Reed Recognized

Back in the 1950s, Gainesville had gained a statewide reputation for the excellence of its police force. Here in Georgia, they were recognized as being among the best of the best.

One of the reasons for this reputation was a Gainesvillian named Bill Reed. Actually, his name was Price Reed, but he was generally known as Bill. Reed had added to the Gainesville reputation when he became head of the Georgia State Patrol. Like the FBI at the national level at that time, the State Patrol in Georgia earned high marks as a professional law enforcement agency.

Anyway, Price Reed decided he would like to join the Washington, D. C. police force, and with the help of U. S. Representative John S. Wood, of Canton, he did exactly that.

Reed had been in Washington less than a year when he was promoted to Lieutenant of THAT prestigious police force. Gainesville's reputation as a base of well-trained, professional police officers continued ... but now at the national level.

✲ ✲ ✲

Congress Should Go Home By Independence Day

Congress would go on its traditional summer hiatus, and the going joke went like this: "Congress is on its summer break so we-the-people are safe for a few days." Or maybe it's not a joke. Anyway, it brings to mind former Senator Howard Baker, of Tennessee, who – in all-seriousness – proposed that Congress should be required to finish its business by July 4 every year. July 4th is Independence Day, but it is also *mid-way* on the calendar, and Senator Baker insisted all Congressmen and Senators should spend as much time in their *home districts* as they do in Washington ... that they should spend as much time listening to their constituents as they do listening to Washington lobbyists.

Our Congressman has been on a brutal schedule this hot month of August, talking with and listening to we-the-people in the ninth district. We're fortunate, for not all members of Congress do that. Senator Baker, a good constitutional historian, pointed out that being a Representative or Senator was never intended to be a full-time Washington job. So why don't all Representatives simply stay back home among we-the-people. I think Senator Baker had it right: Congress should not be adjourned for a summer break. Congress should be through with their business and back among their people for the year.

✲ ✲ ✲

The Legislature Debates The Terrapin Law (1887)

The Georgia Legislature is in session, and it brings to mind the fact that august body once had a unique sense of humor, and played as many pranks as it passed legislation. One of the members of the Legislature in 1887 was one Henry W. Ham, of Gainesville, the editor of the *Eagle,* and well known for his humor.

Mr. Ham was involved in the "Terrapin debate", one of the most hotly debated issues to come before the Legislature in 1887. It seems a Mr. Smith, of Glynn County, submitted a bill to "regulate the capture of female terrapins of a size less than 5.5 inches lengthwise of the shell ..."

Whereupon Mr. Black, of Gordon County, noted there was a lack of knowledge about how to determine the sex of a terrapin, and proposed an amendment requiring the branding of the word "female" or "male" on terrapins when caught.

Then our Mr. Ham amended the amendment to "... establish a department in the public schools to be known as a Department of Terrapinology, to instruct all citizens how to determine the sex of terrapins." Mr. Ham, however, felt the legislation might need to be held up for a decision by the Georgia Supreme Court, as to whether the bill was Constitutional or not. Mr. Ham was concerned the bill might be unconstitutional class legislation since it was giving special rights to the female not accorded to the male.

The records don't show whether this started out as serious legislation or a hoax, but the last thing recorded before Mr. Smith threw up his hands and withdrew his motion was another amendment that mere possession of a turtle should not convict since it was well known that animal, once he or she took hold of a person, would not let go till it thundered.

That was the Georgia legislature in 1887, making about as much sense as some of the animal rights legislation in the today's General Assembly.

The Importance Of One Vote

There have been a lot of very close votes in Congress lately, and a lot of commentary about the importance of one vote, but for some reason the bill that passed Congress in 1940 hasn't been mentioned. The Germans were rolling through Europe, and it was becoming obvious the United States might get involved. There was serious consideration of instituting a peacetime Selective Service Act (you know, the draft), but America had never drafted servicemen during peacetime. Men had been conscripted in the Civil War and in World War I, but not until hostilities were underway. From Lexington and Concord forward, America had always depended on volunteer citizen-soldiers.

But in 1940 the United States Congress passed the Selective Service Act to train draftees for one year. This first vote was popular for two reasons. First, it was not certain the U. S. would enter the war, and the idea that we were prepared would have a chilling effect on Nazi Germany. But more important, jobs were still scarce following the depression, and the draft provided one million new jobs. But when the act came up at the end of one year, and had to be voted on again, there was a different mood in America. The debate in Congress was intense, even bitter, but in the end, the military draft was extended ... by ONE VOTE. So, when the Japanese struck Pearl Harbor, America had more than one million men at least partially trained for war.

✲ ✲ ✲

The New Mayor of Goat Rock

Among the political races taking place this year is a heated contest for Mayor of Goat Rock, and I contend that I won that race hands down. Now, for those of you who may not be familiar with the Goat Rock tradition, about 50 years ago, a local character (Jake Tolbert, if I remember correctly) publicly announced that all people who had just LOST in the local elections would gather at the fictitious Goat Rock for a celebration ... a celebration of the fact they would not have to put up with all those voters who wanted their road paved, or wanted a government job for their kid, or – in those days – wanted to select their kid's teacher. Not only that, the residents of Goat Rock would not be pestered by some constituents to slip a little pork in next year's budget – always for a good cause, mind you. In them olden days, Goat Rock's population grew to include anyone who had ever run and lost an election, and they met regularly at the L & K Café... which no longer exists.

I had some worthy opponents this year for Mayor of Goat Rock. There was Wyc Orr, Bob Vass, and a newcomer named Ashley Bell, who won an election after losing an election and whose Goat Rock voting credentials are therefore suspect, even though he won't take office till January. There were others, but I contend I won fair and square in the very best tradition of Georgia politics. We didn't tell anybody the election was being held, and we didn't tell anybody where they could cast their vote. Not only that, we figured they would all be busy watching the Democrat convention. I got five of my very best friends to vote, and I want you to know, I won the race for Mayor of Goat Rock. The vote was three to two, and winning with 60 percent of the votes is considered a landslide, isn't it?

✲ ✲ ✲

Bob Andrews and The Case of The Stolen Pig

Bob Andrews was one of thousands of GIs who came back from World War II, took advantage of the GI Bill to go to college, and determined to do well in their chosen civilian vocations. Bob had flown his share of B-17 bombing raids over Germany, first as a tail gunner, then in the nose. He chose law as his vocation and Gainesville, Georgia as a good place to practice and hung out his shingle.

At that time, the judge would assign a case to a lawyer if the defendant did not have legal counsel, and the first case assigned to the newly minted lawyer was rather unique. A young man had been charged with stealing his neighbor's pig. What was unique centered around the way the pig was carried off. It seems the defendant and his brother rode a motorcycle to and from work, and every day they would ride by the neighbor's house, located where a gravel road entered a paved main highway. It was a dangerous place for a motorcycle, turning onto a gravel road from a well traveled highway, but the two brothers navigated it safely.

The case charged the defendant with stopping the motorcycle, grabbing the animal, and riding off up the gravel road with the pig as the third passenger on the bike. Bob interviewed the brothers and was convinced they were innocent. He was determined that he would win this, his first case to go before a jury. He walked the area where the event took place. He confirmed the size of the pig. He found character witnesses. He even found a deputy Sheriff who would testify to the danger of riding a motorcycle on a gravel road. He figured his ace-in-the-hole was the fact the pig probably weighed more than 120 pounds, while the defendant weighed only about 150, and the idea of two young men riding a motorcycle holding a squealing pig should immediately create doubt in the juror's minds.

Even so, he didn't want to take any chances, so he prepared a thorough closing argument, and delivered it with gusto. At times he had the jury laughing, and some were laughing in the courtroom, too, for the unique nature of the case had drawn a crowd. Bob Andrews painted a detailed picture of the impossible, ridiculous idea of two young men and a very unhappy pig riding an unstable, slipping, sliding motorcycle up a gravel road. The jury was only out 20 minutes, and returned the desired verdict: Not Guilty.

The judge stood, the bailiff sounded "all stand," and as the door closed behind the judge, there was a hush in the courtroom. Breaking that silence came the voice of the defendant. "Colonel Andrews," he said, "does this mean I gets to keep his pig?"

(True story. Told as only Bob Andrews could tell it.)

CHAPTER 10 – The Great Health Resort of the South

In 1888 a group of Gainesville businessmen came together and published a 68-page booklet entitled:

THE GREAT HEALTH RESORT OF THE SOUTH

And the business center of Northeast Georgia

(Its advantages and resources)

The preface noted it was "the center of the Piedmont region" and further had these things to say: "The score of counties comprising Northeast Georgia are raised on a plateau considerably above the remainder of the state, with an average elevation of from 1,200 to 2,000 feet above the tide water. ... Its perfect climate, inspiring scenery and curative mineral waters have each year brought an increasing number of tourists. The business centre of this region, and the gateway to all its points of interest is Gainesville."

The booklet's Preface goes on to say: "The object of this pamphlet is to present the attractions of Gainesville and the country tributary to it, to all seeking health, and to men of enterprise seeking new fields for investment."

Indian lore from the time before the arrival of the white man tells of Indian tribes coming to these mountains for deer hunting, and for its healthful climate and mineral springs,

Coastal Plantation owners, merchants, and ship captains built summer homes in Habersham County as early as the 1830s to find a pleasant climate, and to escape the "bilious fever" found in Savannah, Charleston, and the plantations. Northeast Georgia was hard to reach, but when a railroad line was opened from Charlotte to Atlanta in 1871, coming through Toccoa and Gainesville, with stops in between, a summer tourism boom began,

As early as 1829, one Adiel Sherwood published a booklet in Philadelphia entitled *Gazetteer of the State of Georgia."* In it he spoke highly of Clarkesville, Clayton, and Gainesville, and stated "there is no purer water, nor any healthier climate on the globe."

Thus it was that from the 1880s til the 1920s, the mountain area of Georgia was a destination for people of wealth all along the Eastern seaboard.

✲ ✲ ✲

THE INFLUENCE OF THE SUMMER PEOPLE

Many people who have come to Northeast Georgia, and especially Gainesville, after living in other small cities, have noted the "welcoming culture" of this region. The culture of many small cities, they say, is too often dominated by one major factory, and/or a few "old families." Those towns find it difficult to accept the "mover inners," and newcomers find it hard to become a part of the community. Not so in Gainesville, and not so in most of Northeast Georgia.

The culture of Georgia's mountain area says newcomers, tourists, and people visiting the health facilities of the region, are welcome. This "welcome neighbor" theory goes back to the era as The Great Health Resort of the South, and for good reason.

Visitors to the mountains had money, and they spent it freely in a friendly and accommodating society. Investment money came into the area to build hotels, and many early investors became aware of the opportunities because they had visited and been welcomed. Even existing businesses helped seek new industry (i.e. the 1888 brochure), a rare circumstance in most cotton mill towns of the South in which mill management did not want another business recruiting their workers.

It was because of well-educated visitors that the Hunt Opera House flourished, and that Brenau's Pearce Auditorium was able to successfully stage summer Chautauquas that drew the likes of Democrat Presidential candidate William Henry Bryan. White Sulfur Springs and the Arlington Hotel regularly brought in bands from New York, and even an art studio once stood alongside an ice cream parlor in downtown Gainesville.

Northeast Georgia's "summer people' came regularly, and became a part of the culture of the area. In

Gainesville, they sent sons to Riverside Military Academy and daughters to Brenau College. The student body at Piedmont College in Demorest had a sprinkling of students from all over the United States.

It is interesting, for the Summer People had a major influence on the culture of Northeast Georgia, and the "welcome brother" foundation laid when this was "The Great Health Resort of the South" carries forward, even today (2010).

THE HEALTH RESORT

Remember the title of that 1888 booklet? It did not say "The Great Resort"; it said "The Great Health Resort."

It began with the Indians. James Mooney, in his 1900 book, *History, Myths and Sacred Formulas of the Cherokees* devotes almost 100 pages to the Sacred Formulas. In traditional Indian history there are references to visits to healing springs in North Georgia, and in stories about White Sulphur Springs, reference is often made to Indian treks to those springs before their discovery by the white man. There were doctors who became nationally famous for their "research" and adoption of innovative medical practices. Dr. Crawford Long, of Jefferson, used "laughing gas" to put his patients asleep before "sawing off" a leg. He is generally credited with the modern sedation practices used in surgery.

There was Downey Hospital, and its nursing school, in Gainesville. There were others; many others.

Gainesville was not just a resort; it was a HEALTH resort. Still is.

☼ ☼ ☼

It All Starts With Southern Hospitality

I was at a meeting the other day, listening to a young lady who is a former Olympic athlete. One of her comments reminded me of a European friend of mine and his theory on why Atlanta got the 1996 Olympics rather than Greece.

"Those of you who live in the American South," he said, "have no idea how valuable your Southern Hospitality is. You have good manners. You are courteous. Not only will you stop to help someone; you honestly seem to enjoy helping them. You are just naturally friendly."

"What happens," he went on, "is that people enjoy being around you."

If our Southern Hospitality is one of the major reasons we got the Olympics, then it seems to me we have a pretty big challenge to live up to in a couple of years when the whole world descends on Georgia.

No matter how good we already are, maybe it would be a good idea for each of us to make a pledge to practice Southern Hospitality on each other between now and 1996 so we will be a little better at it when our world visitors arrive.

✲ ✲ ✲

A Victorian Christmas on Green Street

There is something special about an old-fashioned Christmas ... a warmth, a glow, a mellow time of fellowship and good cheer. And there are certain settings that say "this is Christmas as it should be." Apparently, many people believe historic Green Street is such a venue, for the annual Victorian Christmas on Green Street continues to draw crowds. The homes on Green Street developed their style and charm more than 100 years ago, when Gainesville was the trading center of Northeast Georgia, and when it was a noted mountain health resort, Green Street was one of the first streets in Georgia to have electric street lights, and there was a trolley that ran from the downtown square out Green Street all the way to Lake Warner, near Riverside Military Academy.

For several years now, the Green Street homeowners have decorated their historic homes, and supported by a people who simply like history, have created a new tradition for this history-rich town. This year there were bands playing on some porches, and choirs singing the familiar carols of Christmas on others. There were proper ladies, dressed in styles popular in the 1880s, telling the history of each of the traditionally decorated homes. The event was started with a mile-long parade of Christmas-decorated antique automobiles, and it was ended with the official lighting of the big Christmas tree adjacent to the Chamber of Commerce, the point where historic Green Street begins. The sidewalks, along with the two outside lanes on Green Street itself, were filled with strolling visitors exchanging cheery Merry Christmases. There was conversation and laughter, and the children ... ah, the children with a gleam in their eyes. It is a new tradition that paints a Victorian Christmas on Green Street as it was 100 years ago.

A Victorian Christmas Returns to Green Street

It was a hundred years ago, and there was magic about a stroll down Gainesville's traditional Green Street. There were greenery and red bows and Christmas trees ... and there was a new feature: newly installed electric lights glittered in the classic Green Street homes.

You see, Gainesville during the late 1800s was a resort town ... a place where people came in summer for the cool breezes, and to drink of the health-giving waters from our local springs. There were hotels and fine dining rooms and the great Opera House, and a trolley ran out Green Street and on out Riverside drive to Lake Warner.

At Christmas, as in summer, there were concerts in the Opera House and a live dance band at the Arlington Hotel. There was singing and laughter and yes, there were still chestnuts to be roasted from the North Georgia mountains ... Chestnuts to be roasted by the open fire.

Times change, and Gainesville lost its status as a resort town. Then the Tornado destroyed more of the traditional old homes than it left.

But the other night, it was foggy and cold, and we parked the car and took a leisurely stroll down Green Street, and it was again a Currier and Ives postcard Christmas. The magic is still there.

✲ ✲ ✲

The Elks Club Was Once Mahomme

They tore down the old Elks Club building out on Riverside Drive the other day and cleared some big trees off a huge lot ... and for a lot of old-time Gainesvillians, it brought back a lot of memories. Once upon a time, there was a big home on that lot, and that home became a part of the Elks Club building itself, and that was part of what went down.

Anyway, that home belonged to a Mrs. Whelchel (Ed Dunlap called her "Aunt Cap"), and it was a stately house with a widows' walk on the top. It was high enough, located on the hill as it was, that a person could stand on that widows walk platform and see the Chattahoochee River back before there was a Lake Lanier, but not before there was a smaller dam on the river that backed up Lake Warner.

Mrs. Whelchel's husband died, and she turned the big home into a boarding house known as Mahomme (spelled, I am told, M-A-H-O-M-M-E). At one time, probably in the 1920s, Mahomme became the residence of choice for Gainesville's leading young bachelors, and a lot of businesses and professional practices founded in this town in the 1920s and 1930s carried the name of men who had been proud residents of Mahomme.

One other memory kept bobbing up: Mahomme apparently was a boarding house that had great food, provided by a cook named Floyd Teeter, who was somewhat of a character. Floyd wore English-style riding boots, looking for the world like a World War I cavalryman.

The Elks Club building they tore down the other day had a big room just off the entry, a room adjacent to the bar with a big fireplace . That same stone-faced fireplace was one of the few remaining remnants of the old Whelchel house. But that part of the structure, at least, could remember the days when you could step out the front door and catch the street car to ride to downtown Gainesville, even all the way to the Railroad station. From Mahomme through the Elks Club ... there is a lot of history tied up in that plot of land.

Wanted: Historic Information About Gainesville's Mansion House

I was reading a copy of the Southern Whig the other day, a newspaper published in Athens, Georgia, shortly before the Civil War. There was information about the springs at Madison, and the accommodations in Athens. But the thing that interested me most was an advertisement for the Mansion House, located somewhere in Gainesville, Georgia.

The year was 1841, and the Mansion House had just been expanded and refitted. They had added six family rooms and extensive galleries. And, of course, they pointed out that the water was ... well, let's read from the advertisement:

"The now ascertained properties of the waters of the Gainesville Springs, leaves no longer any doubt of our village and its vicinity being the most favorable location for health in the Southern Country. Its altitude, dry atmosphere, and entire remoteness from any causes whatever that can possibly generate disease, connected with the valuable properties of all the water used by visitors, will at once account for the palpable benefits heretofore received by all those who have spent any reasonable length of time among us, and affords a sure guarantee of future advantage, to such as seek for a summer residence and a view to prevent disease ..."

The advertisement in the Southern Whig continues: "A neat and comfortable bath house will be erected at this Spring, containing half a dozen private rooms for the accommodation of Ladies and Gentlemen. Each room will be supplied with hot and cold baths, at the pleasure of the visitor; one room will be supplied with a shower bath."

Now, we generally think of Gainesville as the great health resort of the South around 1880 to 1920, but this Southern whig ad was run May 14, 1841.

✲ ✲ ✲

Show Girls Remembered At the Hunt Opera House

It was fifty years ago, and Forrest Additon was doing sort of the memory walk I am doing with "Window on Green Street" ... he was remembering bygone days in Gainesville. Only he did his with a column in one of the newspapers, and he called his column: "Do You Remember When?"

Anyway, Mr. Additon started out by asking: "Do you remember what we then considered glamorous show girls at the Old Hunt Opera House?" He didn't set a year for that memory, but the Hunt Opera House burned in 1925, so apparently its show girls were something worth remembering.

The Opera House was large, at least three stories, a brick structure at the corner of Washington and Bradford Streets, right at the corner of the square. Pictures show it to be a classic building, with a lot of fancy brickwork and Victorian design. It was a center of social activity in Gainesville during the era when this town was the Great Health Resort of the South, when it was a mountain resort that had hotels and dance halls and even ... saloons. The trolley ran from the railroad station to the square and out

Green Street to Riverside and on to the river, or rather Lake Warner, and went right by the Opera House. And yes, the Hunt Opera House would have had glamorous show girls.

✲ ✲ ✲

A Risque Moving Picture Comes To Town

Gainesville was still a resort and entertainment town in the early 1920s, so it wasn't unusual that the follies at the Opera House, on the square in Gainesville, would be considered a bit risqué ... risqué at least by the standards of that day and time. After all, more than one report form that era would indicate the chorus girls and the dance line performers that appeared in person in Gainesville were beautiful women.

But then in 1923, the early stages of the "Roaring 20s," an ad appeared in the Gainesville weekly newspaper, *The Herald*, announcing that a new moving picture was coming to town. The name of the moving picture was "Wild Oats,"and it was billed as "the most remarkable photoplay ever shown."

Well, the name "Wild Oats" may tell you more about the content of the movie than you had expected, for the advertisement also noted that there would be separate showings for men and women. The women were invited to attend the Matinee; and the men could come to the night showing. By the way, this film was shown at the Brenau auditorium.

How would you like to see that movie, "Wild Oats" ... for historical research purposes, of course.

☆ ☆ ☆

Gainesville Street Paving: Circa 1884

We've had a bunch of streets being repaved in downtown Gainesville recently, and it reminded me of the mayor's annual report issued in 1884. No, I wasn't here that year, but I did get my hands on that report. Now remember, this was in 1884, and Gainesville was moving into the modern age ... or getting ready to. According to the mayor's annual report for that year: "We have macadamized Washington Street from the public square to and across Green Street ... "In addition, the city had also macadamized that part of Main Street between the public square and Lawrenceville Street. It is probable that Lawrenceville Street today is known as Broad Street, about a block off the square.

Not only that, permanent street crossings were being installed at each corner ... the crossings being made of flat stones purchased (the report said) in Jackson ... probably meaning Jackson County. But probably of more interest to city residents, and especially to the ladies with long, flowing skirts that touched the ground (muddy in rainy weather, and dusty in dry), brick sidewalks were under construction in downtown Gainesville.

Although the hard-surface streets did not turn into a river of mud in rainy weather like dirt streets did, the automobile had not yet arrived, and there was another problem. The wagons, carriages, buggies ... even the street cars at that time ... were pulled by horses or mules, and although there was no concern about air pollution, there was this other problem. As Gainesville grew, the number of animals increased, and they hadn't solved this problem yet. In fact, it would continually get worse until the automobile came into being.

☆ ☆ ☆

Gainesville Expands As A Hospital Center

It was 1950, and Hall County was getting ready to build a new hospital. Gainesville had two private hospitals at the time – the Hall County Hospital, and the more widely-known Downey Hospital – and was recognized as the medical center for all Northeast Georgia ... but this new hospital was something bigger than we had ever seen in the past. The Hall County Hospital Authority had plans on the drawing boards for a totally new, 150-bed hospital with the very latest in operating rooms and equipment.

The U. S. government, in Washington, had a new program in which they were helping finance local hospitals across the nation, and with those federal dollars plus money from state and local government sources, the Hospital Authority had $1,394,000 available. But the cost for the new hospital was estimated at $1,640,000. It was in April – 50 years ago – that the County Commissioners authorized issuance of "revenue anticipation certificates" to push available money over the top, and the contracts were signed ... with work on the new five-story hospital due to start within 30 days.

☆ ☆ ☆

A 1910 Tribute To Dr. Crawford W. Long

I acquired an old book the other day called *A Library of Southern Literature*. As a collector's item,.it's awful, in terrible shape. But the content of that book is incredible.

For instance, in it you will find the words of an address delivered in 1910 on the occasion of the unveiling of a memorial to Dr. Crawford W. Long by the Jackson County Medical Society. It is more than a recognition of the use of anesthesia for surgery; it is a statement about medicine at that time ... expressed in the descriptive language once used by educated Americans. It starts by pointing out that sulphuric ether "...has given science and surgery their innings, and has robbed the operating table of its horrors." The address points out Dr. Long was a country doctor whose work was so immense it became known and recognized worldwide.

And the talk ended by noting that Dr. Crawford W. Long and indeed all doctors of that era (and I quote here): "...at all times and in every way gave their strength to the weak, their substance to the poor, their sympathies to the suffering, and their hearts to God." How's that for great Southern literature?

✲ ✲ ✲

Dr. Raleigh Garner Lived Last Century's History

Dr. Raleigh Garner died the other day. At age 99, he is more than simply a report on the history of the last century ... he lived it. He started the practice of medicine in Gainesville in 1929, a time when doctors made house calls and dispensed medicine out of a little black bag. He delivered a goodly percentage of the children born locally in the 1930s, and was known as an "old fashioned" doctor who knew his patients' personal problems as well as he knew their medical condition.

He was Victorian in his dress and demeanor, so it was appropriate that he lived in the most Victorian home on Green Street. But he also knew how to totally immerse himself in the business of saving lives during times of medical disaster. He was one of the doctors who untiringly saved lives for days on end during Gainesville's tornado of '36. And for three years during World War II, he was a senior medical officer with the Army as the U. S. fought its way from island to island in the South Pacific.

Sometimes people live long enough that we tend to forget their accomplishments; but I'll guarantee you this: anyone researching the history of Gainesville in the 20th century will find ample mention of the contributions Dr. Raleigh Garner made to this town.

This is Gordon Sawyer, from a window on historic Green Street right across from where Dr. Garner used to park his red Cadillac.

☆ ☆ ☆

A Return To Our Roots: A Medical School

Brenau University has announced a feasibility study to see if a Medical College is possible as a part of its Gainesville campus, and that strikes me not only as a brilliant possibility, but also historically appropriate. For those of you familiar with the 1888 promotional book about Gainesville, you will know this town was once called "The Great Health Resort of the South." At that time, people from all over the South, and especially the seacoast cities, came to Gainesville in the summer season for the cool, bracing mountain air; the healing waters of our mineral springs; and to escape the thing they called "the bilious fever "that plagued the coastal areas.

Medicine was different in those days, when experiments by independent physicians served the role of today's research hospitals, and in this area "mountain medicine" had its own unique character. Several doctors and medical clinics in our mountain region gained national recognition for their medical innovations. In nearby Jefferson, Dr. Crawford Long gained worldwide attention for pioneering the use of anesthesia during surgery.

And here in Gainesville, Dr. James Henry Downey gained national recognition when he patented a special table that used suspended weights to hold broken bones in place while they healed. And don't forget, a lot of mountain home remedies, some handed down from the Indians, became legitimate medicine, and a part of medical history. It is fair, also, to say that before 1950, Gainesville's Downey Hospital was not only the leading regional hospital but also drew patients from all over the United States. So for Gainesville to become a major medical center, with its own medical school, strikes me as more than a great idea ... it is a return to our historical roots as "The Great Health Resort of the South."

✲ ✲ ✲

Gainesville and Water, Water Everywhere

The present-day flap with Alabama and Florida about the use of water from the Chattahoochee River is just one more chapter of a longstanding saga of water and its impact on our area.

Early trading roads into the Southern frontier came through Gainesville, and there were two main reasons. First, travelers could cross the Chattahoochee River nearby, and second, there were at least seven major springs in the area that made ideal camping spots.

During the late 1800s, the springs of Gainesville gained a widespread reputation for their health-giving qualities. Each spring had its own unique qualities. People from the coastal areas came here to get away from "the fever" (malaria) and to partake of the pure water and the cool mountain air. Gainesville was one of the first towns in the area to have a public water supply. Water rates about 1900 ran 80 cents a month for a residence housing a family up to five people, and a dime more for each person above five. If you watered a horse, mule, or cow, that also cost you a dime per animal. But if you had a bath tub, that was serious; that would cost you 40 cents a month. Do you reckon the city would cut back on our water rates today if we cut back on our bathing?

✲ ✲ ✲

Roy Cromartie Remembers Gower Springs Neighborhood

I had a great talk about old Gainesville with Roy Cromartie the other day. Roy had been reading my *History of Northeast Georgia*, and it had triggered a lot of memories about the Gainesville in which he grew up. Roy Cromartie was born in 1916, and his family lived on Thompson Bridge Road, sort of across the street from where the Publix Supermarket is now located. Green Street pretty well ended at the intersection in front of the present-day Civic Building, so he and a handful of other families lived in an area that was somewhat on the edge of town. A little further out of town, close to where the Westminster Presbyterian Church is now located, as Roy Cromartie remembers it, was where Byron Mitchell had his slaughter pen. And toward town on the North side of Thompson Bridge Road, on the land where the Publix Shopping Center is located, was the big sand pit. And just toward town from that was another house up on the hill (probably where WDUN is now located, or maybe the cable company offices). The hillside in front of WDUN had Chinquepin trees on it, and of course the Chinquepins were wiped out with the same blight that got all the Chestnut trees.

The focal point of that area of town, along about the early 1920s, was Gower Springs. This was a large and free-flowing spring with high concrete sides, and Roy remembers there were concrete steps leading down into the spring area to make it easy for people to get their water. It was located near where present day Green Street Circle dead ends into Thompson Bridge Road. By the time Roy Cromartie and his young friends explored the area, as only young boys can do, the famous old Gower Springs Hotel ... a favorite in Gainesville's Health Resort era ... had burned, and all that was left was the foundation.

✲ ✲ ✲

One Golf Course Drowns, Another Is Born

It was 1951, and golf was not a major sport in North Georgia. There had been a golf course out near Riverside Military Academy in the 1920s, but the great depression wiped that out. At mid-century, the City of Gainesville had a nine-hole course, a pretty layout near present day Longwood Park, threading down a valley toward the Chattahoochee River. It had a creek meandering through it that acted like a golf ball magnet, which once caused Clifford Martin to say: "I may not be the best golfer in Gainesville, but I'll guarantee you I've got the cleanest golf balls."

Gainesville's course was the only opportunity you had to play golf in these parts, and now it was going to be covered up with water backed up by that big dam being planned down near Buford. While some saw the impending loss of Gainesville's golf course as a disaster, Jesse Jewell saw it as an opportunity. The Chattahoochee Country Club was formed and started acquiring land, way out in the county, for a new course - land they eventually gave the city to develop one of the finest private-public golf courses in the South. And while it was being built, a young golfer from Gainesville's old course got a golfing scholarship to the University of Florida. His name was Tommy Aaron, and he later won the Masters in Augusta.

Industrial Baseball Was Big in the 1930s

It was 1949, and the sports fans of Northeast Georgia were getting excited. It wasn't about football – it would be a few weeks before the Bulldogs kicked off, and Yellow Jacket fans were scarce. It wasn't about the Braves; they were up North in beer country. It wasn't even about the Atlanta Crackers, although they did have a following.

It was about Industrial League baseball, and it looked like the "game of the year" was coming up. The two top teams were New Holland and Commerce, and they were due to play their second game of the year. The first game had been tied at 2-2 at the end of nine innings, and it was in the 12th that Commerce got their winning run. Even so, that game had been protested and still hadn't been settled, and feelings were still tense.

This time Jake Miller would be pitching for the Hollanders and the rest of the starting lineup would be: Lay, Hollifield, Wood, Chapman, Morgan, N. Riley, G. Riley, and Jones. They were expecting a huge crowd on a hot day. Baseball was exciting in Gainesville, Georgia 50 years ago.

✲ ✲ ✲

It Was 1901 And The Circus Was Coming To Gainesville

The year was 1901, and all Northeast Georgia was excited: a major circus was coming to Gainesville. According to the news stories of the time, this circus was – let's quote here: "The Pioneer of Perpetuators of Tented Amusement Institutions."

This massive show was "John Robinson's Ten Big Shows All United" and was considered one of the biggest and best of the traveling shows of that era.

It included four circuses, three menageries, and two stages. There was a herd of performing elephants, and one thousand (count 'em) rare and costly animals. Music would be provided by several bands, and a Fife and Drum Corps. And to add a bit of spice to the whole show, there were one hundred beautiful ballet girls.

The highlight would be a Roman Hippodrome, combined with the Grand Biblical Spectacular entitled "Solomon and the Queen of Sheba."

Let me tell you, I'm not surprised that people hitched up the wagons and came to Gainesville for such an event. I think I would like to see THAT show.

CHAPTER 11 — Of Characters and the Free Press

Where does one learn about the bygone culture of an area? Step one is to go to the local newspaper, for it is the repository of week-to-week information that tells what people did. Yes, it tells who shot whom, whose house burned, and what political body did what. But it also tells you something about what common folk did; what businesses were active advertisers; who was born; who died; who was elected to office; who was sent to jail; and what preacher ate fried chicken at whose home last Sunday.

But the media of the Northeast Georgia mountain area was much more than the official record of normal historical events. From the late 1800s until World War II, this region, dotted with small towns and scattered farm families, had an abundance of weekly newspaper editors who were certified characters; who exerted a powerful influence locally, statewide, and in some cases in Washington.

Every county seat in Georgia's mountain region had a weekly newspaper (or so) beginning after the Civil War.

The paper would be launched when someone came up with enough money to buy the printing press. The paper would start with its first editor/proprietor, but would flop financially. A second, and often a third, editor/owner would take it over before it could gain a foothold and survive. Most county seats, at one time or another, had lively competition with two newspapers.

But no newspaper in Northeast Georgia has had a longer, or more colorful, existence than *The Dahlonega Nugget.*

Dahlonega's first newspaper was the *Mountain Signal,* followed by the *Dahlonega Signal.* The *Dahlonega Nugget* was founded in 1890 and went through a couple of editors before one William Benjamin Franklin Townsend came on the scene as editor in 1897.

W. B. Townsend was a character's character ... and a bit on the crazy side (usually good crazy, but it depended on where you stood on an issue). Anne Dismukes Amerson, who wrote about him and the *Nugget,* in the *North Georgia Journal* describes his writing this way: "Townsend's prose could either be witty or razor sharp, particularly when his words involved a person he considered distasteful. As a result, it was not uncommon for him to be threatened ... with libel suits, but they never seemed to thwart or alter his journalistic style." A local businessman called his style "caustic," but said everybody "dang well read him just as soon as the first paper came off the press."

His wit and wisdom was carried regularly in *The Atlanta Journal* under the heading "Observations From a Peak in

Lumpkin County," and he was quoted often in newspapers all over America, particularly when he "went after" some national political figure. Townsend literally worked to the day he died, and in 1933 his final column had only four words, but they told it all: "Ye editor is sick."

The paper went through several owners and editors before Jack Parks came on the scene about 1950. Parks, who had access and personal contact with several of Georgia's dominant political types, brought back the fire and flavor of W. B. Townsend. Parks retired in 1982. Jimmy Townsend, a nephew of W. B. Townsend, later gained a following as a colorful columnist for*The Atlanta Constitution.*

✲ ✲ ✲

Gainesville was the business center of Northeast Georgia in the early 1900s, and there was a lively local competition between *The Gainesville News* and the *Gainesville Eagle*. Both papers were recognized for good reporting, and no-holds-barred editorial pages ... often with one taking one side of an issue, and the other standing in opposition. Said one local pundit of these two papers: "Reading these two papers on the same day was like watching a ping-pong match, using a hand grenade as the ping-pong ball".

In 1919, Albert Hardy Sr., the editor/publisher of the *Gainesville News*, brought the board of directors of the National Editorial Association to Gainesville for one of their meetings. Mr. Hardy became president of the

National Editorial Association, giving Georgia – and especially Gainesville media – nationwide recognition. (On a personal note: In 1950, I was a young reporter on the *Atlanta Constitution*, and had expressed an interest in "some day" owning a weekly newspaper. Mr. Hardy had a vision of acquiring several weekly newspapers in adjacent counties, buying the first offset press in Georgia, and thus creating the publishing business of the future. It was "Papa Hardy's" dream that brought me to Gainesville. I missed one reality. It was a 20-year plan, and Mr. Hardy was 92.)

Covering controversial news and taking a firm stand on the editorial page has always been a risky business for local newspapers. A big city newspaper can carry an editorial, and the editor doesn't have to live his day-to-day life with the person offended. Not so locally.

Example: The *Gainesville News* reported in September, 1935: "Austin F. Dean, editor of the *Gainesville Eagle,* was badly beaten in the face and over the head by Byron Mitchell, City Commissioner, in the lobby of the Dixie Hunt Hotel Thursday ... The cause of the difficulty was the publication in the *Eagle* the week before of an offensive article about Mr. Mitchell. The two had not met since the article appeared and when Mr. Mitchell saw Mr. Dean he evidently could not restrain himself and struck Mr. Dean a number of times. Bystanders pulled Mr. Mitchell off of Mr. Dean and the latter was carried to a local hospital where his injuries were given medical attention. ... A warrant was sworn out by Mr. Dean against Mr. Mitchell for assault with intent to murder." Talk about characters.... Wow.

☼ ☼ ☼

Dahlonega's Editor Townsend Takes On The Tick Dippers

Every now and then, I run across a bit of history that's good for a laugh, and I came across this one just after reading a far-fetched environmental proposal being put forward by an Atlanta resident about what we should, and should not, be doing in North Georgia. The humorous history comes from last summer's *Georgia Historical Quarterly*, and it has to do with grassroots opposition to tick eradication in the early 1900s. It seems Texas cattle ticks were a problem, so the state passed a law that said anybody who had cattle had to build a dipping vat, fill it with a powerful arsenic dip, and run their cattle through it.

Well, Dahlonega had a newspaper, the *Dahlonega Nugget*, and it was operated by one William Benjamin Franklin Townsend, who was a character, but he knew his local folks. Most everybody in Lumpkin County had a cow or so, but nobody could be charged with owning a herd of cattle. So, Townsend figured for a farmer to go to the expense of building a dipping pit and buying the arsenic goo to go in it, was ridiculous. Not only that, a lot of Lumpkin County's livestock roamed free, and the law said once the cattle were dipped, you had to keep them penned up for a while ... and it was wrong to force his people to go to the exorbitant cost of building fences all over the county. Townsend took a firm, and sometimes hostile, stand and gained national attention by standing up for the little man.

In 1916, Townsend decided to run for Ordinary in Lumpkin County, and his platform was opposition to the livestock dipping law. Not only did he win this election, he continued in office until he died in 1934. In addition, he was elected mayor of Dahlonega a couple of times. I've heard a lot of delightful stories about *Dahlonega Nugget* editor Townsend, but I had never before heard his entry into politics came from his opposition to an environmental law that decreed cattle dipping for Texas ticks.

✲ ✲ ✲

Cousin Arthur Pontificates Circa 1950

We've had a lot of interesting characters in Gainesville, but one of them left a paper trail, for he enjoyed writing about the fun and foolishness in Gainesville, and telling tales about other Gainesvillians, often naming them by name. His name was Arthur Roper, known by one and all as Cousin Arthur, and when he took a notion to write for the local paper, his was usually the best-read piece in that issue, no matter what page it appeared on.

Anyway, Cousin Arthur was pontificating about the wisdom being imparted one Sunday in the Melting Pot Sunday School class at First Methodist Church. According to Cousin Arthur, a well-known elementary school teacher was explaining to her class at Candler Street School the difference between prose and poetry. She began her lesson this way:

"Old lady Jones, she lived on a hill.

And if she isn't dead she's living there still."

"Now, that's poetry," the teacher said. "But if you said: And if she isn't dead, she's living there yet, that would be prose." The teacher then asked her class if someone else had an example, and little Johnny's hand flew up.

And here's what little Johnny said:

"Old lady Jones, she fell in a well,

And if she ain't hit bottom, she's gone straight to …

Hey teacher, you want prose or poetry?"

That was Cousin Arthur in Gainesville, circa 1950.

Cousin Arthur Talks About Worrying

It was 50 years ago, and one of Gainesville's favorite people, Cousin Arthur Roper, was doing a column for the new daily paper in town ,,, the *Daily Times*, or as Cousin Arthur sometimes referred to it, The Daily Terror. Anyway, he had heard a new one from one Ovid Whelchel … or is it Willkie? ,,, a former Gainesville boy then an attorney for the Metropolitan Insurance Company in New York. It went this way:

"There are only two things to worry about," he said.

Either you are well or sick. If you are well, nothing to worry about.

If you are sick, either you will get well or you will die.

If you get well, nothing to worry about. If you died, you have only two things to worry about. Either you will go to Heaven or you will go to Hell.

If you go to Heaven, nothing to worry about.

And if you go to Hell you will be so busy shaking hands with friends, you won't have time to worry.

That was Cousin Arthur in the early days of the *Daily Times*.

✲ ✲ ✲

Community Reporters Cover Their Neighborhood

Before a daily newspaper and radio came to Northeast Georgia, one of the best-read features of the local newspapers was a thing called "Community News." These were columns from the various communities in Gainesville and Hall County, written by reporters who lived in the area, and anything that was going on ... I mean anything ... got reported.

Thumbing through some old papers the other day, and we learned that in Clermont: "Mr. and Mrs. F. M. Head spent part of last week with their parents, Mr. and Mrs. Jim Head."

In Flowery Branch: "Harry Crow, one of our outstanding citizens, has been appointed by Sheriff Ferd Bryan as one of his deputies."

And "The Queen's Court" which reported for Gainesville said: "Mr. and Mrs. Eugene Hollis and family have returned from a visit in different parts of Florida where they attended the Orange Bowl game."

In Sardis: "Mrs. M. J. White, who has been on the sick list, is improving." Alto, Rt. 2: "Mr. Fred Reems, formerly of near Berlin, is now in the grocery business at Jones corner on Route 2. He invites his friends to give him a call when they need anything in the grocery line."

☆ ☆ ☆

A Substitute Columnist Reports From Flowery Branch

One of the most read features of local, weekly newspapers in the 1800s was a report from each of the rural communities in the area. Usually, these were calm reports on who visited whom, who was sick, the latest gossip ... things like that. But there was one week in 1875 when the regular correspondent from Flowery Branch must have been out of town ... or else drunk. Here is the report:

"Flowery Branch is bully – two doctors, one dentist and two ministers; and preacher H, don't live far away if we get in a tight. Flowery Branch has not had a death inside the corporate limits for four years. The father of our little town has fled to the Mountains of Hepsidam or some other dam – we don't care a d__n. Our post master is fat and lovely; you ought to come to see him. George Tumlin, the shingle block man, comes to town occasionally; sometimes Tumlin carries off whiskey and sometimes whiskey carries off Tumlin. We offer a reward for any town of the same size producing as many and as large fleas as Flowery Branch."

And whoever was writing Flowery Branch news this particular week in 1875 decided to do a little county-wide reporting, too, for the column ended this way: "We venture the assertion that Hall County has more large women than any in the state."

✲ ✲ ✲

Murrayville Old Maids Answer the Bachelors

It was more than a hundred years ago ... 1897 to be exact ... and a couple of bachelors in Murrayville had written a letter to the editor of the Gainesville weekly stating they were looking for wives and had heard there were some old maids in the Murrayville area. Which brought a hot reply from at least one lady the next week. Here's what she wrote, and what the newspaper printed:

"There are two young men that live near Murrayville that are nearly crazy to get married. I am told these clodhoppers wrote an article to the *Eagle* that stated that there were six old maids living near Murrayville who were asking the young men to come in and bid them off. Well, now, Mr. Clodhoppers, if you were our only chance we would desire to be old maids. ... You little possum-eared rascals, you need not be talking so grandly, for you are numbered in the bachelorhood ring ... We girls like to have you old bachelors in our settlement for amusement."

✲ ✲ ✲

All The News From Flowery Branch, Circa 1900

I was reading the *Flowery Branch Journal* the other day. If you are not familiar with that newspaper, it was published in the late 1800s and early 1900s. The big news was that in the Hall County Democratic primary Quillian and Pierce had been elected to the Georgia House of Representatives. Stated the Journal: "All the candidates could not be elected – let us feel thankful that it is no worse than it is." In the same news column, the editor noted: "Miss Dottie Troutt, a pretty young lady from Pendergrass, is visiting Myrtis Mahaffey. "Obviously, that editor had an eye for news ... or maybe pretty young ladies.

A new mill, Duncan and Delaperriere, had just opened in Flowery Branch, handling both corn and wheat, but some of the major news was carried in community news columns ... your know, Mount Salem, Chattahoochee, Oakwood, Oscarville, where most news was who went visiting and what preacher ate at whose house. Oakwood was getting a new industry: "Some men from Atlanta and the Puckett boys are fixing to put up a large brick yard (along with a) sewer pipe machine." And maybe the biggest news was to be found in Oscarville: "Hall County (is building) another bridge at the Browns Bridge site. Mr. Nunn, of Hall, bid off the contract at $5 per lineal foot, the total length being 354 feet."

✲ ✲ ✲

A Town Closes Ranks After The Tornado of 1936

I was watching coverage of the dramatic rescue of the trapped coal miners the other night, and listening to how the whole town had closed ranks to support and help the miners' families ... and it reminded me of the news coverage of Gainesville, Georgia, immediately after the Tornado of 1936. I have a yellowed old copy of *the Gainesville Eagle* dated April 16, 1936, and it has some fascinating copy under a section called "Personal Mention."

It goes like this:

Mr. and Mrs. R. F. Christopher are with Dr. and Mrs. B. F. Holcomb on Morningside Drive. Their apartment on East Spring was demolished.

Mr. and Mrs. Ed Roper and family are at the home of Mr. And Mrs. Wilson Smith on Ridgewood Ave.

Misses Mollie and Essie Jarrett left for their home near Gillsville. Their brother, Mr. Gower Garrett, was among the number who lost their life. He was seated in his car in front of a barber shop on South Bradford Street.

Mr. And Mrs. Garland Bennett are with Mr. And Mrs. L. L. Savage on North Street. Their home on Sycamore Street was greatly damaged.

Mrs. Janie Wayne and daughters are with Mrs. J. O. Lay on Academy Street. Their home on Sycamore Street was destroyed.

Mr. And Mrs. Ben Ashe and daughters and Mr. S. G. Garrett are with Mr. and Mrs. J. C. Garrett on West Broad Street. Their home on West Avenue was demolished.

Mr. and Mrs. John Hawkins are with Mrs. J. S. Allen on West Broad Street.

Personal mentions like these filled much of the paper that day.

Gainesville had more than 200 people killed in the Tornado of '36, and almost 1,000 injured. For the most part, the funerals had been held, and the injured cared for. These were the stories from 10 days later, and Gainesville was closing ranks to care for those whose homes had been severely damaged or destroyed.

The Communications Age Arrives In Gainesville

It was 1949, the year WDUN went on the air, and Gainesville was the communication center for Northeast Georgia. Not only did it have two radio stations, WDUN and WGGA, but it also had two newspapers. There was the new afternoon daily newspaper, *The Daily Times*. And there was the *Gainesville News*, an award-winning weekly newspaper published Thursday nights. *The Times* was the only daily newspaper published in this 18-county mountain Congressional District, and the *News* was considered one of the strongest weekly newspapers in the entire state.

Fifty years ago, Southern Bell operated an exchange with 6,055 individual and business telephones. Rotary dial phones were in service, but if a person chose they could call the operator and have their call placed for them ... and many of the old-timers did exactly that, just to have a few minutes chat with "central." There were sixty toll circuits, which meant sixty people in the Gainesville area could make long-distance calls at the same time. Then there was Western Union, which a lot of businesses used for their out-of-town contacts. All of America was edging into the communications age in 1949, and Gainesville was right there with them.

Personality Arrives With Local Radio

The year was 1995 in Gainesville, and there was a right lively media war underway. On the newspaper side, the weekly *Gainesville News*, with a longtime reputation for thorough reporting and strong editorial stands, was faced off against the recently formed *Daily Times*, an outgrowth of the longtime and highly respected weekly, *The Gainesville Eagle*. Editorially, if one paper took one side of an issue, the other paper usually took the other.

And neither paper wanted the other to scoop it with a news story, nor to get caught with a factual error.

On the radio side, the old-timer was WGGA with some radio personalities who had loyal followers. And the brash upstart was WDUN with the newer concept they called Showmanship radio. The media battle was still underway in Atlanta, too, with notorious reporting and editorial battles between the *Journal* and the *Constitution*.

You may not have had as much diversity of cultures in Gainesville back then, but I'll guarantee you ... you had no problem getting a diversity of news and opinion.

✲ ✲ ✲

Sylvan Meyer and Strong Journalism Arrive

Things were changing as the World War II veterans came home; and Sylvan Meyer was reporting the news in the *Daily Times* as it happened. There was a hot debate in local coffee clubs about whether or not this new daily newspaper should report the names of people arrested for drunk driving (nowadays we charitably call it DUI, driving under the influence).

Prior to Editor Meyer, the local papers, most newspapers for that matter, had omitted what they considered to be personal matters, and unless there was a spectacular wreck or someone was killed, drunk driving was personal and therefore not reportable news. But Gainesville had a growing problem with drinking and driving, and if the paper did NOT report an incident, it immediately became the chief topic of conversation at these very same coffee clubs. They gave Meyer credit for one thing, though: no matter who got caught, their name went in the paper. Huffed one local leader: "If his own mother got caught for drunk driving, he'd put her dad-blamed name in the paper."

Gainesville has a tradition of strong journalism ... both print and broadcast, and the new local daily was making itself known.

✲ ✲ ✲

Keep Them Cards And Letters Comin'

It was the early days of radio in Gainesville, and there was a lively competition between the local radio stations for the listening audience which followed local bands. You heard me right: local bands. There were a bunch of them, and they played country music, or gospel, or both, and people would turn out to enjoy them ... and they certainly enjoyed them on the radio. Grady Watson had a band, and so did Opal Thompson ... and when the radio stations weren't carrying local bands, there was the famous Hayloft Jamboree.

Anyway, WGGA had a band led by one Apple Savage, and Apple had a following. He later made his name in politics in Clayton, Georgia, but that is another story. And on WDUN, the new station on the block, there was "Sugar Booger" who was both a character and a

Country Music DeeJay. And no, I'm not kidding you ... the handle he went by was Sugar Booger.

There was also a great competition among the music groups to see who would get the most fan mail, so the appeals to listeners to "keep them cards and letters a'comin' "were almost as frequent as today's appeals for money from Georgia Public Television. Except live country music on local radio was a lot more entertaining.

The Poultry Times: Beginnings

As I remember it: It was the early 1950s, and the broiler industry was blossoming in Northeast Georgia, especially in Hall, Forsyth, and Cherokee counties. National feed and pharmaceutical companies were seeking ways to advertise to this rapidly developing market. The *Gainesville News*, a leading weekly, had brought in a 24-year-old reporter (that was me) from the Atlanta Constitution with an assignment to give the Gainesville paper regional news coverage in order to attract Atlanta retail advertising.

The developing broiler industry fit the regional pattern, so when the second Southeastern Poultry and Egg Convention was held in Atlanta, the *Gainesville News* published a special tabloid featuring the poultry industry. Financially, it was a success, but the 92-year-old senior member of the Hardy family, who owned the News, died, and his three sons had other goals for that newspaper.

With the growth of the poultry industry, the diverse poultry, egg, and turkey organizations, led by the politically connected Georgia Poultry Improvement Association, had come together to form the Georgia Poultry Federation. The leaders of this organization wanted a full-time office and an executive secretary. As a reporter, Sawyer had come in contact with industry leaders. He was offered the new position, and accepted.

Charles Smithgall, the driving force in the other newspaper in Gainesville, had been the voice of an early morning farm program at WSB in Atlanta before coming back to Gainesville, and fully understood the potential of agricultural advertising. The meeting that created the *Poultry Times* included soft-spoken Joe Tankersley, a former Berry College professor now manager of Twin Oaks Hatchery, who represented the Poultry Federation Board; Lou Fockele, publisher of the Daily Times; Gordon Sawyer, executive-secretary of the Poultry Federation; and, briefly, Charles Smithgall.

The agreement created a joint venture between the Federation and the *Daily Times*. The tabloid publication would go to all *Daily Times* subscribers once a week; to all members of the Poultry Federation; and to members of the Federation's various member organizations. Advertising would be sold by the *Daily Times* advertising staff in conjunction with WGGA radio, another Smithgall property. In addition to his duties as Executive Secretary, Sawyer was to carry the title of editor of the *Poultry Times*.

He would write a weekly column, and be responsible for news stories from the various poultry associations. George Porter, a *Daily Times* staffer, would handle the rest. The profit, if there was such (and there was), would be split 50-50.

There was more. It seems fair to say the early developers of North Georgia's poultry industry enjoyed horse trading, especially if they could get "something extra" as part of a deal. The Georgia Poultry Federation's first unofficial headquarters was in the corner of Hall County Agent Leland Rew's office. After the *Poultry Times* joint agreement, the Georgia Poultry Federation was quartered in an office in Smithgall's new Press Radio Center ... rent free. (As a sidelight, that building was purchased from Smithgall some 15 years later by Gordon Sawyer's Sawyer Advertising).

✲ ✲ ✲

CHAPTER 12 – Trouble, Tornadoes and The Great Depression

It has often been said that a person – or a community or nation – can be measured by how well it handles adversity. For Georgia's mountain area, the test began with the Wall Street crash of 1929. But that was only the beginning.

Actually, the stock market crash itself was not a major disaster for individuals in the area, for very few were stockholders. The fact that the Great Depression "swamped all boats" did affect the local economy, however, and that included everybody. Life was lean, and many families were living hand-to-mouth, barely getting by. The summer tourist business was the primary victim of the depression, but it was already in decline.

The largest disaster of the 1920s and early 1930s for Northeast Georgia came in the mountains ... not on Wall Street. It was estimated that 30 to 40 percent of the trees in the mountains were Chestnuts ... majestic trees that often had a diameter of five to six feet. Cutting these huge trees, and hauling them to the sawmill was a major provider of jobs in the mountains.

Then a Chestnut Blight moved over the region, as one forester said "like a fog." The great trees were mostly dead by 1930, and the sawmill at Helen – the largest in the Eastern United States at the time – closed. The ripple effect was immediate. For instance, the main reason for the railroad from Helen to Gainesville was to haul lumber to meet other railroads that would take lumber to U. S. markets and to Savannah for world markets. Even the Chestnuts, a sideline income producer for mountain families, were gone.

The primary cash crop for farmers in the area was cotton, and in the late 1920s the Boll Weevil arrived. Cotton was king in the entire South, and a system was in place that provided a ready market for cotton farmers ... even the small farmers of mountainous Northeast Georgia. Not only that, there was a massive move of New England cotton mills to the South, so the market now was nearby. For many Northeast Georgia farmers, cotton was their only cash crop, so the coming of the Boll Weevil that destroyed the cotton was a deathly blow to the small farmers in the area. Major warehouses in Gainesville that normally would be full to the rafters with bales of cotton at the end of the cotton season, suddenly stood empty.

Even the old standby, moonshine whiskey, took a hit. The Prohibition Amendment to the U. S. Constitution had been passed in 1919 and created an unmeasured, but important new market for this mountain industry. Then in 1933 the Prohibition Amendment was repealed, and legal, tax-paid whiskey took the lion's share of that market away from the moonshiners.

Interviewing a survivor of the 1930s in the year 2000, I listened as he recalled that era as "just one dadburned thing after another." One year, he said, "even the fishing was bad."

Then on April 6, 1936, tornadoes converged on Gainesville, described by national newspapers as "... a prosperous little mountain trading and mill town." The U. S. Weather Bureau said at the time that 203 people were killed, 934 injured, and damage estimated at $13 million. *Northeast Georgia: A History* noted: "Because Gainesville was the business, financial, and transportation center for Northeast Georgia, the entire mountain region had suffered a crippling economic blow."

At the time of the tornado in Gainesville, President Roosevelt was in Warm Springs, Georgia, and three days later, the train taking him back to Washington stopped in Gainesville. The president, it was said, was humbled by the devastation, but even more so by "... the proud spirit of the people."

President Roosevelt pledged to help, and he did. Thus Gainesville became the "New Deal's" Exhibit A in how Washington programs could help local communities and citizens in times of adversity.

The president returned to Gainesville two years later, and as reported by the national news (mostly newspaper at the time, but also with President Roosevelt's favorite media, radio) congratulated the town on its "indomitable spirit" and its progress in rebuilding. Thus began a cultural/political debate that continues to this day: did Roosevelt and his New Deal programs save Gainesville, or did the people – working through volunteer organizations like the Red Cross – "pull themselves up by their own bootstraps."

No matter who won the political debate – those who said President Roosevelt led to the rebuilding of Gainesville, or those proud souls who insisted local people (with volunteers who poured into town to help), did the job themselves, the fact is Gainesville was energetically "back in business" by 1938.

✲ ✲ ✲

Private Savings Banks Pay More Than Postal Savings

The year was 1949, and the local Post Office, then located in what is now part of the Federal Building, was on a growth binge. Postmaster Huram Hancock said postal receipts were up a full 10 percent over the same time a year ago, a combination ... Mr. Hancock said ... of population growth and a strong local economy. It was an era when the back dock of the local Post Office almost always carried the cheeps of live baby chicks in boxes with air holes ... baby chicks being delivered by mail from out of state hatcheries. The Post Office had hired another person, and had to buy a new truck to take care of the growth.

On the other side of the coin, however, Postmaster Hancock reported that Postal Savings were down. Local citizens had about $1,250,000 in savings in the local Post Office, he reported, and that was almost $100,000 below the amount in savings at the same time a year before. At that time, a lot of people saved money at the Post Office, but the going Postal Savings rate was two percent, and the new Savings Banks were paying 3 percent. A lot of people were still saving, but they were moving their money to get the higher return.

✲ ✲ ✲

Home Canning at the Canning Plant

I was listening to Gene Anderson, our County Agent, invite people out to the Farmers Market the other day to get some early tomatoes and corn, and it sent me scrambling to dig out information about another service we once had in Hall County, back when most people had their own gardens.

It was 50 years ago, and the county canning plant at Lula had opened for the season. Local people would come in with vegetables, fresh from their own garden ... some already prepared for canning, but a lot, like snap beans, that needed preparation. Some said they tasted better when snapped just before canning, but the real reason for doing some preparation at the canning plant was the fellowship. Sort of like a quilting bee.

Anyway, it cost you seven cents for a number two can, eight cents for a number three. You prepared the contents, and they did the cooking and sealing. In 1949, the Lula canning plant, which had been in operation 14 years, turned out almost 100,000 pints of food for local citizens to take home and stash away for winter.

Now...I've got a question of you folks; I know we had a canning plant at Lula, and one at Flowery Branch. But where else did we have canning plants in Hall County?

☼ ☼ ☼

Do You Remember When ...?

In the late 1940s, George Finger wrote a column in one of the local newspapers called, "Do You Remember When?" He was talking about the good old days, the things that happened in Gainesville in the EARLY 1900s.

Do you remember, he said: "On Sunday afternoon, lots of people used to gather and watch the old C. J. & S. narrow gauge railroad come in; and get a big kick out of seeing the engine and tender being turned on a turntable located just across the street from where the Pierce Company's shop is now located."

Or do you remember: ":When the old Holzendorf Hotel burned. It stood on the hill just above the famous Gower Springs, just within the main arc of what is now known as Green Street Circle."

"Or when Gainesville had a match factory. It was located on the corner of Main and Myrtle Streets, just north of the old Richmond Hotel, which stood about where Chambers Lumber Company is now located."

That was George W. Finger, talking about the past.

✲ ✲ ✲

Memories From the Tornado of '36: A Homecoming

We had an interesting event in Gainesville the other night. It was called, "The Tornado of '36: A Homecoming," and more than 200 people turned out in lousy, rainy weather to see what it was all about. The program was one of a series being sponsored by the new Northeast Georgia History Center at Brenau University, and these programs ... while the History Center's new building is under construction ... have been held in the Chapel at the First Baptist Church.

The program started with a silent, black-and-white film of the devastation in downtown Gainesville on the day following the Tornado of '36. Parts of Gainesville were literally obliterated on April 6, 1936. And yet, some areas of town, sometimes no more than a few feet from an area in shambles, were untouched. I'll admit it was more emotional than I had expected, both from the nostalgic moments and the humorous ones. B. J. Williams moderated a panel of people who survived the tornado, and it brought on a yo-yo of up and down emotions.

Pierce Hancock talking about the death of his brother when a brick wall fell on the convertible he was riding in. Grace Moore about the agony her father faced as he walked through rubble downtown on his way to Brenau to see if she had survived. Memories of the stores on the square from Charlie Frierson and Mr. Newman. Of Gainesville High from Bonnie Valentine. And the funny moments, like a memory from Clifford Martin of the student who lifted his head out of the rubble at Gainesville High and, spotting the principal, C. J. Cheeves, said: "Mr. Cheeves, do you reckon we'll have our exams today?"

White Marble Courthouse After Tornado of 1936

After Hall County's magnificent brick Court House was destroyed by the tornado of 1936, the county returned to an architectural style first seen in Gainesville's public buildings early in the century. The Gainesville Post Office introduced a white marble architectural style in 1910, and the Federal Building followed the style about 1935. When the large brick Court House and the classic brick City Hall and fire department were blown apart by the Tornado of '36, a decision was made to create buildings that matched the style of the Federal building and the Post Office.

Thus, soon after the debris from the tornado was cleared away, construction was started on a white marble Court House and a complimentary design for the City Hall. The Court House was built at the location of the old brick Court House, and the City Hall directly across Broad Street.

A Court House addition was built in 1976, on space between the original Court House and the Federal Building ... still following the white marble architectural style of the 1910 Post Office, But when the Mountain Center and a new county-city office building were built, the white marble architecture was dropped. Broad Street was closed, and Roosevelt Square was created. And now, we're building again....this time with brick.

✲ ✲ ✲

The Drought Is Not Even Close To The Dust Bowl

It was bound to come sooner or later: a news reporter quoted some supposed scientist who said we in Georgia are in a drought because of ... you've got it: GLOBAL WARMING. Nothing was said about the floods that have plagued the Midwest this year, but I will give this particular reporter credit – he did not quote Al Gore. There is no debate that the world climate is changing, and for that matter, there is no debate that the earth is warming. There are two debate points in all this: first, is this warming being created by man, or is it a natural event? And, second, how rapidly will warming take place?

To the first argument, not all scientists agree that whatever is happening is being created by man. If that is the case, the opponents say, what about the warming period that happened in the Arctic in the last century? Or what about the weather history of Greenland? And to the second point: Al Gore predicts Global Warming will create havoc within a decade, and therefore governments should take control right now. In *An Inconvenient Truth*, Gore predicts that worldwide sea levels will RISE 20 FEET. But the "Intergovernmental Panel on Climate Change," which shared this year's Nobel Prize with Al Gore, predicts oceans MIGHT RISE 7 to 24 INCHES in the next 100 years.

And the next thing we can expect is someone making a statement that this drought is the worst in American history, but the worst recorded drought in our country came from 1931 to 1939, and the current drought in Georgia is not even in the ballpark with that disastrous event. Generally, that drought is referred to as the "Dust Bowl," and it first hit the Midwestern and southern plains in 1931. It continued through 1933 when Franklin D. Roosevelt became president. His administration enacted legislation intended to save the small American farmer, but the drought continued through 1934 and 1935, when Roosevelt initiated severe government programs intended to help farmers. The Soil Conservation Service was founded in 1935 under the U. S. Department of Agriculture, replacing the Soil Erosion Service in the U. S. Department of Interior.

The drought continued through 1936, then 1937 and 1938. It became known as the DUST BOWL because so much topsoil blew away in the Midwest, but before that drought ended, it covered 75 percent of the United States and affected 27 states severely. The rains finally came in the fall of 1939, and not long afterward, the great plains again became golden with wheat. I don't want to belittle the drought we are now having, but please don't call it man-made, and it is not the largest in U. S. history.

✲ ✲ ✲

Northeast Georgia Goes After Jobs in 1933

The year was 1933, and the State of Georgia was celebrating its Bicentennial. Gainesville had chosen this period of time, with the nation in the throes of the Great Depression, to seek new industry, and their target was the North. A promotional edition of the Eagle, a local newspaper, had as its lead headline: "Gainesville is Logical City for Your Southern Plant." The subhead noted: "Advantages Here Are Surpassed by No Other City."

"From the standpoint of healthfulness," the literature said, "Gainesville has no superior." From the standpoint of climate, "Gainesville combines the equable temperatures of the Southern mild winter with the cooler temperatures along the foothills of the Blue Ridge mountains." It told of great education, unlimited hydro-electric power, three railroads, and an excellent market location.

The highlight, of course, was good workers ... dependable, hard-working people.

That was Gainesville in 1933 ... the year the State of Georgia celebrated its Bicentennial.

☼ ☼ ☼

Celebrations After World War II: Labor Day

Gainesville's First Night event the other night brought to mind the way we celebrated shortly after World War II. The biggest celebration in that era was a big Labor Day Festival ... and some people still insist THAT event was the biggest ever held in North Georgia, and they might be right. It took an hour-and-a-half just for the parade to go by. The Marine band from Cherry Point was here; so was the Navy band from Charleston. American Legion drum and bugle corps units from all over Georgia were here. The Shriners section was six blocks long all by itself. The town was packed with people, not only local folks but also visitors from Atlanta to the Carolinas.

That afternoon, there was an air show at the airport; an event that caused great excitement. There were a lot of World War II warbirds - P-51 Mustangs and Navy Hellcats and B-25s - still around at that time, and the pilots who flew them were still young and bold. But this day was special; there was a fly-by of jet aircraft, the first ever seen here. And to wind things down, there were band concerts that night at City Park.

When Gainesvillians celebrated at that time, they celebrated.

☼ ☼ ☼

The Need To Relax in 1933

It was April in 1933, and the U. S. government was creating programs to counter the Great Depression. The *Gainesville Eagle* reported that our town had been chosen as headquarters for "... the Roosevelt reforestation plan." But the *Eagle* also reported Hall County had some things going along just fine despite the depression. Riverside Military Academy and Brenau College were doing okay. The two Pacolet mills were running, and so was Chicopee. And it had just been learned that a new hosiery mill was locating here, with a lot of new jobs. This region had not escaped the hurt from the depression, especially in the farming sector, but life went on, and at times it was even fun.

For instance, an *Eagle* interview with the head of Pruitt-Barrett Hardware, one of North Georgia's largest farm equipment dealers, noted this company also specialized in sporting goods and athletic equipment. The company reported it had "...sold more fishing tackle, guns, golf clubs, etc. (during 1931 and 1932) than in any two previous years combined." Said Mr. Barrett: "The depression has shown people the necessity of relieving the tension of high pressure business with relaxation now and then." That was how Gainesville survived the Great Depression."

✲ ✲ ✲

Winston Churchill Looks Back at "The Gathering Storm"

Following World War II, Winston Churchill wrote a series of books. The book entitled *The Gathering Storm* outlines in 600-page detail, the events, decisions, and diplomatic strategy leading up to the Second World War. At the end of Chapter 17, Churchill chronicles the period in which Hitler was demanding Germany be granted control over certain countries and threatening to invade them if not given his way. This was the period in which Prime Minister Chamberlain met with Hitler for the third time, came home to Britain and declared "...there shall be peace in our time," and the point at which Hitler, now convinced the Allies would not fight, turned his armies loose.

Churchill left some thoughts which, he said, "may be a guide in the future." Let me quote Churchill: "... Ministers assume their responsibilities of guiding states. Their duty is first to so deal with other nations as to avoid strife and war and to eschew aggression in all its forms, whether for nationalistic or ideological objects. But the safety of the state, the lives and freedom of their own fellow countrymen, to whom they owe their position, makes it right and imperative in the last resort, that the use of force should not be excluded. If the circumstances are such as to warrant it, force may be used. And if this be so, it should be used under the conditions which are most favorable. There is no merit in putting off a war for a year if, when it comes, it is a far worse war or one much harder to win. These are the tormenting dilemmas upon which mankind has throughout its history been so frequently impaled."

CHAPTER 13 – Duty, Honor, God and Country

Patriotism has always been a major part of the core culture of the people of Northeast Georgia, a trait that goes back to the very earliest settlers of the Georgia frontier. Historic Fort Yargo still exists, one of a string of blockhouse forts where settlers could go for safety when the Indians went on a rampage. Early towns like Gainesville had a militia company, and the militia drill was part of the excitement during the early 1800's when farm folk came to town for Court Week.

The Georgia mountain area was still considered Indian country during the Revolutionary War, so few men went from Northeast Georgia to fight the British, but the Indians sided with the Englishmen, so settlers on the frontier banded together to "stave the Indians off." After the Americans won their freedom, many veterans of that war took advantage of the Headright system and claimed land in Georgia, some in areas still shown on maps as Cherokee country.

While the small farmers of Northeast Georgia had practically no slaves, and were not enthusiastic about that part of the Civil War, they had little use for a dominant federal government (remember the Whiskey rebellion?). Redwine Methodist Church, located between Gainesville and Flowery Branch, became a point where voluntary Confederate companies were formed. That church still holds a ceremony once a year to honor those soldiers, and eight are buried in the adjacent cemetery. (They will also remind you that Redwine had more volunteers in World War II than most communities, and were loyal supporters of our American military during the Vietnam era.)

There are other historic clues showing a patriotic spirit among the mountain folk in the 1800s. Among those killed at The Alamo, one was from Hall County. Somewhere on the Hall County Courthouse grounds, one can find a marker honoring those local men who served in the Spanish-American War. World War I and II are patriotic stories all their own.

It was not only those who served in the armed forces, either. Those on the home front were also patriotic, and proud of it. Parades, special ceremonies, Fourth of July celebrations ... they were all part of the culture of the Northeastern corner of Georgia.

Patriotism comes naturally to the people of Northeast Georgia. They have a deep-seated love for America, and are not embarrassed to say so. Patriotism is deeply embedded in their culture.

☆ ☆ ☆

World War I – The War To End All Wars

President Woodrow Wilson won re-election campaigning on a pledge to keep America out of "Europe's war." Germany was winning, and except for war material coming across the Atlantic from America, the Germans might have already been the victors.

The Germans were convinced President Wilson meant what he said, that America would not enter that war, and their submarines began sinking American ships on their way to Europe. A populist movement began in America among citizens who felt America had to help win the war in Europe, lest we would find ourselves defending this nation on our own shores. President Wilson reversed his stand, and not only did the United States continue sending supplies to Europe, we also sent two million troops.

At Gainesville's Paul E. Bolding Post 7 of the American Legion, you can view a large 8-foot high block of granite. Markers on three sides list the names of the 816 Hall Countians who served in World War I. And on the remaining side you can find 29 names of those who died in France that we might live in freedom in America.. The monument was erected in 1923 by the American Legion Auxiliary Unit of the Paul E. Bolding Post 7 ... "In honor of the men of Hall County who placed their lives in the hands of their country during the World War."

Lest we forget, those who made their last roll call in Europe were: James T. Bales, Paul E. Bolding, James T. Chandler, Asbury E. Church, Rufus B. Clark, Benjamin Corn, William M. Dobbs, John H. Dowdy, Silas Dunnegan, Robert Elrod, Lee Garner, James W. Jarrell, Hubert Lancaster, Allen Langford, Hubert Ledford, David Marshbanks, D. McKinney, M. Miller, Herman R. Mills, Cecil Neal, Bryant B. Nuckols, Russel G. O'Kelley, Fletcher Smith, Samuel M. Smith, E. S. Southern, George W. Stancil, Frank Wayne, Clyde Wilson, and William C. League.

The World War I armistice was signed on 11-11-11 – The 11th hour of the 11th day of the 11th month of 1918. It was made a holiday under the name Armistice Day.

The national American Legion was founded in Paris by a group of citizen soldiers who saw merit in harnessing for peacetime the immense power the American troops had displayed in "The War to End All Wars."

A Gainesville native, Edgar B. Dunlap, went to Paris, and was a part of the founding meeting. Returning home, he was active in forming posts in Georgia. Atlanta, the capital city, was established as Post 1. Gainesville, as one of the first posts formed in Georgia, became Post 7, a very low number that is a historic honor among Legionnaires.

Each Post honored one veteran, and the Gainesville Legion post officially became the Paul E. Bolding Post 7 of the American Legion, and Colonel Dunlap became its first commander. Paul E. Bolding was a Marine corporal, and the first Hall Countian killed on the battlefield in World War I.

And what about the national organization? The American Legion became the largest veterans organization in the United States, with a well-defined mission. The PREAMBLE to its Constitution, which is repeated at every meeting states: For God and Country we associate ourselves together for the following purposes: To uphold and defend the Constitution of the United States of America; to maintain law and order; to foster and perpetuate a one hundred percent Americanism; to preserve the memories and incidents of our association in the Great War(s); to inculcate a sense of individual obligation to the community, state and nation; to combat the autocracy of both the classes and the masses; to make right the master of might; to promote peace and good will on earth; to safeguard and transmit to posterity the principles of justice, freedom and democracy; to consecrate and sanctify our comradeship by devotion to mutual helpfulness."

World War II – Only two decades later

World War II was well underway before America was abruptly thrust into it at Pearl Harbor. Hitler's armies had first rolled into Poland in September, 1939, and by Thanksgiving 1941, Germany held almost all of Europe except Great Britain. Here in America, Franklin D. Roosevelt had won re-election for an unprecedented third term as the president who had kept us out of war.

Here in Northeast Georgia, some men had been called into service by the first peacetime draft in American history, and a number were home on leave for the 1941 Thanksgiving holidays. Others had chosen to fight, and had volunteered as an American in units like the Flying Tigers in China, or had chosen to help England by joining the Canadian army.

President Roosevelt had started a government-financed Lend-Lease program, and declared that although the United States would not enter the war, it would be "the arsenal for democracy". America would supply war material to Great Britain and others on credit.

Jobs had been scarce in America all through the 1930s, and were now beginning to show up at bomber plants, shipyards along the east coast, automobile plants in Detroit. Many Northeast Georgians, who had been hungry for jobs since 1933, were going where the new jobs were paying premium wages. Many were home for the Thanksgiving holidays.

Gainesville's weekly newspapers were filled with Christmas advertising. Santa had duly arrived in Gainesville, and many parents with small children were going to Atlanta for the annual festival at Rich's Department Store. It was a tender time when almost everyone in Northeast Georgia was getting over their Thanksgiving dinner and turning their attention to Christmas 1941.

There was a Christian manger scene on the square, with live shepherds. The homes on Green Street were being decorated with red ribbons and green swags, with electric candles. The stores had outdone themselves with window displays. The Saturday after Thanksgiving had been a record shopping day in Gainesville and in most other towns in the mountain area. It was peacetime in America, and everyone was focused on Christmas ... the birthday of the Christ Child.

Then, on December 7, 1941, a Sunday, the patriotic mettle of all America was tested as the Japanese launched their sneak attack on Pearl Harbor and the Philippines. A peaceful America was turned upside down, and in an instant, the people of Northeast Georgia became warriors.

Go back and read the weekly newspapers of Northeast Georgia during the fall of 1941, and you will find a culture that focused on local elections, new businesses, church services, Court House events, football games, weddings, and social events. The local papers listed weddings, births, obituaries. The coffee clubs talked about the early days of the chicken business and who was likely to run for Sheriff or the County Commission. Community news columns reported on out-of-town visitors and who took which preacher home for dinner last Sunday (dinner meaning the noontime meal).

That culture was shattered on December 7, 1941, **but most went off to war remembering that culture as the one they were fighting for.**

Now the papers began to list those called up by the draft board ... who had joined the Navy or

Marines ... those accepted as cadets in the Army Air Corps. Community news reported on families that had gone to the Gulf Coast to work in a shipyard, or whose wife had taken a job in the Bell Bomber plant.

Food was given a very high priority, and the budding broiler industry began to blossom. For those not in service, jobs were plentiful and the hourly pay was enticing. Many jobs carried overtime, and for people working in a defense plant, working overtime was patriotic and was encouraged. Women entered the work force, doing jobs never before offered to women. Age didn't seem to matter. Confederate General James Longstreet's wife held a job as a riveter at the bomber plant in Marietta. Southern blacks became GIs, and many of those not in uniform found jobs not available to them before.

Home front people volunteered for Civil Defense, bandage rolling, the Red Cross. Homegrown food was encouraged with Victory Gardens. Government controlled rationing was accepted, and food stamps determined what and how much a family ate. To get gasoline and tire coupons beyond a minimum level, one had to make an application and explain to a local board how this helped the war effort.

✲ ✲ ✲

The culture of Northeast Georgia changed dramatically during World War II, but one trait held firm ... and was intensified: **Patriotism**. The people of Northeast Georgia were proud to be patriotic. They wanted to do their part, volunteering for service, and once there, volunteering for dangerous duty. Mothers proudly posted the blue star flag in their front window, signifying a family member in service, and those who lost a son displayed the Gold Star and were the most highly honored of all.

Duty, honor, God, and Country had always been part of the culture of mountain folks. It was especially important during World War II.

✲ ✲ ✲

July 4: The Day Americans Took a Stand

In the current political climate, it is not acceptable in this country to take a strong stand on anything lest you offend someone who thinks differently. Take a strong political stand today, either right or left, and you will be called an extremist, a radical, a bigot, or worse.

Today is July 4, and today we celebrate the day a bunch of Americans took a radical stand. It wasn't easy. The "politically correct" thing to do was to go along with the King, even though most agreed the King was wrong. The easy thing to do was to NOT speak up for fear you would hurt your neighbor's feelings. The safe thing to do was to stay quiet, for the King had great power and didn't hesitate to use it ruthlessly. And if you quietly went along with the King, you just might get rich.

There were 56 signers of the Declaration of Independence. They were citizens, just like you and me. Most were well-educated. They were prosperous and enjoyed status, power, and wealth. But they believed in freedom and were willing to make a stand. "We mutually pledge to each other," they said, "our lives, our fortunes, and our sacred honor." Most lost their fortunes. Many lost their lives. But not one lost his sacred honor.

Because they believed in the ideals of a free, democratic nation and because they were willing to take a stand, today we are celebrating American Independence Day. THAT'S what July 4 is all about.

✲ ✲ ✲

The Pledge of Allegiance

It was fifty years ago, and on July 4 ... on any other day of the year, for that matter ... we said the Pledge of Allegiance to the American flag without hesitation. It was just part of our life. But then a discussion started about the pledge, not the kind you might expect today. There was a great discussion about whether or nor we should add something to our historic pledge, and we did in 1954. We added, "under God" as a part of that sacred pledge.

"I pledge allegiance to the Flag of the United States of America, and to the Republic for which it stands. One nation, under God, indivisible, with Liberty and justice for all."

Somehow, on Sunday, July 4, it seems appropriate to recite the Pledge of Allegiance ... and in the historic America I know, it seems appropriate to include "under God."

✲ ✲ ✲

"Sandy" Nininger: The First Medal of Honor In World War II

The objective of Memorial Day, which comes up in a few days, is to remind all Americans of the sacrifice made by others that you and I may live in a free land. It seems to me that we have one native son hero who deserves much more honor than we have ever given him. His name is: Alexander Ramsay Nininger, and he was called "Sandy." We know he was the grandson of W. Harve Craig, and that his mother was living at the Craig residence on Park Street here in Gainesville, when he was born. His parents separated, and in time he moved with his father to Ft. Lauderdale, Florida. His high school records there show he was an athlete and a good student. He attended West Point, was commissioned in 1941, and assigned to the Philippines. At the same time that the Japanese attacked Pearl Harbor, they also destroyed all American air power in the Pacific and launched a massive attack on the Philippine Islands. General MacArthur and his troops were pushed back onto the Bataan Peninsula, where they were attempting to establish a defense line.

It was during this action that Sandy Nininger won the Medal of Honor posthumously. One report told it this way: "The enemy attacked, and the army retreated, except for Nininger. He ran straight into the assault, shooting snipers out of trees, hurling grenades into foxholes, bayoneting anybody who got in his way. Three times he was wounded. He scooped up an enemy machine gun and sprayed bullets until, finally, he fell." The Japanese advance was stopped. The defense line was established. And General MacArthur was the one who recommended Nininger for the Congressional Medal of Honor ... thus it was that the first Medal of Honor in World War II went to a native son of Gainesville, Georgia.

☼ ☼ ☼

Paul E. Bolding: A Memorial Day Remembrance

This is the month in which we observe Memorial Day ... the official holiday commemorating those men and women who have offered their lives or given their lives so that you and I may live in a free land. Let's begin with World War I. The U.S. entered that war late. Americans fought for only about two years before that bloody conflict ended, but in that period of time the United States lost 117,465 men, and another 205,690 were wounded. If you drive out to the end of Riverside Drive, in Gainesville, to the place where the Paul E. Bolding Post 7 of the American Legion is located, you can find a huge block of granite, and on three sides of that monument you will find bronze plaques listing all the men who left from Hall County (and I quote here) "...who placed their lives in the hands of their country" during the huge conflict that was called the war to end all wars. Hall County's population was about one-fourth as large as it is now, but on the plaques you will find the names of 816 local men who joined to fight in World War I. And on the final side of that granite block, you will find another bronze plaque listing the names of 29 (and again I quote) "who made the supreme sacrifice." That was 29 Hall County boys who gave their lives in World War I that you and I might be free.

One who died was named Paul Elbert Bolding, the name you will hear any time the local Post 7 of the American Legion is mentioned. Paul E. Bolding, a Marine corporal, had been educated at the old Sardis School and attended a Baptist Church nearby. He came from a respected family. His grandfather built both Bolding's Mill and Bolding's Bridge, structures now under the waters of Lake Lanier. His father had been the County Ordinary. Bolding was sent overseas three months after his enlistment, and was first wounded in action in July 1918. He recovered and rejoined his company. It was in the brutal battle of the Argonne Forest that he was killed in action on October 9, 1918. He was a local boy, and he gave his life in World War I that you and I might live in freedom in this United States of America.

✲ ✲ ✲

Denver Truelove and The Doolittle Raid on Tokyo

Memorial Day was created to remind us Americans of the price paid by patriotic men and women so that you and I might live in freedom in this unique democracy of ours. Let me tell you about something that comes about at one time or another in almost every combat situation. A person steps forward and says, "I need a few good volunteers for a very dangerous but important mission." Such was the case in early 1942 when a call went out in the Army Air Force for volunteers for a highly secret and very dangerous mission. One of the volunteers who stepped forward was a Hall County boy named Denver Vernon Truelove. About all they learned about their mission while training was that it would be led by one Lt. Col. Jimmy Doolittle.

We know now these volunteers began intensive training in twin-engine B-25 bombers, mostly learning to take off in a short distance and to hit targets with bombs from a very low altitude. In time their planes were loaded on a Navy aircraft carrier, and they learned from Colonel Doolittle that their target was to be Tokyo ... in the heart of Japan itself. They were to take off from the aircraft carrier, bomb Tokyo, and end up somewhere in China. Lt. Denver Truelove was the bombardier-navigator in plane number five over Tokyo, and his bombs scored direct hits on a power station, oil tanks, and a large manufacturing plant. After that, the plane was to head for the Chinese coast.

Low on fuel, with darkness closing in, plane five made land, and the entire crew bailed out. They landed safely and were greeted by friendly Chinese. Remarkably, of the 80 who flew over Tokyo on April 18, 1942, 69 eventually made it out of China. Of the 11 lost, three were killed exiting their aircraft, three were executed by the Japanese, one died of malnutrition and mistreatment in a Japanese prison, and four were repatriated at the end of the war after 40 months of captivity.

A recipient of the Distinguished Service Cross, Denver Truelove returned to duty and was killed in action over Italy two years later. Remembering men like Denver Truelove is what Memorial Day is all about. He made our freedom possible.

John Yarbrough: The Hurry Up and Wait of War

It was early 1945, and headline news reported the Allies were pushing the Axis hard on all fronts. But if you ask the World War II gang, all will remember days, sometimes weeks, when the greatest challenge was to find something to do to keep from being bored stiff.

In Europe, for instance, John Yarbrough was with an Army unit on one side of a river facing a German force on the other, but for days all had been quiet. So John and some of his buddies decided to learn to ride the motorcycle assigned to their company. The only road was along the river, in full view of the Germans, but so what? It was Yarbrough on the motorcycle, making a shaky ride, when a shell exploded on the road directly in front of the bike, and despite all John could do, he tumbled into the rubble.

Later, the Americans realized these German artillerymen were excellent marksmen. They didn't miss. So, they too had probably been bored and spent the rest of the day laughing about that crazy GI they had sent tumbling on his motorcycle. A few days later, things got serious. The Americans crossed the river, and soon afterwards, the war in Europe ended. John Yarbrough was an Alabama boy, but you will remember him here in Gainesville as Cap'n Chick ... the long-time editor of the Poultry Times.

✲ ✲ ✲

American Legion Post 7 Organized in 1919

It was at the end of World War I that an organization of American veterans, called the American Legion, was formed in Paris, France. And it was shortly after that a Post was formed in Gainesville, Georgia. Said the local paper on August 6, 1919,

"The organization stands for the betterment, socially and morally, of our returned soldiers and sailors, and will be beneficial to the community as well as the members." It was estimated there were at least 200 Hall County men who had served in the Armed Forces during World War I and were thus eligible to belong to the American Legion.

Present at that first meeting, according to the paper, were Edgar B. Dunlap (who became the first Commander of Post 7), Pete Craig, Hammil Palmour, George D. Day, Ashford Daniels, R. F. Cavender, Leonard

C. Cinciolo, Edwin A. Smith, Roy A. Newman, William J. Phillips, Oris Lathem Jr., William A. Longstreet, Garland Tumlin, Haywood Pearce, John Pearce, Thomas Pearce, Clifton Goforth, and Claud B. Barrett.

A committee was named to form the constitution and bylaws and a meeting was called, to be held at the Court House, on August 16, 1919 ... and it was hoped every veteran in Hall County would come in and join.

✲ ✲ ✲

The Red Poppies of Flanders' Fields

The good ladies of Post 7 of the American Legion Auxiliary were distributing poppies to honor the veterans of both World War I and World War II. The poppy tradition had started shortly after World War I and was a program started by the American Legion to raise money for the benefit of veterans and their families and especially for those who needed physical rehabilitation or financial help.

The poppy came about, it is said, because of Flanders Fields ... a famed World War I battlefield covered with red poppies mixed with the red blood of wounded soldiers ... a reminder of the serene beauty that could follow the grimness of war ... a reminder of the price paid by some for the freedom we all enjoy ... a way to honor those who served and to remember those who fought but now need our help.

The ladies of Post 7 Auxiliary will again be distributing poppies today, November 11, mostly at the Veterans Day ceremony which starts at 11 a.m. at Roosevelt Square. By tradition, the poppy is never "sold," but also by tradition, people wearing them have made a contribution to the "Poppy Fund" ... as recognition that they remember and honor those who served our nation in wartime.

✲ ✲ ✲

150 Man-Years of Legionnaire Leadership

A small group of past commanders of Post 7 of The American Legion, gathered at the post home the other night to honor three of their own - Tom Hodge, Bob Adams, and Roy Tumer. Each of these three men have given more than 50 years of leadership to the local Legion, but more interesting – each of them was commander of Post 7 more than 50 years ago, and they have been part of the glue that has held that great organization together since the end of World War II.

The local American Legion was formed shortly after World War I, but here locally it reached its zenith with the return of the troops from World War II. It was the center of local energy that saw to it that American patriotism was strong immediately following World War II. There were parades and special veterans events. A post home was acquired at the end of Riverside Drive ... a post home that was destroyed in a tragic fire and then rebuilt. A constant stream of youngsters were sponsored to both Boys' State and Girls' State. Some of the best Legion baseball in the South was sponsored locally by Post 7, and the Ivey-Watson baseball field was promoted and partially paid for by this local Legion post.

This local group of Legionnaires stood strong for our American military and constantly supported our troops ... even during the Vietnam era when much of America had turned against them. In recent years, we have been reminded of the importance of the Fourth of July with the largest fireworks display in Northeast Georgia; of Veterans Day with a ceremony at the eternal flame in Roosevelt Square on November 11; and of Memorial Day with a parade, with last year's parade being the largest ever held in Gainesville.

The Army Air Corps Arrives in Gainesville: 1936

I was watching a plane land at the local airport the other day ... an open cockpit biplane, logically an antique ... coming in smooth and slow, and it reminded me of one of Jim DeLong's favorite memories as a Gainesville teenager. It seems it was the winter of 1936, and the town was unexpectedly caught up in a snowstorm ... the kind that had large snowflakes falling heavily enough so that visibility was becoming a problem. To the surprise of everybody on the ground, and to the delight of a bunch of teenagers, a flight of noisy twin-engine biplanes showed up, almost at treetop level.

In 1936, low flying airplanes were relatively rare, so you can imagine the astonishment and excitement as the thundering planes went over. It turned out there were eight of the planes ... World War I style Army Air Force bombers – possibly Keystone or MB-2 planes – the kind that had fabric covering and guy wires holding the wings firmly in place. DeLong and his friends realized the planes were trying to get down out of the foul weather, and they headed for the airport. Now, the Gainesville airport in 1936 had one hangar and the runway was grass, but for the times it was a pretty good facility. By the time the locals got there, the planes were landing, big cumbersome biplanes with twin engines hung between the wings and with open cockpits. The pilots climbed out, wearing their classic leather and sheepskin suits, complete with boots and goggles.

It was one more exciting day in Gainesville as Jim DeLong and other local high schoolers ferried the pilots into town to spend the night at the Dixie Hunt Hotel. Only a few years later, DeLong would become a World War II pilot, and would fly more than 70 missions over Europe ... in a much, much later model bomber.

✲ ✲ ✲

A Day of Infamy: Have We Learned Anything?

Today is December 7, and imagine with me, if you will, that it is December 7, 1941. War was raging in Europe, led by a German madman named Adolph Hitler. Here in Gainesville, Santa had officially arrived as usual on Thanksgiving, so the holiday shopping season was underway. Green Street was decorated, as were the stores. Families were making Christmas goodies and mailing Christmas cards. President Roosevelt had been re-elected to an unprecedented third term with the theme "He Kept Us Out of War." FDR said it was okay for America to be "the arsenal of Democracy" – to furnish the ships and tanks and planes for the Allies - but never again would he send our "boys" to fight across the Atlantic.

On the other side of the world, Japan had taken part of China and had joined Germany and Italy to form the Axis. But Japan was way across the Pacific and was considered a nobody ... a nation of slant-eyed people who couldn't fight their way out of a paper bag. Anyway, Japan had two of their highest ranking officials in Washington talking with us, opposing an embargo, and the news said talking was all we had to do with them. History now tells us the Japanese were convinced we would not fight, and based on that, they had a plan. If they could cripple our fleet at Pearl Harbor and destroy those 35 new B-17 bombers and the 107 P-40 fighter planes in the Philippines, Japan could take the entire South Pacific before we could wake up and regroup.

I had been out playing with a bird dog pup that Sunday afternoon, and when I came in, I found my Dad glued to the big radio in our living room. What's up Dad?" I asked casually. "Our lives have just changed", he answered. "We are at war." That was December 7, 1941, and I ask you: Have we learned anything from that day of infamy?

☆ ☆ ☆

The 50th Anniversary of D-Day

It was 50 years ago this morning that American troops began to land on the beaches of France on D-Day – the first day of that bloody and awesome return to Europe that allowed you and me to live in freedom.

A lot of Gainesvillians were there at that time: Jim DeLong, flying cover; Roy Turner landing in a glider; George Austin hitting the beach.

And we have a lot of Hall Countians over there right now, celebrating the 50th anniversary of D-Day: Bub Dunlap, Bill Gignilliat, Ellis and Ann Keener, George and Ann Thomas, Roy Turner is back, and Ed Dunlap, who served in the South Pacific. Probably a lot of others, too.

And we have four guys with two jeeps who will do the landing and travel the battle route. Dick Stribling, Lee Martin, Jack McKibbon, and Sam Butner, who designed Lakeshore Mall. Their jeeps landed at Portsmouth a couple of weeks ago; and they along with 750 other vehicles have now been taken across the English Channel.

I, for one, am glad Hall County is well represented on the beaches of Normandy this morning, and I am especially pleased they will be facing friendly greetings this time ... rather than the withering, hostile fire they met there ... 50 years ago ... today.

☆ ☆ ☆

What Is Anzio? A Rembrance.

Something came up not long ago about Anzio, and a younger person among us asked: "What is Anzio?" And I remembered the news reports about landings at that coastal Italian town called Anzio – an end around which would allow us to move on up the Italian boot in World War II.

I was stateside at the time – itchy to get in the fray – and what I did not know was the destroyer I would later serve on was shelling German gun emplacements in the hills above Anzio. And a high school football star class-mate of mine was running up the sandy beach. The destroyer's shells didn't knock out all the gun emplace-ments, and a German 88 shell exploded in the face of J. C. Church. It was weeks before I learned about it, but I cried.

I hope we'll never forget the price some have paid for our freedom, those of us who lived through it, and those who – thank God – never had to face it.

War is different when it is very personal. Church, old buddy, on this Memorial Day, I remember that you gave your life for us ... 50 years ago at Anzio.

✲ ✲ ✲

Richard Kidder: A Japanese POW Survivor

I was asked a question the other day that was, in my opinion, very valid. It went something like this: With all the World War II veterans available, how did you choose Richard Kidder to write a book about? The person asking the question was not being critical; he was simply curious. And my answer: I heard Richard Kidder had been a prisoner of war for more than three years. I had heard many years ago about the brutality of the Japanese toward their POWs, and I figured this was a story that should be preserved, one way or another.

You see, 37 % of the Japanese-held POWs died AFTER they were captured. By comparison, only two percent of German-held POWs died in prison camps. The great majority of American troops who fought in the Pacific went out there after the U. S. started fighting our way back up the Pacific Island chain toward the Japanese homeland.

Richard Kidder was in the Philippines when the war broke out, so he faced off against the Japanese at Manila, then on the Bataan peninsula, then on Corregidor, where he was finally captured. Add that to his POW experience at Cabanatuan POW camp in the Philippines; on a Hell Ship to Japan itself; in a POW slave labor camp in Osaka; and in another POW camp in Tsuraga. Thus the name of the book: *Richard Kidder: WWII SURVIVOR; Manila to Bataan. To Corregidor. To Cabanatuan POW. To a Hell Ship. To Umeda Bunsho POW in Osaka. To Tsuraga POW, To Home, Alive* ... I challenge you to read it and see if you don't think it's a story that needed to be told while Richard Kiddler was still alive to talk about it.

✲ ✲ ✲

Bob Hope: For GI's, The Name Speaks For Itself

A lot is being said about Bob Hope, and a lot should be said. He was truly a great American. But there is something interesting about how we remember this man. He was a comedian, a celebrity, a Hollywood type, if you will, even though Hollywood played second fiddle to the great days of radio. He made people laugh, but very few of us can remember specific jokes or lines. Maybe it is because there were too many of them, for when he took to the stage ... any stage ... everyone knew there was going to be a running series of one-liners, odd-ball jokes, and crazy stories that poked fun at famous people ... and before the program was even underway, the audience was rolling in laughter. And, I might add, it was superbly funny without being filthy dirty. He was a funny man.

But I ask you this: what is your first image of Bob Hope? And I'll bet it is not a TV show, or a movie with Bing Crosby, or even the sound of radio. I'll wager your first image of Bob Hope is just like mine: It is Bob Hope the American comedian in front of a group of American military men in some God-forsaken spot in the world, breaking their monotony with laughter, having fun with them out there where they are fighting for our freedom, poking fun at their commanding officers with the help of those good men, saying to our troops wherever they were that those of us back home honored them and thanked them.

☆ ☆ ☆

Veterans Day and the Sound of a B-17

Charlie Frierson said he knew what it was the moment he heard it fly over. It was the guttural sound of the four big radial motors of a World War II B-17 ... a distinctive sound that jogged the memories of anyone who ever heard the big guys fly over ... a sound and a distinctive high-tailed design that even 50 years cannot erase.

Out at the Gainesville airport, the B-17 landed, and out of the woodwork came World War II types and fly-boys of every war. Bob Andrews took a role .. a noisy but pleasant trip, a far cry from the trips he took over Germany 50 years ago, first as a tail gunner and then in the nose.

The visit in Gainesville of a vaunted Flying Fortress was timely, for today, November 11, is Veterans Day, the day we honor all of those who have fought for their country ... and especially those who have died that we might live free. Today at 11 O'clock, the American Legion will hold a ceremony at the Eternal Flame at Roosevelt Square. It is the veterans' way of reminding us all that America is worth fighting for ... that the price they paid, in lost time and in lost lives, was not too high.

✲ ✲ ✲

Looking Forward To A Historic Reunion

I ran into a friend of mine the other day. He was headed for his car in the parking lot, and he was carrying his

World War II uniform. He's one of the few guys I know who can still get in that uniform, but that's another story. Anyway, I asked the obvious of him and his wife: "Where ya' going?"

It turns out he was headed for a reunion of his World War II bomb group. This particular veteran was a B-29 pilot in the big war, one of the select group of airmen who were bringing Japan to its knees even before the atomic bombs were dropped. These were men who, day in and day out, rolled out of their bunks, put on their flight gear, got their briefings and, knowing full well some might not come back, flew off toward Japan to end a war ... not only to preserve the kind of culture we believe in but also to see to it those Americans back home were safe. They took the war to Japan so the Japanese would not bring the war to America.

Right now, America is edgy because we have been attacked at home. But once again, we are pushing the war offshore. Once again, some brave Americans are rolling out of their bunks (most in other parts of the world, a few right here at home), putting on their flight gear, getting their briefings, and flying into harm's way so we in America may live in safety, and hopefully, without fear.

A Celebration in Greece

Here in the United States we tend to think of World War II as something we were intended to win, and we cannot accept the idea we might have lost and been run over by an alien army and ruled by ruthless dictators. It is something we simply can't visualize.

Not long ago, a group of us sought out and found a neighborhood restaurant in Athens, Greece, where the locals go ... and there was a noisy but fun table of 23 Greek men there. They were of the class of '53, getting together for a reunion. And when one of them learned we were Americans, he said quietly to me: "Thank you, Yankee."

For me at least, it was a touching moment, for these, you see, were men whose country had known the hell of being overrun in war ... who knew what living under a dictator was all about ... who had seen their homes destroyed and friends killed ... who regained their independence 50 years ago because a bunch of American kids, barely older than they were at the time, went to bat for their freedom.

Here in America we are celebrating the 50th anniversary of victory in World War II, and locally, the American Legion is leading that remembrance. They're celebrating in Greece, too.

✲ ✲ ✲

The Spanish-American War Finally Ends

The other day, Republicans in Congress, seeking ways to cut taxes, officially ended a 100-year-old tax we have been paying to finance the Spanish-American War.

About the time that war started, telephones were the new technology, and something like 1,500 had been installed. So Congress figured a small tax on those new phones wouldn't hurt anybody and would raise some needed money for the fighting in Cuba. They put a 3 percent tax on telephone bills about the turn of the last century.

The war ended, and here in Gainesville we eventually installed a marker that read: "Dedicated to the veterans of 1898-1902 / By Department of Georgia / National Auxiliary United Spanish War Veterans / the 15th Annual Convention / May 15-17, 1938." The plaque includes a quote from President McKinley, "You triumphed over obstacles which would have overcome men less brave and determined." Go look at it; you will find it in front of the Court House Annex. Then in 1976, Hall County honored 96-year-old J. M. Reese. Pat French interviewed him for the local paper. Reese had gone into the Army in 1899 at age 19 and went first to Cuba, then on to Manila Bay.

I agree it's about time we quit paying taxes on THAT war.

✲ ✲ ✲

Two Local Events Feature Civil War History

Some scholars don't think of Northeast Georgia as a major part of Confederate History, but it is, and this weekend we will have a couple of events that will remind us that we deserve a solid chapter in the story of the Civil War. Friday and Saturday, the Longstreet Society will hold its annual bivouac at the location of General James Longstreet's hotel here in Gainesville. It is an event for Longstreet historians and others interested in Confederate history, who will gather at the remnants of the 1880's hotel to paint it and fix it up and to honor the General as a part of American history, both during and after the Civil War. General Longstreet was the second-ranking General in the Confederate Army of the East ... the person General Robert E. Lee called "my old war horse." He is buried here in Alta Vista Cemetery.

Then on Sunday, the James Longstreet Chapter of the United Daughters of the Confederacy will commemorate the 100th anniversary of the statue that stands in the center of the downtown square. It is the replica of a front line Confederate soldier that we fondly refer to as "Old Joe."

The Civil War is long since over, and we are proud to be Americans. But for many of us, this history is very personal. For instance, my great-great-grandfather fought in the Confederate Army of Northern Virginia, and he died in a military hospital (if you can call it that) in Lynchburg, Virginia. More than 600,000 men died in that conflict – from both North and South. Its history is a part of America, and it is worth remembering. This weekend we all have a chance to learn more about this area's involvement in it....

☼ ☼ ☼

People Come From Everywhere To Study Longstreet

Richard Pilcher took a local group on a Longstreet tour of Gainesville the other day, the kind of tour he has done a number of times for people who do not live here. It was interesting, not only because it was about Confederate General James Longstreet, who lived his last years in Gainesville, but also because friend Pilcher gave us a glimpse of how outsiders view Gainesville when they come here to study Longstreet.

We started at Longstreet Café, near where his original Gainesville home was located, and went from there to the Old Clark House, across from the Olympic Rowing venue. It was here that Longstreet entered our area immediately after the Civil War. This leads one to speculate he came from Appomattox down the Great Wagon Road, then into Georgia on the Unicoi Turnpike, and down from the Sautee-Nacoochee area to Hall County. We spent some time at the site of the original Longstreet home at the top of the hill adjacent to the City swimming pool at City Park. It is there you will find the statue of the General.

We rode by his house on Green Street, the one where his second wife started the local Catholic church, and probably the one from which General Longstreet rode his mule to town to serve as the local Postmaster. And a surprise: we stopped where a relative's house was once located, where there is now a parking lot. It was there that General Longstreet died. And, of course, we went to the American flag at Alta Vista Cemetery, where he is buried and where most of the visitors come to shoot their pictures. There is a growing interest in the American Civil War, both in the United States and especially in Europe, and for those students, Lt. General James Longstreet, General Robert E. Lee's second in command, and the one Lee called his "Old War Horse," is of great interest.

✲ ✲ ✲

History Says America Is Unafraid To Protect Its Own

In many ways, it is discouraging to read in the American press that George W. Bush is taking America in a totally new diplomatic direction in our relations with the Muslim world. It says we have not read our history, or maybe we want to rewrite that history. Try this bit of information: it was about 1800, and American ships were being captured by the Barbary states of North Africa – Algiers, Tunis, Morocco, and Tripoli (which is today's Libya). The ships and their cargo were being sold, and the American crews were being sold off as Christian slaves to Muslim masters. The British Navy was no longer protecting American ships because we had declared our independence from England.

America was spunky in those hectic days and determined to protect its own. Even though the European countries did not join with us, the United States declared war on the pirates, built some fine fighting ships – the Constitution, the United States, and the Constellation – and brought the United States Marine Corps into being. When Thomas Jefferson became president, he promptly dispatched a fleet, without Congressional approval, by the way, to force the Barbary pirates to lay off Americans. We did not cower down and seek diplomatic solutions; we sent the fleet straight to the Mediterranean.

Over the next four years, the new United States Navy blasted the harbors of Algiers, Morocco and Tunis. When the Tripoli government got arrogant and captured one of our ships, Captain Stephen Decatur sailed straight into Tripoli harbour, burned the captured ship, bombarded the fortified town, released the American prisoners, and boarded the pasha's own fleet. Then in 1805, the Americans put together a force of Americans, Arab rebels, and mercenaries, marched across the desert, and took Tripoli's second city, Derna. At that point, Marine Lt. Presley O'Bannon of the United States Marine Corps hoisted the stars and stripes over the captured city. For those timid souls who think America is in the Middle East for the first time or going there without support from other countries for the first time, let me suggest you study our history and sing the Marine Corps song where it says "to the Shores of Tripoli."

☆ ☆ ☆

Standing Up For Freedom and Democracy

America has never been popular with the elite rulers of the world – the kings, the dictators, the military opportunists ... the people who rule as they wish while the commoners bow down or else. That is the nature of our democracy - it doesn't trust an all-powerful government. Not only that, we want to sell the rest of the world on our kind of democracy, the kind that allows people to rule. Dictators and ruling families don't like that idea at all. But their people do, and therein lies a problem for the United States.

At the end of World War II, after we had deposed dictatorial rule from the likes of Hitler and Mussolini and Tojo, we in America took it upon ourselves to sell the world on democracy. Actively opposing democracy was Communism. The difference in governing style was very obvious. In a democracy, we-the-people rule, while communist states are ruled by a small group of dictatorial individuals, supposedly on behalf of the people. The United States government even created a worldwide radio operation to promote freedom and democracy.

And if you will compare national governments around the globe now, as compared with governments based on democratic principles 50 years ago (that is democratic with a small d and not the party), you will find we have made a great deal of progress. And we made much more progress when Communist Russia came apart. But we hear from our elite media and liberal politicians that America is not liked by many nations and that we need to quit pushing democracy and freedom so aggressively. And I ask you: Is being loved by countries run by dictators and tyrants more important than freedom for all mankind? Have we lost our zeal for democracy?

CHAPTER 14 – Coming Home and The Baby Boom

For those who had lived through World War II – both in service and on the home front – it appeared the war ended abruptly. Germany surrendered first, and after celebrations and parades, all America turned its attention toward the defeat of Japan. There was still a war to be fought, and everyone knew by now that the Japanese were brutal warriors.

Battle-hardened GI's were being transferred from Europe to the Pacific. Some were being sent by ship directly through the Panama Canal; others came through the U. S. Those lucky enough to come stateside got leaves, and homecoming celebrations broke out all over the Georgia mountains. Those whose sons were already in the Pacific, and those whose sons were going straight back to war, were happy for those who made it home for a brief leave, but ...

It was a bittersweet time, for there was still a war to be fought, and after all-too-short leaves, the heroes of Europe were joining the heroes of the Pacific to "finish the job." What would a D-Day be like in Japan? How many would be killed? How long would it take? It was a time of high anxiety.

America quickly buttoned down again to its wartime culture. Young men (and now young women) were joining the military, and Northeast Georgia was again a leading area for volunteers. Women returned to jobs in aircraft plants and other occupations once considered "men's work." Families again were glued to their radios, following the news hour-by-hour as their men deployed to the Pacific, and especially as new American invasions were announced, ever closer to Japan itself.

The photo of an American flag being raised on a mountain top on Iwo Jima brought cheers, just as telegrams to some families brought tears. There was no indication the Japanese would ever surrender. None.

Then came the news of a huge bomb that leveled an entire Japanese city. It was an "atomic bomb," and all across Northeast Georgia people went to their World Atlas to find the city named Hiroshima. Then, only a week later, another atomic bomb leveled a city named Nagasaki. And just like that, VJ-Day was announced, and the war was over.

Street celebrations throughout America quickly turned to the next job at hand - getting 13 million GI's home. A point system was established to release GI's from service. One got points for the number of months in service, for combat, for wounds; and for other things. Those with the most points would be released first.

Prisoners of war in Japan had first priority. There was fear the Japanese would execute American POWs and great relief when the news came out that the POWs were being handed over peacefully. Every family in Northeast Georgia with a son or daughter in the military learned to calculate points and were delighted when they found some returning military man was being sent home or discharged with points that matched their family member.

Looking back as a historian, the end of World War II and the transition from a wartime culture to peace seems remarkably smooth. But at the time, it seemed to be pure chaos. Most took advantage of a Red Cross service when they hit the West Coast and called home. Many Northeast Georgia boys (that is what we GI's were called then ... remember?) who were released on the West Coast simply stepped out on the highway and started hitch-hiking home. Their parents had no idea where they were until they walked in the front door. For 13 million GI's, many who had never held a civilian job, it was a happy, yet anxious, time.

Many immediately got married, and the Baby Boom was underway (in that order).

The GI Bill gave all of them an opportunity for the college or special education they might not have received if peace had prevailed during the 1940s. Veterans asked themselves: do I want to take advantage of the GI Bill, or should I jump right into the job market and get a head start on all of those other guys getting out of service?

Wartime jobs evaporated. The American free-enterprise machine that had built products for war proved its flexibility by immediately transitioning to cars, washing machines, diapers, and a thousand other consumer items.

For two groups, especially, there was great hesitation to go back to the pre-war culture.

First, should women keep high-paying jobs they had done so well in wartime, or should they drop out of the job market and stay home to tend to family matters? This was a major cultural clash, especially in the rural areas of Northeast Georgia.

And second, what about the blacks? At the beginning of World War II, all of the South and much of the rest of America, was segregated. In the North, labor unions were mostly white. For the most part, the American military was segregated in 1940. As the war progressed, blacks were given more responsibilities, and it became apparent they could do some jobs denied them in a segregated society. Throughout America, blacks who had served in the military were not interested in returning to the lifestyle – the CULTURE if you will – they knew prior to World War II.

In Northeast Georgia – and all across America – individual decisions were being made that would determine the POST-WAR CULTURE. In Northeast Georgia, there was a strong pull toward the mountain culture that existed before December 7, 1941.

✲ ✲ ✲

The Baby Boom Begins

The war was over, GI students had mostly graduated, and you've never seen so many little people running around Gainesville in all your life. It was the beginning of what we now know as the Baby Boom. You see, during World War II, some 13 million men ... all of them the right age to start families ... had gone off to serve their country. Now they were home, and it seemed like every young couple in Northeast Georgia was making up for lost time.

Many veterans had taken advantage of the GI Bill and gone to college or learned a trade, and they were now getting jobs. The great American war machine was shifting from war goods to consumer goods – strollers and playpens, cars, refrigerator, and yes ... washing machines. Among other things that were different then were diapers. They were cloth, and you didn't throw them away. You washed them and boiled them, and not always in the washing machine. If you don't understand all this, ask your mother or grandmother how it worked.

Things were changing dramatically, and no change was more dramatic than the arrival of all those kids.

✲ ✲ ✲

1950: Hall County Statistics

It was 1949, and as the year wound down, the Chamber of Commerce was sending out information about Gainesville and Hall County. ... Hall County had a population of about 42,000, and Gainesville was close to 14,000. Both had grown more than 20 % during the previous 10 years, and Gainesville, with a growth rate of 26.8 %, was listed as one of the fastest growing small cities in America.

There were three banks with $13.8 million in resources and one Savings and Loan with $2.2 million. The information stated the city had eighteen white churches and eight Negro churches and twelve civic groups.

✲ ✲ ✲

Gainesville Grew Rapidly During WWII

World War II had been over for five years, and there was a continuing debate about whether or not some towns should continue rent controls. You see, during World War II, the Federal government set up a rent control system to keep people from going up on rents. When the war was over, it was up to local governments to do away with rent controls, but even then it required an okay from Washington.

Gainesville and Hall County were trying to get out from under the Federal rent control program, so there was a guy from Washington in town doing a survey. His report noted that Hall County's population in 1940 was

34,822, and he estimated the population in 1949 was a whopping 44,000. Farm population was 13,771 according to the report, and Negroes made up 9.6 percent of the people. Inside the city limits of Gainesville - that is, inside the one-mile radius - were 10,243 people in 1940 and 12,000 in 1949. If you reached out to a two-mile radius, 22,000 of the 44,000 people lived in that area. The report also noted that 3,200 people worked in six large mills just outside the Gainesville city limits.

The Washington bureaucrat determined Gainesville needed 150 to 200 new rental units, and rent controls were dropped.

☼ ☼ ☼

The Coming of Buford Dam

There was growing concern in Gainesville in 1950 about a dam that apparently was going to be built down the river near Buford. When the Grand Jury wanted more facts, it came out that 539 Hall County farms would be covered by the new lake. Only three bridges would be built to replace 16 that would be covered. 25,000 of the 45,000 acres in the reservoir were to be in Hall County. To quote the Gainesville News: "An Enabling Act passed by Congress several years ago allows the government to flood an area by merely giving property owners notice that a dam is going to be constructed ... and to settle with the owners at the leisure of the government." This was getting serious.

Atlanta had been promoting the dam and lake, for flood control reasons they said. So the local Chamber of Commerce invited the Hon. Elbert Tuttle, President of the Atlanta Chamber, to be the featured speaker at its 40th Annual Banquet. The whole theme of his talk that night was that the dam would be good, and that Atlanta would assist with any problems it might cause in Hall County.

It had not been named Lake Lanier yet ... but that lake was the main topic of conversation in all Hall County.

✲ ✲ ✲

Gainesville, Georgia: A Champion Home Town

It was 1949, and Gainesville had just won high honors in the statewide Champion Home Town competition. The Champion Home Town Contest was a program sponsored by Georgia Power Company. It emphasized the things that make a town a better place to live and work, and Gainesville had won a coveted third place ... narrowly beat out by Camilla and Toccoa.

The idea of the Champion Home Town competition was to encourage the small cities of Georgia to do the things which would bring them new industry and which would improve living conditions, make their cities more beautiful, improve educational opportunities ... It was quite a program, and it made a difference in the state of Georgia. The Champion Home Town committee worked all year to encourage citizens, businesses, government – everybody - to do the things needed to win. Winners were chosen on the basis of a massive scrapbook documenting the progress.

The committee in 1949 was headed by James A. (Bub) Dunlap, and serving with him were R. A. Brice, John W. Jacobs, Jr., Ed Jared, and Sylvan Meyer. Gainesville was officially a Champion Home Town in 1949, and in my book, it still is.

☼ ☼ ☼

Hudson Super Six Hits The Market

There was excitement among the people of Gainesville. The new Hudson Super Six automobile was being introduced in Northeast Georgia by Gainesville Hudson Sales, Inc. It had already been advertised in Life and *Look* magazines, of course, so people knew what it looked like. But here it was, the "modern design for '49'," right here in Gainesville.

Right after World War II, a few of you will recall, the major automobile companies reactivated the designs they had at the first of the war, and simply started cranking new cars out. Anybody who wanted a new car had to get on a waiting list, and anybody who wanted a car "right now" usually took a high mileage used car and paid through the nose for it. It was strictly a seller's market, and getting your hands on a new car - that is, a car that wasn't about to fall apart - was more important than design.

But then came the Hudson and the Studebaker, and Wow! America was in love with its cars again ... They wanted something big, fast, and modern, and the Hudson had set the new standard.

Incidentally, if you wanted to call Gainesville's Hudson dealer, the phone number was 158. And, yes, you could dial it. 158.

✲ ✲ ✲

Civic Leaders – Post World War II

Gainesville has a history of strong civic leadership, and that was just as true fifty years ago as it is today. Take a look at 1948.

In the business area, the President of the Gainesville Chamber of Commerce was J. Larry Kleckley. Carl Lawson was president of the Jaycees, or the Junior Chamber of Commerce - to give it the full title it tended to carry in those days. Miss Mary Lucy Lilly was president of the Business and Professional Women's Club.

Leading the civic clubs were Lester Hosch, president of the Rotary Club, and Adger Whitfield, president of Kiwanis. Paul Hampton was president of the Lions Club, David A. Rankin president of Civitan. Harry Holland president of the Optimists, and Miss Vada Kent president of the Pilot Club. Mrs. S. C. Moon was president of the Garden Club Council, and Conrad Romberg headed the Civic Music Association.

✲ ✲ ✲

A Trip To Atlanta, and the Old Dutch Mill

Late in the 20th century, there was no expressway to Atlanta. No I-85, no I-985. What we had was a reasonably good two-lane identified as U. S. 23 ... now U. S. 13. Gainesvillians going down to the State Capitol, I am told, allowed about 50 minutes to travel the 52 miles from downtown Gainesville to the parking lot at the Capitol. We drove fast, did not have seat belts, and did well to get 11 to 12 miles per gallon. But that's another story.

With this in mind, and headed for Atlanta anyway the other day, I decided to drive the old way. It was a right pleasant drive. Not a whole lot of traffic. Good two-lane highway with adequate places to pass. It becomes solid metro Atlanta much, much farther north than 50 years ago, of course. It is not a scenic drive nowadays. Even sorta junky at some places.

It dawned on me, though: where is the Old Dutch Mill? Fifty years ago, there was a restaurant, a blue and white replica of a Dutch mill - windmill and all - and we ALWAYS stopped there ... at least for coffee. What happened? Did they tear it down? Surely not.

Tech-Georgia Thanksgiving Football

It was Thanksgiving Day 50 years ago, and one of this state's greatest traditions was about to occur. In 1949 they were getting ready for the 17th annual Scottish

Rite benefit football game, an always popular freshman game between Georgia's BullPups and Georgia Tech's Baby Jackets. In those days, you see, college freshmen could not play on the varsity. So the freshman game raised money for the Scottish Rite hospital. Strong legs will run, they said, so weak legs may walk. It was one of the South's most respected sporting events.

Well, 50 years ago, the BullPups won the Thanksgiving game, 18-0, and Gainesville's own Jack Roberts caught a 22-yard pass for the first score of the game. By the way, he also played on defense.

In the big game on Saturday, Georgia Tech won a thriller 7 to 6. In the colorful sports writing of the era, here's how UP sports writer Edwin Pope described it: "The game was legalized mayhem (with) a wild flurry of interceptions and fumbles ... Georgia Tech's resilient engineers absorbed Georgia's primitive punches and stabbed out a 7-6 victory." That was Thanksgiving weekend 50 years ago.

Statewide Flower Show Winners From Gainesville

It was 50 years ago, and as we went into the Christmas season, there was a great emphasis on home decorations for the holidays. The talented members of the Association of Flower Show Judges of Northeast Georgia were holding a major competition to garner new and dramatic ideas for home table arrangements for Christmas dinner.

The event was widely publicized and was held at Atlanta's prestigious Capital City Club with its marble floors, wood-paneled walls, and crystal chandeliers ... and its classic Christmas decorations were already in place. The event drew crowds.

Well, as it developed, two Gainesville ladies won first and second with their Christmas decorations, and thus Gainesville got high statewide recognition for its Christmas ideas and floral design. The winners were: first place, Mrs. Charles Hardy, and second place, Mrs. Claude Carter.

From Gainesville, the Atlanta story was covered by *The Daily Times*' Women's Editor, Jane Eve Wilheit.

The Television Revolution Begins

It was mid-century, and television was the most exciting thing that had happened since the atomic bombs that ended World War II. It was absolutely amazing, this idea you could sit in your own house and look at - not just listen to, mind you - but look at AND listen to, all kinds of stuff. The programs were mostly from radio with a TV camera stuck in somebody's face. And then there were the sports programs. I mean you could sit at home and WATCH football and baseball. It was a true miracle.

Of course, not everybody could afford a television set, but everybody had an antenna ... even some who didn't have a TV yet. If you had enough money, you bought a TV mounted in what looked like a nice piece of furniture, sort of like a cut-down sideboard. But what most of us had, when we could finally afford it, was a black metal box, about two feet square (I mean 2 x 2 x 2) sitting on a little metal rack that would let the TV turn. The screen was sort of roundish and probably about 14 inches wide at best. The picture was black and white – well, really it had more snow than black - but you could see the picture pretty well. We had three channels in Gainesville, all from Atlanta. But how exciting it was at mid-century in the Queen City of the Mountains!

Moss Hill – A New Apartment Complex Opens

It was 1950, and there was a housing shortage in Gainesville. The guys were back from World War II, many had taken advantage of the GI Bill and had finished college, and families were forming. Not only that, but the broiler business was booming, Gainesville was growing, and new people were moving to town. So it was big news when Gainesville's first large apartment development opened.

The project was developed by Odis Moss, and it was called Moss Hill Apartments. The news story said there were 24 "bright, airy units" ... all on the ground floor. The story continued with this information: "Rooms are large and the units well planned for space and efficiency." The apartments were nice, but the rent was steep. The rental at Moss Hill Apartments was $60 a month for a three room apartment, and $75 for five rooms, water furnished." The entire development cost around $200,000, and it was built by Carroll E. Daniel.

Looking back, the people who first moved into Moss Hill very nearly became the Who's Who of Gainesville during the second half of the 20th Century.

CHAPTER 15 – A Segregated Society Until The 1960's

Look at a map and it is obvious mountainous Northeast Georgia is in the heart of the American South. And if one looks only at the final votes of the 1861 assembly which approved Georgia's withdrawal from the United States of America, and it appears Georgia was solidly for secession. The records of the debate, and the early voting, say differently. Had Georgia been two states – North Georgia and South Georgia – it is possible North Georgia could have remained with the Union ... at least for a while. In fact, one county in the far northeast corner of the state never did agree to become a part of the Confederacy, and to this day its name is Union County.

For the 100 year period from the 1860's to the 1960's, the black person's experience in Northeast Georgia was somewhat different from those in the plantation culture of South Georgia. Only a handful of plantations were located in the mountain region, and they were small by comparison to the plantations along the coastal area of the eastern seaboard. The small white farmers of the mountains were hardscrabble poor people ... way too poor to own slaves. Their dislike for the federal government was much stronger because the feds were trying to control, and tax, moonshine whiskey. They did not particularly oppose slavery, but neither did they vigorously support it.

And yet, once Georgia did agree to join the Confederacy, men from the mountains joined the Confederate army in large numbers, and because they could shoot straight at a long distance, and showed no fear in battle, they were considered among the most prized front-line soldiers that wore the gray.

Many white Northeast Georgians died in the Civil War. Go visit the historic cemetery at Redwine Church, near Oakwood in South Hall County. Many Confederate volunteers went to war from that church, and as the cemetery confirms, many came back to Redwine's cemetery as their final resting place.

Were Northeast Georgia's small farmers defending the institution of slavery? Possible not. But intentionally or not, they did set the stage for political opposition to Republican-imposed Reconstruction after the war, and for total alliance to the Democrat Party for 100 years.

There were always blacks who were accepted, and respected, in the business community, even though they were not accepted in the social or political cultures. Before the Civil War, in the Gold mine era, there was the Free Jim mine, owned and operated by a free black man who was considered an astute businessman.

After the Civil War and Reconstruction, there is the great story about how Georga Stephens, a black man who owned and ran a tailor and pressing shop, who loaned the Gainesville school system payroll money to finish a school year circa 1920, And after World War II Dr. E. E. Butler had a thriving practice in Gainesville, and was involved in many community activities. One of the main streets in downtown Gainesville is named E. E. Butler Boulevard. (The other is Jesse Jewell Boulevard).(More came to light after the 1960's – see Volume II when it is finished. And, yes; there were a number of characters, and even a few crazies.

Some say the black-white culture of Northeast Georgia was "softer" because the black population was less than ten percent. Others pointed to the cooperation between the races, noting that after the Tornado of '36 there had been blacks on the local board of the Red Cross (which, they point out, was not the case in Atlanta). Still others pointed to the folklore that Northeast Georgia had been an early stop on the Civil War era "underground railroad" which spirited black slaves to the North. Fact or fiction? Who knows?

Probably the best picture of the black experience in Northeast Georgia comes from two books and a booklet about some dedicated educators who peacefully – but with determination – gave young Negros a better life in segregated Northeast Georgia.

First, a 2004 book by Linda Rucker Hutchens and Ella J. Wilmont Smith entitled *Hall County, Georgia,* a photographic history, stands out. This book is one in Arcadia Publishing's Black America series, and it gives a great view of how the black community looked and lived in the first half of the 20th century.

The second book is entitled *A Chance For Change: Sharecropper to Landowner.* It is a histo-autobiography of J. R. Rosser, Sr. compiled by J. R. Rosser, Jr. and edited by Audrey Rosser Milo. It is the story of a black man who lived the entire 20th century, and his rise from farm hand to an admired educator who provided an education to black children in Habersham and surrounding counties.

The story of Beulah Rucker is told in a booklet entitled *The Rugged Pathway* that was written by Beulah Rucker Oliver. It was about a dedicated lady and her industrial school, a lady who was determined to help her "race" lift itself to unlimited heights through education and determination.

THE NORTHEAST GEORGIA BLACK EXPERIENCE – 1865– 1960

Let's start with this concept: Pre-Civil War black history in the mountains was different from that in coastal plantations. The large plantations of the South had a few "house slaves" and many "field slaves." Black historians make this clear. From the beginning, most slaves in Northeast Georgia were "house slaves." Mountain whites were mostly too poor to own slaves. It is appropriate, also, to separate slave ownership in Northeast Georgia from Northwest Georgia. The Northwest side of Georgia, south of Chattanooga, had a number of Indians (mostly mixed-bloods) who owned black slaves, primarily to work in rich, flat, valley land. Don L. Shadburn's book, *Cherokee Planters in Georgia 1832 – 38,* names prominent Cherokee slaveholders in eleven counties of Northwest Georgia, some who took their slaves with them to Oklahoma on the "Trail of Tears."

In the culture of the plantation South, field slaves were laborers who worked in the fields or at an enterprise like a sawmill, or even a Gold mine. House slaves did household chores, cooked, or worked in a small business, but they also helped raise the children. In many cases they were educated, saw to early education of their owner's children, and were encouraged to educate their own children. Besides job distinctions, here also was a distinction among the blacks according to how dark-skinned a person was.

Northeast Georgia had a higher percentage of house slaves to field slaves than South Georgia, and it seems fair to say that house slaves, mostly females, were treated differently, even before slavery was abolished.

There was another reason the white population of Northeast Georgia had a different attitude toward slavery: competition. From *Northeast Georgia: A History*: "Linda Gale Housch, a young graduate of Spelman College, researched black history in Northeast Georgia in 1969 for the *Daily Times* and painted the following picture: 'It is very interesting to note at this point that although the white small farmer in the Northeast Piedmont region of Georgia (including Hall County) did not especially love the black man, he did not love the white planter, either'. ... In his book *Make Free*, William Breyfogle cites that the white man in the Northwest Piedmont often considered himself the victim of having to compete with slave labor and a slave economy."

Fast forward to 1900. The Culture in which blacks and whites lived in Northeast Georgia did not change much after the Civil War. Blacks were free, and could come and go wherever they wished at random. After President Lincoln's death, Congress enacted "Reconstruction" legislation, mostly designed to punish the South, not only for slavery, but also for trying to break up the union. Although it was aimed at Southern whites, it also led to disenfranchisement of the blacks.

After the war, Confederate General James Longstreet retired to Gainesville. He publicly identified himself with the Republican Party, and a friend of Ulysses S. Grant. Throughout the South, he was quickly branded a "scalawag". At the same time, Northern Congressmen, realizing addition of blacks to citizenship would give the South more members of the House of Representatives, brought blacks into citizenship as three-fifths of a person. The federal government took control of the railroads and set rates that allowed Northern manufactured goods to move South cheaper than the same goods could be shipped north. Manufacturing in the South was stymied. Under the dominance of Northern legislators and newly forming labor unions, the South was doomed to be only an agrarian area. Manufacturing, with its many new jobs, was allocated to the Northeastern United States.

Southern Democrats took control of Southern politics through poll taxes, county unit voting, and party primaries. When the courts knocked down one impediment to black voting, another popped up. One of the barriers came when the legislature passed a law saying no one could vote who could not read. The story went the rounds that one Registrar got a French newspaper, and when a black came in to register to vote, he would be handed that newspaper and asked to read it. On one occasion a black man came in to register and was handed the newspaper. The black man said, "Certainly I can read that." "Okay," the Registrar countered, "what does it say?" The answer was quick and loud, "It say ain't no black boy gonna vote in this election this year." Sad ... but things like this did happen. This segregated society held sway in Northeast Georgia, and throughout the South, for one-hundred years.

There were separate schools for whites and blacks... a very difficult problem for those counties with very few blacks. In the mountains regional black schools were established, and students were bused to the school from several surrounding counties. There were separate black and white restrooms in the Court House, and separate drinking fountains. There were separate eating establishments, and separate churches.

All sports were segregated for both high schools and colleges. Of course, this was not just in the South. Big

League baseball was segregated, even though no Big League baseball cities were located in the South. The United States military was segregated up to, and including, most of World War II.

This is history. It was the culture of Northeast Georgia up until the 1960's.

✲ ✲ ✲

Beulah Rucker and "The Rugged Pathway"

I ran across a little book the other day – a book my friend Lovie Smith sold me ... probably five years ago. It was a reprint of a little booklet called "The Rugged Pathway," a piece written a number of years ago by Beulah Rucker Oliver.

For those of you who do not remember Beulah Rucker, she was a pioneer in education for black students in these parts and built and operated the Industrial School on Athens Road with nothing more than hard work, sheer determination, and an unconquerable faith in her Maker.

The booklet is a short and very humble story of her life. But it tells more than that. It tells of her excitement about education and her belief that her "Race" – as she referred to her people – could, with education and determination, lift itself to unlimited heights.

The reason the booklet is being reprinted is to help with a foundation that will carry on Beulah Rucker's tradition. It is a book worth reading and a cause worth supporting. Lovie Smith, by the way, is the long-time

Scoutmaster of the historic black troop 15, which was started in 1936 by the Gainesville Kiwanis Club.

✲ ✲ ✲

Three Who Cared: Beulah Rucker, E. E. Butler, and Ulysses Byas

For those of you who like local history, the cover story of the current edition of the Georgia Historical Quarterly is entitled "Three Who Cared: Beulah Rucker, E. E. Butler, and Ulysses Byas – Twentieth-Century Trailblazers in Education for African-Americans in Gainesville, Georgia". It is a scholarly historical article, well-documented, and written by Winfred E. Pitts – a person I don't know but would like to – who is an assistant professor at Southeast Missouri State University in Cape Girardeau.

Let me tell you ... this 30-page story is a classic, and it is written about three people who deserve to be remembered in the history of Northeast Georgia. It's obvious we cannot cover the full 30 pages, but let me summarize it by quoting the last paragraph.

"These three African-Americans, Beulah Rucker, E. E. Butler, and Ulysses Byas, left indelible prints on the educational landscape of Gainesville and Hall County," Pitts says. And he goes on to say: "At a time when African-Americans in northern Georgia had very few opportunities for formal education, the courageous Beulah Rucker sacrificed to provide educational access for those who would have no other chance for an education.

E. E. Butler, as an African-American community leader and school board member, no doubt opened the door for future black Gainesville individuals such as Mayors John Morrow and Myrtle Figueras. And although in 1969 Ulysses Byas was not chosen to be the principal of the newly integrated Gainesville High School, his leadership has been an example to the several black principals who have since served in the city schools system. Citizens of Gainesville and Hall County, both black and white, owe a debt of gratitude to these three who cared enough to blaze a trail for others to follow"

The Regional Black High School in Cornelia

There once existed a State of Georgia "Office of Negro Education," and it had a problem with the mountain area, not because there were too many blacks to educate, but too few. To make it still more difficult, they were clustered – a section in Gainesville, another section in Cornelia, and Bean Creek in White County. Some counties had no blacks at all, and many counties did not have enough black students to warrant a school.

In the book *A Chance For Change*, J. R. Rosser, Sr. tells the story of the "regional" school in Cornelia this way, "It was a brick school built for Blacks as an effort to avoid desegregation of the White high schools. Four counties had pooled their building funds several years before and built a school on the edge of the Black community in

Cornelia." Banks, Habersham, White, and Rabun counties bused their black students to this "regional school."

J. R. Rosser, Sr. was principal of the regional school in Cornelia and became a respected community leader throughout the integration era.

The book I mentioned is entitled *A Chance for Change: Sharecropper to Land Owner* and is a fascinating chronicle of an educated Black man's journey through life in the 20th century, as well as a story of his ancestors back to 1813. It is the best view of the Black experience in the mountain area of Georgia that I have found. It is frank and honest, without bitterness. It also brings forth the dramatic difference between the culture of Blacks in Northeast Georgia and those in the historic plantation areas.

My Vote For The Greatest Marching Band

I don't know who decided it is "politically incorrect" to say our black friends just naturally have rhythm, but I was called down the other day for saying so on the air. The white lady that chided me for my rhythm comment intimated it was racist and that I was guilty of "stereotyping." Well ... I think it is a compliment. I do think African-Americans – if that is the term you want me to use – have a God-given gift of rhythm, and I think it is great. It is an integral part of their culture, and I think it is wrong to try and take it away from them. It is probably impolite of me to instinctively pat my foot when a black church choir starts singing, but I do, and to be honest, I don't think gospel music is gospel unless the choir is moving.

And while we're at it, I think the greatest marching band I ever saw and heard was the E. E. Butler High School Band. When you consider the fact that Gainesville and Hall County high school bands have a history of great music, and that the University of Georgia band is one of the best in the nation, saying the E.E. Butler band was the best is quite a statement ... but I just said it, and I'll stick by it. The band director was one Rufus Tucker, and he had no problem recruiting a large number of students for his band.

In the 1950s, Gainesville would have a parade at the drop of a hat. People would come from all over the area – white and black – and they would line the entire parade route just to see that great band dance by. It wasn't just the baton twirlers out front that showed rhythm, although they put on a show of their own. The entire band played great music, and they marched with a rhythm no one else could match. They had rhythm. And they still do.

✲ ✲ ✲

Colin Powell Had Fond Memories of Northeast Georgia

A lot of changes are taking place in Washington as George W. Bush begins his second term as President, but probably none is more dramatic than the retirement of Colin Powell, a black man, as Secretary of State, and his replacement by Condeleeza Rice, a black woman who grew up in nearby Alabama. The position of Secretary of State is generally considered the third most powerful office in any administration, and I think it is fair to say Colin Powell was a great one during difficult times. It also seems evident that Condeleezza Rice was just as effective.

After his retirement from the Army and before George W. Bush appointed him as Secretary of State, Colin Powell wrote a book about his life called "My American Journey," and one of the key points in that book was how far America has come in race relations during his lifetime. There is a photo in the book, made in 1958, of thirty young soldiers attending Ranger School. The cutline reads, "Smiles of relief from young second lieutenants who have just finished the final field exercise at the Ranger school mountain training camp in Dahlonega, Georgia."

In the book, Powell tells about attending church in Gainesville. You see, in the late 1950s, Southern churches were segregated, and Gainesville offered the nearest church he could attend. The Army furnished him with a vehicle, and Powell said he enjoyed attending church in Gainesville. One quote from his book says: "There I sang and swayed with the rest of the Baptist congregation." Beyond that, however, he did not identify which Baptist Church he attended.

Colin Powell is a remarkable man who has held some of the most powerful military and political offices in America, and I am especially pleased that his memories of Northeast Georgia were pleasant.

✲ ✲ ✲

CHAPTER 16 – Reflections on 10 Core Values

Family / Religion / Honesty and Integrity / Work / Independence and Moonshine Whiskey / Politics / Patriotism / Education and Common Sense / Property / Inherited Culture and Psalm 121

In this book you will find a gazillion clues about the CULTURE of Georgia's mountain area in the "Good Ole Days." Many names and stories are included. Many were left out ... there is way too much material to include them all. (I accept responsibility for those used and those left out).

But when one boils it all down, what were the "core values" of the Good Ole Days in the mountains of Georgia? What was the culture of our fathers? I have selected 10. See if you agree.

#1. FAMILY. First and foremost came the family. The father was the breadwinner and the head of the household. The mother was ruler of the home and the person responsible for preparing the children for adulthood. Divorces were rare and frowned upon. To be born out of wedlock was a disaster. The family consisted of one man, one woman, and their natural or adopted children. That was it.

#2. RELIGION. Protestant Christianity was fundamental to the culture of Northeast Georgia. It came with the earliest settlers - Baptist, Methodist, Presbyterian and Episcopalian - not Catholic and not Jewish. Muslim was something foreign that the missionaries had to put up with. The men sat on the governing boards of their churches, and the women of the church saw to the education of the children, and helped the church give to the poor and oppressed. Quite often men and women attended separate Sunday School classes. And every child knew John 3:16 because it was the shortest verse in the Bible, and they always had to recite verses from the Bible in Sunday School.

#3. HONESTY and INTEGRITY. One of the most devastating things that could happen to a family was for one of its members to be considered a "consummate liar." It wasn't just the one person; it reflected unfavorably on the entire family. Business deals, large and small, were sealed with a handshake. "You can count on his doing what he says he will do" was a high compliment - maybe the highest.

#4. WORK. To be "industrious" went back to the Jamestown Colony: "If you don't work, you don't eat." In the Georgia mountains, a man was measured by the job he held or the farm or business he ran. To be tagged as lazy was about as low as a man could get. A strong work ethic was drilled into the children. When cotton mills and other industries came into the area, mountain folk were found to be hard workers, loyal to their company, and their vocation. Congressman Phil Landrum gained a solid following in his mountain district when he co-sponsored the Landrum-Griffin bill, an act considered anti-union at a time when unions were sweeping across American industry in the North.

#5. INDEPENDENCE and MOONSHINE WHISKEY. These two traits blended with "self-reliance" to say, "I don't want anybody telling me what to do, or not do, so long as it doesn't hurt somebody else. I can do it on my own, thank you." There was (and is?) a rebellious tone to the culture of the mountains, going all the way back to the illegal-but-socially-accepted Moonshine Whiskey industry, and the rough-and-tumble Gold diggers. We knew our Sheriffs were aware of some shady things that went on, yet we happily voted for "our Sheriff." This "I'll-do-it-myself" attitude also brought on a spirit we would call entrepreneurial today, creating business activities called "Creative Capitalism" in this book.

#6. POLITICS. For more than a century following the Civil War and Reconstruction, Georgia was one-party Democrat except for the furthest Northeast corner of the state, where one could find a handful of elected Republicans. And yet, all during that 100-or-so years, the Georgia 9th was one of the most conservative

Congressional districts in the nation. The inherent distrust for big government went back to the moonshine wars of the late 1800s when the revenuers (the federal government) and the moonshiners (we-the-people) clashed.

It continued in the 1930s, when local Democrat leaders told President Roosevelt "we will take your money, but don't press us on how to vote for the Supreme Court bill. Georgians don't scare." President Roosevelt had told the Georgia delegation he would cut off Washington money unless they supported his effort to pack the Supreme Court. All local officials were elected in the Democrat primary (for there were no opposition Republicans running in the General election). And the Southern Democrats successfully rigged their primary to keep blacks out of power.

#7. PATRIOTISM. Despite a willingness to speak out against policies of the democracy they cherished, when their government was challenged by outside forces, or inside powers, these mountain men were among the first to volunteer for service. They were patriots and proud of it. During the Civil War, some counties stood with the North. And although they had little acceptance of slavery, many took a stance with states rights and served with the Confederates. Volunteers of Northeast Georgia were represented at the Alamo and in the Spanish-American war. Large numbers went to France in World War I, and among the volunteers for World War II was the first Medal of Honor recipient of that epic conflict. Energetic American Legion posts sprung up after World

War I and grew exponentially after World War II, keeping patriotic holidays like Memorial Day, July 4, and Armistice Day a solid part of the culture of the area during the time now called the Good Ole Days.

#8. EDUCATION and COMMON SENSE. An education did not come easily for children of the scattered small farms and communities of the mountains, but it was important in the minds of early settlers. They equated it with future success in life for their children and were willing to pay a heavy price to get it. Stories are legend about children walking miles to school, and most of them are true. Small community high schools were started and boarding schools established to meet the needs of a growing population. Colleges were begun, with some of them still existing today. The goal, however, was not to create scholars but to prepare youngsters for success in life, in business, in the church, and in the American democracy. They were taught "common sense," and there was another term, "makin' do." When you did not have something, you could use your mind to "make do" without it.

#9. PERSONAL PROPERTY. One of the early settlers of the mountain area is quoted as saying (probably over the barrel of a long rifle), "My land is my kingdom, and my home is my castle. Don't mess with it." The mountains of Georgia were not settled by wealthy land owners from the coastal areas of Georgia and the Carolinas. They were settled by poor European immigrants (mostly Scotch-Irish) who came down the Great Wagon Road after landing in Philadelphia or Baltimore. The battle over who owned the land of the Georgia mountains brought on the Trail of Tears, among other things. The right to own property was, and to some degree still is, part of the "sacred right" secured by the Revolutionary War and written into the Bill of Rights of the U. S. Constitution.

#10. INHERITED CULTURE. The people who settled in mountainous Northeast Georgia throughout the Good Ole Days came with a cultural background of their own, and that culture permeated the culture of the area through World War II ... maybe even longer. They were the Wesley brothers and the Methodist church; the British and the rule of law; the people of Scottish descent and their ability to make good whiskey; the Morse brothers and their knowledge of sawmilling; people from all corners of the globe who came seeking a fortune from Gold.

In the history of the United States of America, the mountains of Northeast Georgia were a melting pot, taking from many cultures and blending to make a stronger culture than any single immigrant brought into the region. For all, ownership of land was a measure of wealth and success. For all, rule by royalty was the enemy. .For all, the American dream that allowed a hard-working individual to become wealthy was worth fighting for. For all, freedom of religion was worth living for. And ... for all, this rough little corner of Georgia was a dream come true.

And for all who created Northeast Georgia's culture, there was Psalm 121:

I will lift mine eyes unto the hills
From whence cometh my help.

✲ ✲ ✲

When The Holy Bible Was Basic In Everyday Life

There is a Men's Bible Study Group that meets at lunch here in Gainesville on Thursdays. The other day there was some kind of a mix-up, and the room where they usually met was in use. They had arrived early, so they took one section of the public portion of the restaurant and proceeded with the meeting as customers filled the rest of the tables.

This group is not affiliated with any one church or denomination, and no one seems to know when or how it started. It is open to anybody who wants to walk in, and for the most part, their review of the Holy Bible sheds light on decisions to be made in the business world. Some things seem to come up at every meeting - the Golden Rule; the 10 commandments; the Parable of the Talents; the 23rd Psalm.

Now, back to that particular meeting in the midst of regular customers from all walks of life. It should be no surprise that this Men's Bible Study Group always opens and closes with prayer, but this particular day one man with a deep bass voice decided to pray in the middle of the meeting. He was thanking God for all the blessings we have as Americans, and an interesting thing happened. A hush came over that rather large room. People in the serving line paused and lowered their head. A couple of guys with caps on took them off. And when the prayer ended, loud Amens were heard throughout that restaurant.

✲ ✲ ✲

Helping The Man By the Side Of The Road

"He's a dried-up old devil that looks like a prune. If the average-sized man were a silver dollar, he'd be the sales tax."

The man talking was slouched across a table in the composing room of the *Gainesville News*. His voice was quiet, not irritated, and he was talking about his new-found friend, Baldy.

Hub Black was not what you would call an aristocrat. He wasn't a great church worker. He only shaved on Sundays, and in his own words, dressed like an unmade bed. But in his own humble way, Old Man Black made great strides toward promoting Peace on Earth, Good Will Toward Men.

There's no way of knowing how many men Hub put on their feet. Certainly he would be the last man to keep count or to believe he had any part in it. But there were a great many. And most of them he found just the way he found Baldy.

This guy Baldy was in the pool room across the street from the *News* one day. How the old printer met him is not quite clear, but no one was surprised, for Hub met no strangers.

Baldy was broke. That sufficed for Black. He bought the old man lunch, and to top it off, bought him a pack of cigarettes. Most folks would have left it right there, but not Black. He cussed the old fellow roundly and paid for a meal that night.

One week would surely have stopped it. Not for Black. He fed Baldy for a week ... two weeks ... even a month or so. Then one day Baldy turned up with a job, and the old man proudly bought his own meal. It had taken two months living off Hub Black, but he had regained confidence in himself and gotten himself a real job.

Hub Black is a respected man in his community, and he knows that there are other respected men who temporarily hang out in pool rooms, begging for food. And one day he believes they can return to society and be useful citizens.

For Hub Black had his own battle with the bottle. And, in the worst of it, when the depression hit, Black found his own self-confidence in a pool room. Now he owns his own home and is happy with his wife Hattie and considers his grandchildren a blessing.

And yet ... across the street in the pool hall, he finds a calling. For there he finds men who have shrunk to the value of a sales tax, and he must re-build them to their full, silver-dollar value.

✲ ✲ ✲

Abraham Lincoln's Values and Political Beliefs

Serious historians generally credit George Washington and Abraham Lincoln with being America's two greatest presidents. This year marks the 200th birthday of Abraham Lincoln, and thus we are hearing some of the history that earned him this recognition. Mostly we hear that he did away with slavery and held the United States together when it was split apart ... and that is appropriate.

Among his writings, we hear the Gettysburg address, but we seldom hear that he was the first Republican president and that he clearly stated values and free-enterprise principles that are the foundational beliefs of today's conservatives. For instance, Lincoln clearly stated 10 political beliefs that we, in my judgment, would do well to adopt today. Here they are ...:

... You cannot bring about prosperity by discouraging thrift.

... You cannot strengthen the weak by weakening the strong.

... You cannot help small men by tearing down big men.

... You cannot help the poor by destroying the rich.

... You cannot lift the wage earner by pulling down the wage payer.

.... You cannot keep out of trouble by spending more than your income.

... You cannot further brotherhood of men by inciting class hatred.

...You cannot establish sound security on borrowed money.

...You cannot build character and courage by taking away a man's initiative.

... You cannot really help men by having the government tax them to do for them what they can and should do for themselves.

Abraham Lincoln

✲ ✲ ✲

Winston Churchill and Brave Horatius

It has always interested me that many great leaders have a short poem, often from the classics, that serves as their guide – a brief but concise statement of what they stand for.

Winston Churchill was such a leader. He was a fighter. He knew what he stood for. And as long as England drifted aimlessly just prior to World War II, he was not given a high leadership position.

But when Britain's back was to the wall, they called on Churchill, and he served them well. While a schoolboy, he memorized a couple of verses from Macaulay that served as his constant inspiration, and it tells you something about the man and why he won the Second World War. It goes like this:

Then out spake brave Horatius,
The Captain of the Gate:
"To every man upon this earth

Death comes soon or late.
And how can man die better
Than facing fearful odds,
For the ashes of his fathers,
And the temples of his gods?

✲ ✲ ✲

Boy Scout Values At Mid-Century

In doing research for the photographic history of Hall County, I came across a picture of one of our Boy Scout troops of 1950 ... and the thought struck me, "Boy, this community really got a bunch of quality leaders out of this troop." With the advantage of 20/20 hindsight, it seems pretty obvious the Boy Scouts had it right then, and they've got it right now. How many of you can repeat with me, "On my honor I will do my best to do my duty to God and my country, and to obey the Scout law; to help other people at all times; to keep myself physically strong, mentally awake and morally straight."And while we're at it, the Scout Law referred to above said then and says now a Scout is: Trustworthy, Loyal, Helpful, Friendly, Courteous, Kind, Obedient, Cheerful, Thrifty, Brave, Clean, and Reverent found a home and to be makes one wonder: 50 years from now, what will we say this generation taught our kids?

✲ ✲ ✲

Don Brewer and Baseball Sportsmanship

One of my local heroes, Don Brewer, recently wrapped up his 20th season coaching the American Legion's Post 7 baseball team. His record is legend, enough so he was named Georgia's Coach of the Year by the Legion. In the past decade, his teams have won the state title 5 times.

He has sent an incredible number of youngsters to college on baseball scholarships, trained high school and college coaches, sent players to the major leagues. By every measure, Post 7 has had one of the premiere American Legion baseball programs in the South.

But the thing I like most about it, and probably the reason I hold Don Brewer in such high esteem, is what he and his cohorts teach young men about Sportsmanship. Their teams know, repeat regularly, and live by a 7-point Code of Sportsmanship in which each player says, I WILL ...

...keep the rules ... keep faith with my team-mates ...keep my temper ... keep myself fit ... keep a stout heart in defeat ... keep my pride under in victory ... and finally, keep a sound soul, a clean mind and a healthy body.

Don Brewer coaches winners – on the baseball field and in life. I hope he goes on coaching forever.

✲ ✲ ✲

Military Booklet Contains The 10 Commandments

The other day I came across one of those 100-page booklets used to train junior officers just before World War II. This one was about "character guidance," and the book carried a title all servicemen knew very well: "Duty–Honor–Country." This book teaches about authority, character and personal discipline. It also teaches about some things I'm not sure would be taught today.

For instance, it refers to some "Natural or Inalienable Rights." The right to life, including the right to self-defense and the right to make a living. The right to marry, to found a home, and to be a free person. The right to own property and to remain free and unmolested in its enjoyment.

But along with our rights, this mid-century military booklet says, we have some moral obligations. And guess what you will find in this U. S. Government book as "The finest summary expression of these moral obligations." ... You will find the Ten Commandments ... all 10 of them, with no editing and no apologies.

This military leadership training manual says: "The Moral Law is the foundation of National Law, and of our Republic." And it makes this commentary - "It is on these principles that our Republic was founded."

✲ ✲ ✲

Jesse Jewell Said: GO TO IT

It has been almost 60 years since I was a young twenty-something in Gainesville, among a raft of veterans back from World War II. It was an interesting time, and we all were encouraged to have a CAN DO attitude. There were a number of motivational speakers that appealed to us, and little booklets that encouraged us to GO TO IT.

The reason this came to mind was because I was cleaning out some files about the history of the poultry industry the other day and came across one of these motivational booklets, and on the front of it were these words: "Compliments of Jesse Jewell." The message was by one E. F. G. Gerard, and inside it said it was in its 27th printing. I don't remember his giving me this pocket-sized booklet, but it doesn't surprise me.

It starts out saying, "Only fools say it can't be done." Then it talks about Men of Action and The Will To Win. It picks up with Common Sense and commands one to Drop That Inferiority Complex. There is a page explaining this: "Give to the world the best you have, and the best will come back to you." There is a section on enthusiasm ... one of Jesse Jewell's abiding characteristics. It includes the Power of Faith, and Ideas, and finally this, "It makes no difference who you are / Or where you are or why / Here's the secret to success / Always keep aiming high. / Not a thing on earth can stop you / If you'll try with all your might / You CAN do it, if you'll GO TO IT / And you'll always come out just right."

That was Jesse Jewell, probably about 1955.

✲ ✲ ✲

Sir John Templeton: Six Keys To Success

I ran across an article the other day that quoted Sir John Templeton, founder of the Templeton Funds and a pioneer in Global Investing. The author was commenting on a book Sir John had recently written and in which he points out that people can be successful no matter what the circumstances. And what does he say it takes to be successful? Here are his keys:

1. Be grateful for what you have.
2. Be enthusiastic about everything you do.
3. Make sure your job is your career.
4. Realize that success is a journey, not a destination.
5. Learn as much as possible from those around you.
6. And finally, perseverance is the difference between success and defeat.

✲ ✲ ✲

Thomas Paine: Voice of the American Revolution

We often talk about the bravery of the men who signed the Declaration of Independence, and we in Georgia revere Button Gwinnett, George Walton, and especially

Lyman Hall. But in this year 2001, when politicians and citizens seek information from the media to help us make up our minds, it seems appropriate we remember a journalist who, more than any other man, was the voice of the American Revolution.

According to the magazine *American History*, "When Thomas Paine published 'Common Sense' in 1776, he put into words what large numbers of patriots had been thinking – that America should declare its independence from Britain by whatever means possible." He denounced the English Parliament and said that "...in America the law is king."

Within a year after Thomas Paine wrote the little 47-page pamphlet called "Common Sense," more than 500,000 copies were in circulation (an amazing number for 1776), not just in private hands but also in bookstores, libraries, taverns, wherever.

There were many great leaders in the Revolution, but Thomas Paine was the voice that mobilized American public opinion in favor of freedom from Englsih rule.

Independence Day Was Just The Beginning

Tomorrow is July 4. Independence Day - July 4, 1776 - was the day we declared our independence from England, but there were 11 years of blood and tears before the Constitution was written and two more years before it was ratified by the states. The Revolutionary War was fought, and against all odds, it was won. Common law had evolved in England on the tradition of liberty, property and contract, and using this as their foundation, the Founding Fathers' vision said, "...that all men are created equal, that they are endowed by their Creator with certain inalienable rights, that among these are life, liberty, and the pursuit of happiness – That to secure these Rights Governments are instituted among Men, deriving their just powers from the Consent of the Governed." And at the ending, it said, "...and for the support of this declaration, with a firm Reliance on the Protection of Divine Providence, we mutually pledge to each other our Lives, our Fortunes and our sacred Honor."

Think about that. These were successful, wealthy men. They signed that document, and in so doing pledged their all, and many gave their all. We fought wars with other nations and fought one war with ourselves to maintain the nation they founded with their blood. It was almost a century before we put together a pledge that we-the-people could take. It goes this way, "I pledge allegiance to the flag of the United States of America, and to the republic for which it stands. One nation under God, indivisible, with liberty and justice for all."

One does not have to study much world history to realize we have been handed a unique and wonderful nation, and that we have a heavy responsibility to hand it intact to the next generation.

✲ ✲ ✲

Memories From The 1930's

At one point, while researching for this book, I asked a number of people at random: what comes to mind first when you are asked about your memories of the 1930s? Most would take a minute or so to figure how old they were at that time, and then there were some immediate answers ... not one, but several. The great depression was rarely mentioned. The gathering storm that became World War II was mentioned by a few men. For the most part, these people - most of them teen-agers or younger in the 1930's - had top-of-mind memories about the daily life they lived. Some memories were fairly universal among those who answered ....

.... We never locked our doors. In fact, the screen door was usually the only one ever closed in summer.

...There was no question about it - Dad was head of the household. But, somehow, Mom always got her way.

....We ate dinner at noontime and supper at night.

.... Turn off the lights and shut the door. Were you raised in a barn?

....Eat everything on your plate. Don't you know there are poor little Chinese kids going hungry?

.... Getting a whipping at school and dreading going home because I knew I was going to get another one when my Daddy got home.

.... Getting dressed on Sunday and then having to sit around till time to go to church so I wouldn't get my clothes dirty. Do you remember grass stain?

There were a lot of other memories telling how we looked and how we lived in the years just before World War II. It is interesting that most of the things mentioned as I asked about their childhood memories were little things that are no longer a part of the life of today's more urbanized children. Things like these examples ...

... When I was real young, my grandparents let us know in no uncertain terms that playing cards and dancing was a sin. My folks did both, but not when our grandparents were around.

.... Going barefooted the day school let out, and staying that way all summer. We even played kick-the-can barefoot.

..... Jukeboxes.

There were a couple of honkey tonks around, and we would slip off and go to them. One was across the county line toward Dawsonville, or was it toward Cumming? The other was north of Gainesville, on the road to Lula.

.... Every boy had a BB gun. And every girl wore bobby socks.

.... Goin' way back, we used to really have fun with corn cob fights in the old barn on rainy days. Wet corn cobs from one of the stalls was illegal. Do you know what it feels like to get hit with a wet corn cob?

Those were indeed the good old days.

✲ ✲ ✲

Three Tame Ducks

A Challenge to a College Graduating Class -

There are three tame ducks in my backyard,
Dabbling in mud and trying hard
To get their share and maybe more
Of the overflowing barnyard store
Satisfied with the tasks they are at
Of eating, sleeping and getting fat,
But whenever the free, wild ducks go by,
In a long line streaming through the sky,
They cock a quizzical eye
And flap their wings and try to fly.
I think my soul is a tame old duck,
Dabbling around in barnyard muck,
Fat and lazy, with useless wings;
But sometimes when the North wind sings,
And the wild ones hurtle overhead,
It remembers something lost and dead,
And makes a feeble attempt to fly.
It's fairly satisfied with the state it's in –
But it ain't the duck it might have been.

And May The Wind Always Be At Your Back

I have had a good bit of comment about my closing line for my "Common Sense Chronicles" on WDVN … "may the wind always be at your back."

I picked that up many years ago in the Navy and have used it off and on through the years. To me, it was a friendly farewell carried forward from the days of sailing ships ... from the old salts who could quickly tell you a trip was easier and safer if the wind came from astern, and much easier than the constant hassle of tacking and turning when the wind came at you from port or starboard.

Then I got this note from my longtime friend Lou Fockele that said: "I am haunted by the hunch that goes, "May the wind be always at your back." And Fockele style, he started the search to get at the truth. It turns out, he reports, it is an old Irish Blessing, and it goes like this:

May the road rise to meet you,
May the wind always be at your back.
May the sun shine warm upon your face.
May the rain fall softly upon your fields.
And until we meet again
May God hold you in the palm of His hand.

God Bless you all, and May the wind always be at your back.

✲ ✲ ✲

ENDNOTES and BIBLIOGRAPHY

Much of the material in this book comes from research found in three sources, and first used by the author in "Common Sense Chronicles", a series aired on WDUN, the Northeast Georgia radio station, and published as columns on *AccessNorthGeorgia.com*, the internet newspaper. The primary sources:

1. Hall County Library. This local library has a wealth of published and unpublished documents about the Northeast Georgia mountain region. Especially valuable are the local newspapers housed there.
2. *Northeast Georgia: A History* This author did extensive research in writing this 2001 book. Both material from this book, and especially from unpublished notes, were often used in *Characters, Crazies and the Culture of Northeast Georgia.*
3. *A North Georgia Journal of History*. Edited by Olin Jackson. There are five volumes in this series, collections of articles drawn from the *North Georgia Journal* (This author was Chairman of the Board of this publishing company for several years). It

continues as *Georgia Backroads*, and Dan Roper, of Rome, GA is the publisher.

And then there is Zell Miller. A former U. S. Senator and Georgia Governor, Zell Miller has written books of national importance about politics. But I nominate "Old Zell", the mountain character who never mentally left the mountains, as the Dean of Historians for this region. In his book about *Patriotism, Values and Character* he speaks of a culture his mountain folk are willing to fight for. He speaks of the political values he grew up with, and how they have changed, in *National Party No More: The Conscience of a Conservative Democrat.* He also writes about Brasstown Valley and their old mountain ways that are *Purt Nigh Gone*. My personal favorite is *Corps Values: Everything You Need to Know I learned in the Marines.* You won't find many direct quotes from Zell Miller's writing in this book, but I sincerely hope it conveys the "tone", the "feeling", the love, the deep belief in mountain values set forth by this Dean of Georgia's mountain history.

Almost every chapter will include "Chronicles" taken from family books, genealogical information, or information given to this author by individuals. Is some of it "made up? Well, maybe. There are some tall tale-tellers in these here mountains. Try Boney Tank. Many more come from interviews with "old timers" that I interviewed as far back as

1950 when I was on the news staff of *The Atlanta Constitution*, or 1955 when I was editor of the *Poultry Times*. I have been a history nut for a long time.

Then there are the published books … some you have heard of, most you have not.

Brice, W. M. – *A City Laid Waste*. (the story of Gainesville's 1936 tornado) Self Published. 1936.

Burrison, John A. – *Bothers in Clay: The Story of Georgia Folk Pottery*. 1983.

Cain, Andrew – 1978 -- *History of Lumpkin County for the First Hundred Years.*

Dabney, Joseph – *Mountain Spirits*. 1974

Dorsey, James E. – *The History of Hall County, Volume I and Volume II*. 1991 and 2010.

Ehle, John – *Trail of Tears: The Rise and Fall of The Cherokee Nation*. 1988.

Garrett, Franklin M. – *Atlanta and Environs: A Chronicle of Its People and Events*. 1954.

Gedney, Matt –*Living on the Unicoi Road. 1996.*

Humperley, Marion R. – *Indian Heritage of Georgia.* 1994.

Jackson, Olin A. – *A Northeast Georgia Journal of History*. Four volumes – 1989, 1991, 1995, 1999..

Kephart, Horace – *Our Southern Highlanders.* 1913.

Lane, Mary C. – *History of Piedmont College*. . 1993.

Lumsden, Dr. Thomas N. – 1989 -- *Nacoochee Valley: Its Times and Places.*

Muir, John A.–*A Thousand-mile Walk To The Gulf*. 1916.

Noble, Ben and Jackson, Olin – *Lakemont, Georgia: The Early Years* . . 1989

Otwell, W. Larry – *The Gold of White County, Georgia* 1984

Rensi, Roy C. and H. David Williams – *Gold Fever: America's First Gold Rush* . 1988

Ritchie, Andrew Jackson – *Sketches of Rabun County History*.1948

Robinson, W. Stitt – 1979 --*The Southern Colonial Frontier 1607-1743.*

Rouse, Parke, Jr. – *The Great Wagon Road: From Philadelphia to the South* .1995

Sawyer, Gordon – *The Agribusiness Poultry Industry*. 1971

Scruggs, Caroll Proctor – *Georgia During the Revolution* 1976

Shadburn, Don L. – 1990 -- *Cherokee Planters in Georgia 1832-1838* .

Webb, J. A. – *The History of New Holland, Georgia, and Pacolet Mfg. Co.* 1985

White, George – *Historical Collections of Georgia* . 1854

White, Max E. – *Georgia's Indian Heritage* . 1988

And there were other sources: *The Atlanta Constitution, The Gainesville Eagle, The Gainesville*

News, Poultry Times, and finally the magnificent Gainesville 64 page promotional booklet published in 1888.

Gordon Sawyer
2011

✲ ✲ ✲

--30--